CHURCH OF MARTYRS

PETE FUSCO

This book is a work of fiction. All names, characters and places are either products of the author's imagination or are used only for literary effect. No reference to any real person, living or deceased, is intended or should be inferred.

ISBN: 1500469157
ISBN 13: 9781500469153
Library of Congress Control Number: 2014921549
Createspace Independent Publishing Platform
North Charleston, South Carolina

Other books by Pete Fusco

"Moondog's Academy of the Air"

And, dying, bless the hand that gave the blow.

John Dryden

This book is dedicated to my parents. My father would have gotten a big kick out of it. My mother might not have approved.

ONE

When the Church of Martyrs could no longer pay its own way, Rome summarily defrocked it, repossessed its sacredness and left it to the mercy of the punitive Cleveland weather. The church fell derelict, an extinct volcano abandoned by its deities. Only the current congregation of rats and pigeons were present that night to witness the infrequent human visitors.

Eddie hid in the confessional. A few minutes before, he had been asleep on the downstairs couch in the rectory. Men speaking Italian on the second floor awakened him. Eddie, fluent in Italian, heard a man say there was no one upstairs, that they had come a long way to kill someone who wasn't there. He rolled off the couch and ran out of the rectory into a cold March rain wearing only boxer shorts. One of the men spotted Eddie leaving and watched him enter the side entrance of the church.

The heights and reaches of the century-old Church of Martyrs offered many good places to hide, especially at night. Eddie knew them all. He also knew that a confessional was not one of them but it was close and the broken glass beneath his bare feet made running any further impossible. He slipped into the penitent's side of the confessional as the men entered the church. His choice of hiding place might have worked, but for protesting pigeons disturbed from roosts atop the confessional. Their squawks guided Eddie's pursuers like a beacon.

"E casa, Signore?" One of the men knocked on the side of the confessional and asked if Eddie was at home. The Comedian's buddies laughed.

"Dica la Sua confessione ultima, Signore." The Comedian, on a roll, urged Eddie to make a last confession, a suggestion that amused the others even more.

Eddie, not sure if he was trapped in a nightmare or a confessional, thought to short-circuit the event by tapping into it. He had only to step out of the confessional and out of the nightmare. He would awaken back on the lumpy couch. Eddie placed his hand on the confessional's brass Crucifix doorknob and traced the worn figure of Christ's body with his thumb. It felt real, as did the continuing a cappella gripes of the resident vermin. The rain that funneled through the leaky church roof into the confessional was too wet, too cold. Nor could Eddie ignore the pain from the glass shards embedded in his feet. The toes of his right foot throbbed. He had smashed them into something hard—his best guess was the base of one of the marble statue plinths—as he ran past it in the unlit church.

Eddie released the knob, not willing to chance his dream theory and hasten his fate just yet. He fought to keep from broadcasting his pain and fear though he was certain most of the west side of Cleveland could hear his clacking heart.

"Lasci noi dramma 'Apri la Porta' come su televisione. Ciascuno sceglie una porta. L'uomo che sceglie la porta corretta puo uccidere l'occultamento dell'uomo interno." The Comedian told his pals that their victim's predicament reminded him of an Italian television game show called *"Apri la Porta,"* Open the Door, and suggested an improvised version of the game, just for fun. Since they weren't certain in which side of the confessional—priest or penitent—Eddie was hiding, the Comedian and another of the men would each choose a door. The winning contestant on the television show merely got to spray the person behind the door

with whipped cream; the winner that night would get to murder the occupant.

"Dovremmo fare un piu salariale." In a deep wheezing that barely passed for a voice, one of the men challenged the Comedian to a wager. Comedian and Wheezer agreed on a thousand dollars.

A thousand dollars? Even in a dream, that's a lot of money.

The two men argued over how their victim would die. They settled on the knife; it was not only quieter and more interesting but more *tradizionale.* The Comedian ordered a third man to back them up with his pistol.

Eddie heard the sloshing of water and the grinding of glass on the floor outside the confessional. He guessed the Comedian and Wheezer were moving into position in front of their chosen doors. Eddie heard the close presence of labored breathing and assumed the Wheezer had picked the penitent's door. He also heard what sounded like two switchblade knives opened in rapid one-two cadence.

"Qui e la sua penitenza. Terro presto i suoi testicoli nelle mie mani." In a strained voice, the Wheezer said he held the victim's sharp penance in his hand. He also speculated on what else of Eddie's he might soon hold in his hand. As the others laughed, Eddie heard a lighter and smelled cigarette smoke.

Realization that the men considered him such a lightweight that they could indulge in whimsical diversions, even a cigarette break, before dealing with him deepened Eddie's fear. He leaned back on the bench, rested his head on the rear wall of the confessional and swallowed hard.

The Wheezer added yet another sporting touch. He suggested they open their doors one at a time to heighten the suspense, like the contestants on the television show. He told the third man to flip a coin to determine who would go first.

A sliver of light spilled into the confessional through a crack around the edge of the doorjamb. Eddie wiped away a steady stream of cold sweat running into his eyes, leaned forward and focused through the narrow opening. He couldn't see Comedian or Wheezer, both of whom stood too close to the confessional. He was only able to see the third man, a small wiry figure who stood three or four yards back with a flashlight in one hand, pistol in the other. The gunman tucked the flashlight under his arm and searched his pocket for a coin, which he flipped into the air.

"Mune di coda!" The Comedian called tails. The coin clanged like a manhole cover on the terrazzo floor. The gunman verified the outcome with the flashlight and announced the winner by name: *"Emile!"*

The flashlight beam disappeared, reappeared for a moment and disappeared again as the gunman swept the flashlight from one door to the other like a theatre spotlight. The two *Apri la Porta* contestants snorted an appreciation of their friend's showmanship. Eddie fully expected an accompanying drum roll. He gripped the Crucifix doorknob with both hands and braced for a struggle.

Creaking of the ancient door-latch mechanism on the *priest's* side of the confessional filled Eddie with an absurd sense of relief. *Emile must be the Comedian. He won the toss and he's opening his door first. The priest's door. The wrong door*! Eddie cherished his reprieve, the extension of sweet life however brief. He knew a bloodthirsty, wheezing bastard with a knife stood outside the penitent's door. And, of course, there was the little guy with the pistol. The end of the game was only postponed, the outcome inevitable. Eddie knew he'd soon be the unwilling prize in the game of *Apri la Porta,* imported, late night, you-bet-your-life-church-in-ruins version.

"I hava you now! You mine! Theesa too easy!" Without a trace of his earlier humor, the Comedian's voice sliced through the inkiness of the confessional.

What did he say? I hava you now? Who the hell's he talking to? Who's sitting in the other side of this confessional? Who else is going to die in this God-forsaken church with me? Or is this another of his bad jokes?

Releasing one hand from the doorknob, Eddie pulled at a loose corner of the rotting wood and silk screen that allowed priest and penitent to hear but not see each other. Through an opening about an inch wide Eddie confirmed that the Comedian was not joking. The priest's compartment *was* occupied. A large man stripped to the waist sat upright and motionless, either already dead or, more likely, frightened stiff. His face and body were bloodied. Eddie guessed the stranger was one of the Briggs Hill neighborhood homeless. He had probably been beaten up and had sought refuge from the cold and rain in the church.

You would have been better off in the rain tonight, buddy.

Eddie also caught his first glimpse of the Comedian. Tall, brawny and dressed in dark clothing, he stood just outside the open confessional door, rolling a knife in the palm of his hand. The flashlight beam illuminated the blade like a signal mirror. Eddie released the corner of the screen, not out of indifference to the fate of the luckless individual in the priest's compartment but because of the revulsion he felt at the prospect of witnessing a dress rehearsal of his own death.

Eddie closed his eyes and summoned his nerve. He had to scream out that the person on the priest's bench was not the man they were after, was not the man they seemed so eager to murder. As Eddie opened his dry mouth to shout an appeal for the stranger, a wail penetrated his claustrophobic private berth on the Nightmare Express. The wail came not from inside the confessional but from *outside*.

Even as Eddie argued with himself over whose voice he heard, the heavy oak confessional began to reel back and forth, almost tossing him off the bench. A stray elbow knocked a jagged hole in the screened partition, allowing Eddie a much better view into the priest's compartment. The scene, illuminated by the flashlight beam, defied all logic. Except dream logic.

The stranger on the priest's bench had reached forward and thrust what appeared to be a small garden rake into the Comedian's throat. Jets of blood squirted from the wound and flowed down the seated man's outstretched arm, which Eddie thought seemed abnormally large. The Comedian held onto the doorjamb with one hand to keep from being pulled into the confessional; he thrust his knife repeatedly at the seated man's chest. A chiseling sound, that of steel against an unyielding surface, echoed through the church. From his ripped throat, the Comedian gurgled a single word laden with surprise and terror: *"pietra!"*

Did he say "pietra?" Stone?

The flashlight beam bounced back and forth from the seated man to the Comedian, as if the person holding the light sought to determine whose blood flowed in the confessional. Perhaps his pal was only clowning again, only *pretending* to be in trouble, simply spicing up the finish of *Apri la Porta* with a few more laughs. Eddie saw the Comedian was not clowning and was, in fact, fighting for his life in the close combat of the confessional. With the hooked weapon stuck fast in his throat, the Comedian lost his grip on the doorjamb and fell forward into the lap of the occupant.

The Wheezer appeared behind the Comedian. He threw his cigarette to the floor, clamped his knife between his teeth and pulled on the Comedian's legs in an attempt to extricate his comrade, now a human tug-of-war. The harder the Wheezer pulled, the deeper the hooked weapon sank into the Comedian's throat, compounding his suffering. The man on the priest's bench could not be budged; he reined the writhing Comedian, along with the Wheezer, into the confessional across a floor made slippery by his victim's blood. The Wheezer conceded to the greater force; he released his grip on the Comedian's legs and stepped back. The knife fell from his mouth.

The gunman stepped into Eddie's view. Flashlight in one hand, raised pistol with silencer in the other, he shouted for the Wheezer to stand clear. The gunman hunched and stared over the pistol sight with a dark, pitiless eye.

Eddie edged as far away from the open partition as possible; muted shots hit the seated man in the chest and face, including several between the eyes. Incredibly, the bullets ricocheted off the target. A deflected shot whistled past Eddie's ear and drilled through the thick oak of the confessional wall.

When the shooting stopped, the sound of panicked vermin and rain falling on the church roof mixed with the Comedian's unabated, desperate stabbing, the sound of steel against...*pietra*?

The gunman moved closer to the confessional, close enough for Eddie to see the confusion—but not fear—in his darting eyes. He fired two more shots point blank into the seated man's face and two into his chest. The shots had no more effect than the first salvo.

The bulletproof stranger wasn't yet finished with the Comedian. Eddie watched him grasp his quaking, blood-drenched prey by the back of the neck with a shovel-sized hand. In no great hurry, he dislodged the hooked weapon from the Comedian's throat, removing along with it a red glob. With a flick of his wrist, he turned the Comedian face up and sank the hook into his chest. He drew the weapon slowly toward the man's groin. Muscles snapped and separated from bone; intestines flowed from the Comedian's opened stomach cavity. The stranger repeated the action several times in a mechanical, metronomic pumping.

Eddie averted his gaze. He could not, however, escape the Comedian's cries of pain and incredulity, which sounded distant coming from his shredded throat. The cries soon faded to whimpers of submission and despair, which were in turn followed by guttural rattles that signaled the bittersweet promise of death. The sound of the Comedian's knife against—stone?—slowed from a machine-gun tempo to sporadic, feeble pokes.

"Maledizione Lei a inferno, Lei bastardo!" The Comedian managed a barely audible curse, inviting the bastard killing him to burn forever in hell. The victim's defiance at the threshold of death won Eddie's disinclined admiration.

The seated man tossed his victim from the confessional like a petulant child bored with a toy. As the Comedian twitched away his last bit of life on the church floor, the stranger on the priest's bench turned and looked through the broken priest-penitent partition at Eddie with gem-hard eyes, unreflective of the barbaric violence he had wrought.

Despite the obvious setback for the opposition, Eddie renewed his grip on the doorknob. He heard the click of a magazine being released from a pistol and another snapped into place. The math was not difficult: two armed killers against an unarmed, near-frozen soon-to-be victim in boxer shorts.

The brutality in the priest's compartment and the unyielding killers hardened Eddie's fear to anger. He vowed not to die without a fight. If or when the Wheezer opened the confessional door, Eddie intended to lunge, grab him by the neck and not let go until one of them was dead. As for the gunman, Eddie hoped his ally in the priest's side of the confessional was up for more action.

Eddie watched the Wheezer reach down to the dead Comedian. He brushed away the rats that had begun to gather and touched the Comedian's face, perhaps to convince himself that the person inside the confessional had actually killed his friend. He brazenly reached inside the priest's compartment and touched the face of the seated man, who did not react. The Wheezer seemed unsure of what he felt. He spotted Eddie looking at him through the broken priest-penitent partition. Enraged, the Wheezer spun to his left toward the penitent's door.

"I kill you witta my bare hands, you sonabitch!" The Wheezer sucked air into impaired lungs in three or four noisy stages like a person struggling to inflate a balloon. Seething and gasping, he gripped the doorknob.

Again the confessional rocked as Eddie strained to hold the door closed against the Wheezer, unexpectedly strong for someone who worked so hard just to breathe. The Wheezer pulled the door open inch by inch. Eddie looked into the priest's compartment for help but the seated man stared straight ahead, seemingly disinterested.

"I could use some help here, damnit!" Eddie yelled. "Don't quit on me now. If you're not going to help, hand me that rake, or whatever it is."

The stranger did not respond.

Even as Eddie wondered how much strain a century-old doorknob could withstand, it broke off in his hand. Eddie fell back, striking his head hard against the rear wall of the confessional. He heard the Wheezer fall to the floor on the other side of the door. Eddie repositioned the Crucifix doorknob in his hand, converting it to a weapon. He waited for the Wheezer to enter.

The Wheezer growled a long string of curses as he got up from the floor. Still growling, he slammed into the closed confessional door with a force that splintered the thick oak and sent a shower of wood fragments over Eddie. In an instant, Eddie was face to face with the killer, whose head stuck *through* the confessional door. The two men stared at each other, inches apart.

Eddie raised the Crucifix weapon and prepared to stab the Wheezer in the eyes when he realized that his attacker seemed no longer interested in killing him. The Wheezer shrieked in agony and diverted his attention to his right shoulder, which was somehow pinned to the door. A moment later the Wheezer's lower body also slammed hard against the door. Through the splintered wood Eddie watched the Wheezer's arms flail behind him, the image of a scarecrow on a windy day. The more he struggled to free himself, the deeper the jagged wood penetrated, barb-like, into his face and body. With his head wedged in the door, the Wheezer rolled his eyeballs to the corner of their sockets, trying to see behind him and learn the source of his pain. His deep wheezing jumped two registers to that of a high-pitched, out-of-tune harmonica.

Eddie watched the gunman step forward and pull at several long thin objects that protruded from the Wheezer's back. The effort seemed to only increase the Wheezer's agony. The gunman stopped trying to help his comrade.

Something out of the darkness, with the hiss of a very fast bird in flight, struck the Wheezer in the back with a momentum that propelled him ever deeper into the confessional. His frenzied caricature of a face touched Eddie's. The Wheezer suddenly stiffened, quit struggling, sucked air into his lungs one last time and expelled it in a long sour chord. Eddie watched life drain from the Wheezer's eyes, eyes that remained open after death, staring at Eddie in disbelief.

Eddie, equally disbelieving, stared back. Explanations raced through his mind. Had the Wheezer, in an uncontrollable fit of anger brought on by the bizarre death of the Comedian, attempted to body slam through the confessional door? Had he fatally impaled himself in the process? What had hit him from behind?

Afraid to do anything, Eddie sat rooted and quiet for several minutes. He heard only squealing rats, fluttering pigeons and the rain. No question that events had turned against the evening's luckless *Apri la Porta* contestants, but Eddie was slow to declare victory. There was the remaining problem of that little prick with the pistol.

But as Eddie watched through the shattered confessional door, the gunman inexplicably dropped his pistol and flashlight, turned away from the confessional and gazed at the transept wall, which was out of Eddie's view. The gunman fell to his knees in a puddle of rainwater and made a hurried Sign of the Cross.

Now what? What could he be looking at? Those old statues?

After several long minutes, still shaking from the cold and his brush with death but guardedly optimistic that the danger had passed, Eddie pushed on the confessional door. The door was attached only by the bottom hinge and required great effort to open because of the Wheezer's body. Eddie emerged on his tiptoes to prevent the glass shards in his feet from burrowing any deeper.

The gunman's dropped flashlight shined on the remains of the dead Comedian, whose flesh and insides extended away from his body in dark red strands alive with rats. The beam reached just far enough into the priest's side of the confessional to illuminate a pair of crude sandals on the mystery man's feet, as oversized as the rest of his body.

"Thanks for the help, buddy," Eddie said. "You okay in there?"

There was no reply. Eddie didn't expect one.

"Okay, so you're the strong, silent type," Eddie said. He joked only to calm himself.

Keeping an eye on his kneeling attacker, Eddie chanced a look at the Wheezer. He was curious as to what had killed him and why his body remained affixed to the confessional door. Eddie picked up the flashlight and directed it at the corpse.

Three arrows protruded from the Wheezer.

Arrows? What? Who could have shot arrows?

The sight of the anomalous arrows soothed Eddie. Here was the first solid evidence of a nightmare, albeit a very *real* nightmare that refused to end.

Eddie took an equivocal step toward the kneeling gunman. Even though the man had dropped the pistol, it remained well within his reach. The gunman, however, seemed unconcerned about the weapon; he was preoccupied with something on the transept wall. Without taking his eyes off his adversary, Eddie picked up the pistol and tossed it halfway across the church. He aimed the flashlight at the wall to learn what held the surviving killer's rapt attention. Eddie expected to see nothing more than the freakish statues of early Christian martyrs placed there when the church opened in 1902.

Except one of the martyrs was missing! Saint Blaise! The middle statue plinth, on which Blaise had stood for over a hundred years, was empty. Eddie now knew why the man in the priest's compartment looked so oversized. It was Saint Blaise, all seven scary feet of him, complete with the wool-combing hook used to rip his body apart when he was martyred in the second century.

"Make no mistake about it, Mr. Saint Blaise, on your best day you were the stuff of nightmares," Eddie said in a voice mostly breath. "What a fitting end to the nightmare of the century! Saint Blaise, no less!"

A noise in the confessional caught Eddie's attention. He turned, prepared for anything. Anything, that is, except the sight of Blaise getting up from the priest's bench. The martyr stepped over the dead Comedian and walked toward his statue plinth. Large pieces of flesh and muscle that executioners had torn loose from Blaise's limbs and body dangled as he walked. Broken glass crushed into powder under the statue's enormous weight. The rats, afraid of nothing and afraid of everything, deserted the dinner table and scattered.

Blaise returned to his plinth. He ascended it with a vitality that made Eddie gasp. The saint faced forward and struck his familiar pose. He reverted to statuary, his palms upturned beseechingly in an ironic pretense of helplessness. The blood-covered wool-combing hook rested idly in his right hand as it always had. The transmutation from life to stone took only seconds and struck Eddie as unremarkable, like an old film reel winding down, frame by frame, to a frozen image.

Eddie aimed the flashlight beam on the statue. He looked for movement, a sign of life in the wrathful face that had always made Saint Blaise—and the other six statues of the Church of Martyrs—so unappealingly different from statues in other churches. There was no movement.

The kneeling man clutched his hands together, praying. He was small and reminded Eddie of the dozen or so marble angels once arranged on either side of the main altar before a going-out-of-business auction relocated them to private gardens and chapels. In the corner of his eye, Eddie detected movement from the statue next to Saint Blaise, that of Saint Sebastian.

Eddie redirected the light in time to see Sebastian, his body festooned with the arrows of his martyrdom, come to life with a series of jerking, birth-like motions. The coarse rope that bound the martyr to a post behind him loosened and fell to his feet.

Sebastian came down from the plinth. As he moved, the arrows scraped against each other inside his body. Sweat dripped from the saint's contorted face, as if the arrows continued to torment him some eighteen hundred years after his death. Sebastian walked toward the confessional. His path took him close to the kneeling man, who scurried out of the way on his hands and knees like a Church of Martyrs rat.

Eddie, smiling at the notion of walking dream statues, stood his ground as Sebastian passed. Feathers of an arrow that pierced the saint's neck brushed against Eddie's face. They felt real. Sebastian stopped behind the body of the Wheezer. He withdrew the three arrows from the corpse with the ease of a player retrieving darts. The Wheezer's body remained stuck in the confessional door.

Arrows in hand, Sebastian returned to his plinth, which he mounted with a leap so agile that Eddie thought he might have briefly flown. The martyr replaced the arrows, not without monstrous pain, judging from his face, in jagged existing wounds on his chest and stomach. The rope lying at Sebastian's feet slithered upward and bound him by the waist to the post. The saint returned to lifelessness, his eyes fixed on Eddie in a look at once familiar and estranged.

The gunman, who on his knees seemed so small that he could have been mistaken for a child, spoke in a weak voice, tears streaming down his face.

"Statue di pietra, prego a Lei per la mia vita!" He petitioned the statues for a favor: his life.

Eddie braced for the next round of the bottomless, dimensionless nightmare. It didn't take long. A noise, like that of metal clanging against metal, spurred Eddie's senses. He directed the flashlight at the kneeling man, alert, even anxious, for the slightest provocation. He prepared to leap and pound him with the flashlight.

The man, never removing his gaze from the statues, waved pleadingly at Eddie to divert the flashlight beam away from him.

The would-be assassin's lower jaw hung open as if he beheld the inconceivable on the transept wall, or rather, *more* of the inconceivable on the transept wall.

Eddie shined the light on the statues again. The metallic sounds came from the iron chain connecting Saint Stephen's wrists, which had been shackled before he was stoned. The martyr raised his hands to his face and viewed the chain with the one eye not completely swollen shut—the victim's face was always a favorite target of those who cast the stones. Stephen seemed disoriented and annoyed, a hibernating bear waking from a long sleep. He looked around the church, then at Eddie and next at the kneeling man.

Stephen bent over and chose a grapefruit-sized stone from a pile at his feet. He stood and held the stone in front of him with the fingertips of both hands before raising it over his head. The chain between the martyr's hands rattled, the dominant noise in the church, the dominant noise on *Earth* at that moment. Stephen's expression, never exactly amiable, turned ferocious, retaliatory; his face darkened from its usual ashen gray to purple. The saint's robe of tattered sackcloth moved in ghostly slow motion as he trained his eye and stone on the kneeling ex-gunman a few yards distant.

Easy target. Guaranteed kill.

Eddie lowered the flashlight. The beam caromed off the floor and cast an immense image of Stephen onto the transept wall behind him. The saint's arms stretched to the church ceiling like telephone poles. The stone grew to the size of a beach ball. The kneeling man turned his gaze to the floor and picked up the pace of his prayers.

Eddie had a roar in his head, nothing associated with any thoughts, just a roar. His mind was a revolving door that whirled blindingly from nightmare to reality. The church seemed to be falling in on him, the air so charged with chaos as to be almost unbreathable.

"Nel nome del Padre, il Figlio e lo Spirito Santo, Dio per favore perdonami." The kneeling man, pathetic in his passivity, made the Sign of the Cross again and begged God's forgiveness in a weak, tearful voice. He remained bowed forward, apparently resigned to execution.

Eddie intervened. Not out of pity but because he had seen enough dream blood, enough dream death. He stepped between Saint Stephen and the gunman and raised an unsteady hand to arbitrate in boxer shorts with a very pissed-off animated monster of a statue.

"Don't! Please don't kill this man! *Per favore non uccida quest' uomo*!" In a halting voice, Eddie asked Stephen in two languages to show mercy.

Bad enough you think you see the statue moving, but now you're talking to it. In Italian even. What an idiot you are!

Saint Stephen's arms remained above his head, his wrists cocked to propel the stone. Unblinking eye shifted from kneeling victim to Eddie and back to victim. The saint began to roll the stone contemplatively in his fingertips.

The statue seemed to be thinking about it.

A moving statue was one thing but a moving, *thinking* statue elevated the horror in the church to an unendurable level. Eddie backed up to the communion rail and leaned against it to keep from collapsing. His stomach alternately churned and cramped. He resisted a great need to vomit.

Along with the kneeling ex-gunman, Eddie awaited the outcome of his petition to judge, jury and executioner. Graphic evidence of the statues' ability and willingness to kill lay only a few feet away. Nor was it lost on Eddie that the statues might not be happy until they had murdered everyone in the church, including himself. What singular death awaited him?

And if these three characters ran out of ideas, there were three more statues in the other transept and even a seventh, hidden away in the chapel. Each had different weaponry: beheading sword, butcher knife, flaming gridiron, disemboweling apparatus. Eddie's mind was alive with the possibilities.

After a few moments, Saint Stephen's face softened from predatory to the more familiar one Eddie recognized, a mix of displeasure and livid impatience with the world. The saint leaned over and replaced the stone back on the pile at his feet. He stood and returned to painted statue, not a fold of his garment out of place. Nothing belied Stephen's previous murderous intentions. Rainwater coming through the leaky roof splashed off the martyr's bald head, rolled down his beard and fell to the church floor in a mournful beat.

The gunman stayed on his knees for several minutes before raising his head to look at the statue. When he saw that Saint Stephen was again inanimate stone and paint, he fell prostrate in the filth on the church floor and began to sob. He prayed and gave thanks in Italian faster than Eddie could make out the words.

Eddie swung the flashlight beam across the three statues several times. No further movement. Only the statue of Saint Sebastian, oozing a too-red liquid from the wounds in which he had replaced the arrows and the too-red liquid on Saint Blaise's wool-combing hook alluded to their participation in the night's activities.

The foghorn of an ore boat making its way across nearby Lake Erie cut through the aftermath of bedlam in the Church of Martyrs like a cheap alarm clock. Pining and insistent, the horn smothered the spared man's prayers.

As the danger to Eddie's life ended, the merciful numbness that had accompanied his fear faded. He felt fully the pain in his cut and bruised feet. He shook in the cold, shook even more when he saw he was splattered with the blood of the two men who had joked of killing him. He winced at the stench of animal droppings in combination with the sickening-sweet essence of a century's worth of incense and burned beeswax. As well as another smell, the unfamiliar but unmistakable odor of fresh blood and slaughtered flesh.

The appalling carnage had not been a dream. Illusion surrendered to reality.

Unconditionally.

"No! Goddamnit! This can't be!" Eddie's voice bounced around the high walls of the empty Church of Martyrs. The physical and emotional volcano building within him erupted. Eddie dropped to his hands and knees and vomited a half-dozen times. He raised himself off the floor and limped on rubbery legs and cut feet toward the marble steps of the main altar.

The would-be killer, still flat on the church floor, looked at Eddie. He managed several mewling "*grazies*!"

Eddie replied with the first and only thing that came to mind: "Go to hell!"

TWO

Eddie brushed trash from the altar steps and sat down. As he tried to comprehend his experience with the statues, he addressed a more immediate problem: the kaleidoscope of glass slivers in his feet. He pulled at a large curved green shard which hurt more coming out than it had going in. He wiggled the throbbing black and blue toes of the foot that he had smashed into a statue plinth while running at full speed. To his relief, the toes were not only all still attached but responded, if sluggishly, to mental commands.

Now and then Eddie cast an unconcerned glance at his former attacker, who raised himself off the floor and backed away from the statues, his head bowed. He signed himself again, turned and walked slowly toward Eddie.

"Why did you want to kill me? Who are you?" Eddie said. His voice was calm; he was over the fear but not the resentment. "Do you speak English? *Parla Inglese*?"

The man didn't reply. He seemed interested only in silently adoring his deliverer, as if unworthy to speak in the presence of such a deserving person whom the very saints of heaven had rescued. Whom the very saints of heaven had *obeyed*! Eddie was about to inquire again, in Italian.

"I speak pretty good English. You save my life, *Signore. Grazie.*"

"Never mind the *grazie*. Tell me, why did you want to kill me?" Eddie shined the flashlight on the man's face.

"Is what I do, *Signore,*" apologetically, blocking the light with a hand.

"What are you, some kind of rent-a-killer? Are you an assassin? *Assassino*?"

The man nodded his head. Yes.

"You and your dead pals behaved more like clowns tonight than assassins."

"Even *assassino* need to have fun sometimes, *Signore.*"

"So do statues, apparently. Who sent you? Who wanted me killed?"

"I not know. I just do what I told, *Signore*. My friend Emile, the one killed with the...hook, he the boss. He the only one who know who want you dead. I just little fish."

"You didn't look like a little fish when you were shooting at that statue."

The man looked at Saint Blaise with remorse. "Please no remind the statue, *Signore.*"

"I'll remind anyone I want! Why are you even still here? Those statues don't seem to like you guys. I'd think you'd want to get as far away from this church as possible while they're on break. I can't stop you with these feet."

The man didn't answer. He tilted his shoulders back and pointed to the statues with a finger held close to his chest.

"So? What about them?" Eddie's voice rose.

"The statues want me to stay, *Signore.*"

"I didn't hear them say anything. Don't tell me they *talked* to you."

"With the eyes *Signore,* with the eyes. I not know why, but I know this is what they want. I want to run. Oh, how I want to run from this place. But I have to stay." He looked again at the statues and sighed in resignation to their fierce silent directive.

Eddie hissed against the pain as he drew a fragment of iridescent blue glass from the ball of his left foot; he shivered from the cold.

"You need some clothes, *Signore*. You freeze to death."

"Nice of you to care. I'm already frozen. Are you going to answer my questions?"

"I try, *Signore*. I try."

"Did you see those statues kill your two pals or am I going crazy?"

"You not crazy, *Signore*. I see it too. Poor Emile and Latillo!"

Except for the troubling recollection of the gunman mercilessly shooting a victim in the face at point-blank range, Eddie might have found the compact Italian comical, especially the mop of curly hair and overgrown mustache that wrapped his upper lip like an untrimmed shrub around the corner of a building. The killer's hardened mad-dog eyes, which had burned with premeditated malice when he took aim and fired at Saint Blaise, were now meek. No, more than meek: cowering. The transformation was nothing short of, well, *miraculous* was the word that came to mind. The wiry little guy was clearly not the same person who had entered the Church of Martyrs. Neither, thought Eddie, was he.

"The only thing I know for sure is that I'm alive—kind of—and those two men are dead," Eddie said. He glanced at the corpses and cringed. His gratitude to the statues was offset by lingering horror.

The gunman signed himself again in the direction of the dead bodies. "*Dio mostra misericordia*! You think God show Emile and Latillo mercy, *Signore*?"

"How should I know? The statues sure as hell didn't!"

"Will you give my friends the last *Sacramenti*?"

"What makes you think I could do that?" Angrily.

"You a priest. No?"

"How the hell do you know that?"

The gunman glanced nervously over his shoulder at the statues. He seemed fearful that Eddie's displeasure might summon them back into action.

"I know this from my friend Emile, the one killed with the..."

"Yeah, I know, the one killed with the hook," Eddie interrupted. "Who told him I was a priest?"

"I not know who tell Emile this."

"Well, I'm not a priest anymore."

"Why you live in the priest's house?"

"I run a women's shelter here. Not that it's any of your damned business."

"So you no can give *Sacramenti*?"

"No! I'm no longer licensed to do that stuff. I don't believe in it any more. It wouldn't count. Besides, those men tried to kill me."

"I try to kill you too but you talk to *Santo Stefano*. You ask him to spare me. You ask him 'no kill this man.' You ask him in Italian even. Remember?"

"Don't remind me. I might change my mind yet."

"You think the statue understand you English or you Italian? Probably you English. You Italian not so good."

"Yeah, like you English," Eddie mocked. "Quit trying to change the subject. Now, you don't know who wanted me dead. Fine. Who do you work for?"

The gunman started to answer but seemed unable to finish the sentence. "Please give me some time, *Signore*. When I tell you who I work for, it is my death sentence."

"Can't let that happen, can we?" said Eddie. "Do you know *why* someone wanted me dead?"

"I not know, *Signore,*" he answered hesitantly. The man stiffened. Somehow he knew his answer would end Eddie's patience. He was right.

Eddie exploded. "You don't know!? You mean you kill people and you don't even know why you do it or who in the hell you do it for!?" He vented everything: his brush with death, the unfathomable statues, the pain in his feet and, most recently, the little man's inadequate answers. Eddie's ranting alarmed the man, who again checked the statues. He fidgeted like a defendant whose trial wasn't going well.

"Quit worrying about those statues, I can't bring them to life. But I might try if I don't get some answers out of you." Eddie scanned both transepts. "Let's see, which one of the boys looks like he needs a little exercise? How 'bout Saint Bartholomew over there? That butcher knife he's holding looks pretty sharp. Shouldn't take him too long to skin a little guy like you."

Eddie whistled at Bartholomew like he was calling a dog. He made conjuring motions with his hands, all just to torment the man. It felt good.

"Please no make joke about statues, *Signore.*"

"Joke? Do you hear me laughing?"

"Please, *Signore*. You need me."

"Need you?" Eddie roared. "For what? Why would I need *you*? Why would I need a sawed-off greenhorn who doesn't know anything?"

"I not know *why* you need me, I just know you need me."

The man's apparent remorse and sincerity played on Eddie. He relented a bit. "As soon as I can walk on these feet and work up an acceptable story, I'm going to the rectory and call the cops. That doesn't scare you?"

"I afraid of nothing, *Signore.* Except the statues. They want me to stay. I no leave."

"If you fear nothing and you want to stay, then you're going to *have* to talk to me, damnit! I'll ask you again: whom do you work for? You *must* know that!"

The little man rubbed his eyes, stalling for time. He looked at the statues and whispered, *"La Mano di Cristo, Signore."*

The answer was so faint that Eddie couldn't hear it against the background of the rain.

"What? I didn't hear you. Speak up!"

"La Mano di Cristo," the man repeated, a bit louder than before but still in a whisper.

Eddie stopped picking at glass while he rolled the Italian words around in his mouth. "*La Mano di Cristo*? The Hand of Christ? Is that supposed to mean something to me? What're you talking about?"

"*La Mano di Cristo* is what I am...was, *Signore*."

"Never heard of it. The Hand of Christ? Sounds like something the Knights of Columbus would dream up. Is that it? Are you with the K of C, the entertainment committee maybe? I mean, after all, you guys were pretty damned funny."

"No entertainment, *Signore*. Just death, murder—*di morte violenta*."

"Who runs this...*La Mano di Cristo*?"

"Please no get mad when I tell you. Okay?"

"Go ahead, try me."

"Is the Church." Again in a whisper.

"The Church!? As in the *Catholic* Church?"

"Si. Chiesa Cattolica."

"The Catholic Church has assassins?"

"Si." With an Italian shrug.

"You're nuts! *Matto*!" said Eddie.

"I swear on the saints, *Signore*."

"That kind of talk can get your ass killed around this place. Have you forgotten already?"

"I no forget. Please, *Signore*. You ask and I tell you. *La Mano di Cristo* is what I am. What I *was* until *Santo Stefano* spare me."

"How come I've never heard of this *La Mano di Cristo*?"

"Very secret, *Signore*. Very old, very dangerous. Be happy you never hear of it before. Be sorry you hear of it now."

Eddie paused for a moment to consider the notion of such a secret organization. There were way too many holes in the story, chief among them the idea of killing on the whims of the Church.

"How does your *La Mano di Cristo* justify murder for the Church?"

"Dispensa, Signore." Again in a whisper.

"Quit whispering! The rats aren't going to tell anyone. *Dispensa*? As in dispensation for your sins? And who, if I may ask, gave you this dispensation to kill?"

"Il Papa."

"The pope? The new pope? Celestine the Sixth? He gave you dispensation to kill me? He's supposed to be a pretty nice guy. Wants to give away all the Church's money. I don't buy it."

"No, no. Not new pope, *Signore*. Pope who live many hundred years ago give *dispensa* to *La Mano di Cristo*. For all time."

Eddie knew that popes during the Crusades had granted blanket dispensation for mayhem and murder to crusaders engaged in winning back the Holy Land for Mother Church. They were free to kill anyone in their path who was not a Christian and even Christians if they disagreed with the pope—*especially* if they disagreed with the pope. Eddie allowed that long before the Crusades, during the Church's formative years, it certainly would have been handy to have a discreet, swift and conclusive method of dealing with enemies.

And Eddie knew the rules: if a pope had once granted dispensation to a secret society of assassins, it would still be in effect since a pope's infallibility and dictates are eternal.

"You hurt bad, *Signore*? You feet bleed a lot."

"I'll live. Tell me more about *La Mano di Cristo*."

"I already tell you everything I know, *Signore*."

"My brother, my twin brother, died a week ago from food poisoning in Rome," said Eddie. "His name was Donald Russo. His funeral is in a few hours here in Cleveland. He was a priest, worked at the Vatican Bank. You boys have anything to do with that?" Eddie didn't want to believe his brother's death was anything but accidental. He readied for whatever answer he might receive. He would not have been surprised by anything.

"You brother die in Rome? Oh, no, *Signore*, I know nothing about you brother. I swear on my life, on *Santo Stefano*!"

Eddie considered the answer. Everything the man said so far was perplexing and unacceptable. But Eddie could not understand why the killer, who came so close to leaving his brains on the church floor, would lie within view, earshot and a stone's throw of some very irked statues.

"How big is this Hand of Christ gang?"

"*La Mano di Cristo* around the world. But in small group only, just three men. Sometimes we meet other group, work together. We never learn names of others. Emile say we go today to Mexico, to Mexico City. We meet other *La Mano di Cristo*. Some new job. Big job, he say."

"What's going on in Mexico City? No, wait, let me guess. You...don't...know!" Very sarcastically, emphasizing each word with rising voice and finger jab in the direction of the man's face.

"You right, I not know."

"Of course you don't!"

Eddie stood and tested his feet one at a time. "I've got to go call the police and get dressed. I can't stop you from leaving if you want to. You're too damned nuts to ever be convicted anyway."

"I stay here."

"Oh, I forgot. The statues *told* you to stay. And, besides, I *need* you," Eddie scoffed. "Stay if you like. Incidentally, how is it a bad ass like you knows that the statue that wanted to bean you is Saint Stephen?"

"I good Catholic, *Signore*." Proudly. "All *La Mano di Cristo* good Catholic. We do what we do because it is right for the Church. But now I not so sure. I know about *San Sebastiano* and the arrows and *Santo Stefano* and the stones. What is name of the other one, the one with the...hook?"

"Blaise, *San* Blaise to you. What's *your* name?"

"My name Sergio Beneviaggio."

"You're kind of small for a killer, aren't you...Sergio Beneviaggio? Eddie realized after he said it how stupid the observation must have sounded.

"*Assassino* come in all sizes, *Signore*. Everyone no can be tall like you."

The man's simple earnestness began to disarm Eddie. This Sergio guy could have passed for an extra in a Renaissance painting, an awed bystander witnessing a biblical event from the corner of the canvas. Eddie sensed that, for the time being at least, he was stuck with him, like it or not. After all, what was the word of a jaded ex-priest compared to that of sainted martyrs? Eddie smiled without meaning to.

"Why you smile, *Signore*?"

"I was just thinking what a lousy night this has been for us cynics."

"I no understand."

"I no understand either," Eddie aped. "Tell me, when the boys from *La Mano di Cristo* mob learn I'm not dead, will they try again?"

Sergio nodded. "They come back. Kill me for sure. You safe. The statues protect you."

"You're sure about that, are you?"

"I sure, *Signore*."

"Well, in the meantime, I'm going to have to trust the somewhat less dramatic Cleveland Police Department. Eddie completed glass-testing his feet with a halting, springy dance. He started to leave for the rectory when he spotted someone standing at the open side door of the church. The figure, silhouetted by streetlamps in front of the church on Brewer Avenue, seemed hesitant to enter. Or waiting in ambush.

THREE

"Looks like bad news travels fast among the Hand of Christ gang. Is that another one of you goons?" Eddie asked Sergio in a muted, confrontational voice. He pointed to the side door.

"No, *Signore*. Only three of us. I not know who that be."

"Are you positive?"

"I swear on *Santo Stefa...*"

"Okay, okay, don't start that again. I'm going out the sacristy window. I'll circle around the church. You move in on him from inside and we'll nail the bastard. Cabeesh?" Eddie handed Sergio the flashlight. "Can I count on you?"

"Now and always," Sergio said. He slipped the flashlight into his side coat pocket, reached into another pocket and produced a switchblade. He opened the blade with an expert motion that made Eddie very glad the little guy was on his side. He hoped. Not as awe-inspiring as a seven-foot rampaging statue, but he'd do for now.

Eddie worked his way on tiptoes behind the altar, like a circus poodle trained to walk on its back paws. He entered the sacristy, climbed outside through a window conveniently removed by neighborhood vandals and circled the church. Frigid rain mixed with sleet felt like needles on his bare skin. He licked at the revitalizing water and gloried in Cleveland's March weather at its persistent worst. Even the pain in his feet felt strangely comforting, a reminder that he was still alive. Temporarily, at least.

Eddie reached the corner of the church and peeked around. The solitary figure remained motionless at the side door. Eddie took a deep breath and covered the distance to the late-night visitor in a few hobbled steps. Not in a mood to hold back, he delivered his best below-the-knees tackle. He knocked the stranger to the ground so easily that he thought he might have received increased power from his earlier experience.

"Caught you, you bastard!" Eddie yelled. He got set to deliver a string of blows the way he did in his youth when he had been goaded into a fight.

Sergio raced to his aid but the fight ended before it began, as soon as Eddie realized that the body under him was far too yielding, the waist too small, the chest too...*female.*

Oh shit! Will this night never end?

"Get off me, you son-of-a-bitch!" A handful of fingernails found Eddie's arm and a foot caught him square in the groin as he stood.

"Ahhh," Eddie groaned. He pulled up his boxer shorts, which had fallen to half-mast.

"I'm sorry, lady, really I am," Eddie said in a reedy voice, pulling up his shorts. The new pain in his groin made him forget his other injuries.

"Stay away from me!" the woman said. She stood and backed away. She spotted Sergio, who took up a position behind her, knife in hand. She made a move for the street in front of the church.

"Don't let her out on the street! And get rid of that knife!" Eddie said. He wasn't sure who the woman was but didn't want her alone on the streets of Briggs Hill in the middle of the night.

Sergio dropped the knife and ran after the woman. He grasped her shoulders from behind and received a sharp elbow in the chest for his efforts. She broke free and bolted for the street. Sergio ran her down again.

"Please, no go on street. Is not safe. We not hurt you. Come back, please."

The woman seemed to consider her options for a few moments. She stopped resisting Sergio and allowed him to lead her by the arm back to Eddie.

"I suppose I don't have much choice but to take my chances with you lunatics," she said to Eddie, who stood outside the door of the church, blocking the entrance. "Maybe you aren't smart enough to get out of this rain but I am!"

The woman made a move to enter the church. Sergio stopped her. He took the flashlight from his pocket, switched it on and aimed it at her. It proved a provocation. She pulled the light away from Sergio with such insistence that he let her take it. She shined the light first on Sergio then on Eddie.

"Lady, please believe me, you have nothing to fear here," Eddie said.

"Then get out of my way. I'm getting out of the rain."

"Let's go to the rectory," Eddie said. "It's just a short walk."

"This will do fine for now," she said. She walked around Eddie and entered the church. He and Sergio followed. Eddie considered taking the flashlight from her but the weapon-like way she held it made him think better of the idea. She'd probably hit him on the head with it. He had sustained enough injuries for one night. Maybe she wouldn't see anything.

"Why did you knock me down?" she asked once inside. She seemed more inquisitive than frightened.

"We had a little, uh, trouble here tonight and I thought you were someone else. Sorry about the tackle. May I ask why *you're* here?" Eddie said, shaking rain out of his long dark hair while trying to act nonchalant.

"I was looking for the women's shelter. The cab driver told me that this was the closest shelter he knew about. Is this the women's shelter?"

Eddie's face brightened at the mention of the women's shelter. "But this *is* the women's shelter, the Church of Martyrs Women's

Shelter. I'm the director. This man here is my...assistant. The shelter's located at the back of the courtyard in the old convent."

"Do you welcome all the women like this?"

"No, not at all. Actually, you're the first to show up since we opened a week ago."

"I can see why you don't have any other women here. I could have gone back to my ex-husband if I wanted to get knocked over. This is my first time at a shelter but I would say there's room for improvement."

"No argument there," Eddie said.

"You still haven't told me why you're running around in the rain sneaking up on people in the middle of the night in silly blue-striped boxer shorts," she said.

"Like I said, we had a little trouble in the church, a break-in. I had to leave the rectory in a hurry to investigate. Later, when I saw you standing at the side door, I thought *you* were sneaking up on *us*."

"Break in? Are you kidding? Who'd want to break into this place? Dracula?"

Eddie ignored the question. "Let's go over to the rectory where I can get some clothes and call the police."

Eddie's impatience to leave the church seemed to pique the woman's interest. She shined the flashlight around the trashed interior. Rats squealing over the Comedian's body drew her attention. She aimed the light at the sounds.

"Please don't do that," Eddie said.

"Is that what I think it is?"

"Yes, it is. It's a dead body. It would be best if you didn't see any more," Eddie said. He made a move for the flashlight. She swung it out of reach. Again, he decided not to push the flashlight issue.

"Lady, come to the rectory. I'll call you a cab—on me!—and send you over to another shelter. There's one a few miles from here on Lorain Avenue. I worked there before I opened my own shelter. Nice people, not like Sergio and me. Lot better neighborhood. Food's better, too. They have an indoor pool!"

The woman did not respond to Eddie's offer. She redirected the flashlight beam, which next illuminated the Wheezer's body stuck in the confessional door.

"There's another one! What happened to these people?"

"They killed each other," Eddie said, too quickly. "Got in a fight and killed each other. They were professional bad asses, probably drug guys. No great loss, frankly."

"They killed each other? How convenient! So how did you get splashed with so much blood?"

"Lady, please. Don't get yourself involved. Trust me, you really don't want to know anything more about what happened here."

The woman by chance swung the light on the statues of Stephen, Blaise and Sebastian, igniting flashes of tortured madness in jeweled eyes set into bleached, distorted faces. Viewed from the low angle, the statues seemed to hover above their plinths like raptors. The woman's mouth dropped open and she stepped back. She seemed to forget the dead bodies for the moment.

Eddie had seen the reaction many times. Cynical and faithful alike had always balked at first contact with the scowling, brutalized icons of the Church of Martyrs, especially at night. The woman moved closer. She studied the statues with the flashlight. Her breathing quickened. She seemed unable to break away. Yet another victim, Eddie thought, of the old statues' unaccountable seductiveness.

"These are some very strange statues," she said.

"I agree, *Signora*," Sergio said.

"You have no idea how strange," Eddie said in a choppy voice. The muscles across his stomach pulsated. "Look, lady, I've got to go to the rectory and call the police."

"Then quit talking about it and go! And put some clothes on while you're at it. Bring back an umbrella if you really want to help."

Tired of arguing with the woman and fearful that the weather might accomplish what *La Mano di Cristo* had failed to do, Eddie left. He hollered over his shoulder at Sergio, "Keep your mouth shut about you-know-what! Cabeesh?"

Outside, the rain once again refreshed Eddie's brain and allowed him to better assess the situation. An unwieldy equation to be sure, this mix of ex-priest, lethal statues and three members of *La Mano di Cristo,* make that two dead paid-up members and one ex-member with title to the quickest metamorphosis to virtue since Saul. Eddie fought a nagging, unanswered anxiety and tried to convince himself that his brother's recent death in Italy was not part of the same equation.

Eddie called the police from the downstairs phone in the rectory. To keep them from showing up too quickly, he reported a break-in. He did not mention the dead bodies. The police would find them soon enough. They would take their time responding to a break-in in an abandoned church. He lied only because he needed the extra time to get the stubborn woman out of the church. He went upstairs to wash.

As Eddie cleaned away the blood and filth, he looked out the bathroom window at the Church of Martyrs, which he now and then cruelly referred to as "a dead church too damned big to bury." Unable to find the bottle of iodine that had fallen out of the medicine cabinet at least once a day for the fifteen or so years he had lived there, he splashed *Old Spice* aftershave on the cuts. It made him admire mystics who walked on hot coals. He slapped on some Band Aids, dressed in the warmest clothes he could find, dug up an umbrella among the tons of junk fighting a space war in the rectory and rushed back to the church.

The woman appeared agitated. "What about these statues?"

"Sergio, what did you tell her?" Eddie said in a disgusted voice. He fought with the umbrella for a few seconds then gave up and threw it unclosed to the floor. He glowered like the statues at Sergio, waiting for an answer.

"Not too much, *Signore.*"

"When you left, this man became terrified of the statues," the woman said.

"Serves him right!" said Eddie. "Did he say anything?"

"He said the statues like him a little bit but they like you very much," said the woman. "What the hell is he talking about?"

"Sergio doesn't know what he's saying. He's had a bad scare, that's all. And he's about to have another one if he doesn't keep quiet."

"I know what I see, *Signora,*" said Sergio, who calmed down after Eddie reentered the church.

"Sergio, please shut up! If not for me, then for your old buddy *Santo Stefano,*" Eddie said. He turned to the woman. "You have a choice: stay here or let me get you a cab and send you to another shelter."

"I want to hear more about these statues," she said.

"Are you serious!?" said Eddie. "There's two dead bodies over there and you want to hear about statues?"

"Yes! And don't ask why, I just do," she said. "Your friend told me you know all about them."

"Thanks a lot, Sergio," said Eddie, who watched the woman move closer to the statues, the flashlight beam leading the way.

"Be careful," Eddie said, wryly.

"Why?"

"Some of the parishioners believed that the statues would steal your soul, or something like that, if they caught you staring at them."

"I can't imagine anyone staring for very long. What kind of a church was this?"

"You have to ask? Catholic, of course. Only a Catholic church in an Italian neighborhood would have tolerated statues that dispensed guilt like a candy machine."

"Did these men ever exist?" the woman said. "Did they really die this way?"

Okay stubborn lady, a real quick tour and then your butt is out of here. If I have to carry you!

Eddie began the way he once did for the Church of Martyrs' school children, perpetually fascinated by the grisly methods employed in the saints' martyrdoms.

"This guy is Saint Stephen. He was the first of Christ's followers to be martyred. He was shackled, then stoned to death. The one in the middle is Saint Blaise. They tore Blaise's flesh from his body with iron hooks used for combing wool. The extreme torture was meant to deter others from becoming Christians."

"It would have given me second thoughts, that's for sure," she said.

The woman stepped in front of Sebastian. She moved the flashlight beam up and down the saint's arrow-bristled body. Shoulder-length tousled hair framed a handsome face too grave and angry for someone so young, a face steeled against suffering by the power of faith and obsession, the essential and inseparable ingredients of martyrdom. Sebastian was nude except for a gauzy loincloth, which gave the statue a carnal quality some parishioners had found objectionable, even wicked. The martyr stood defiantly upright and unconquered on arrow-pierced legs, an act of will that even in stone and paint seemed beyond heroic, beyond human.

"Who is this?" she said.

"This is Saint Sebastian," said Eddie. "He was Emperor Diocletian's personal protector. His charity to the poor tipped off the emperor that Sebastian had converted to Christianity. Diocletian had him shot with arrows; the archers were told to prolong death as long as possible to give Sebastian time to renounce Christ. The arrows didn't kill Sebastian so they beat him to death. Witnesses said he never so much as flinched."

"The world could use more men like this," said the woman, whose expression told Eddie that, while perhaps intrigued and stirred, she did not entirely understand the motivation for such morbid self-sacrifice. Eddie watched, startled, as she reached up and touched the martyr's foot.

"What made you do that?" Eddie said.

"I don't know. I guess there's something about this old church that makes everyone a little crazy."

"That would be true of *all* churches," Eddie cracked.

"How come you know so much about the statues?"

"I was once in the statue business." Exhaustedly.

"You *still* in the statue business, *Signore*," Sergio said. "We now *both* in the statue business."

"You're welcome to my share of the business, Sergio."

Eddie turned to his first potential client. "Lady, you really shouldn't be in the church when the police get here. It wouldn't do much for your anonymity. Speaking of which, what's your name? You don't have to tell me if you don't want to."

"My name's Pat, Pat Adams. Do you have a name or should I just bow my head and call you '*Signore*?'"

"Gimme a break! My name's Eddie, Eddie Russo."

"Sorry, but I couldn't resist," she said.

Eddie noticed that the woman's eyes, so distrusting when she arrived, had acquired a splash of sparkle. He attributed the improvement to Sebastian and envied the saint's way with the ladies.

"Are you staying?" Eddie asked.

"Yes. I'm not sure why, but I want to stay," Pat said. "I must be as crazy as you two! Besides, it's late and I'm worn out."

Eddie picked up the umbrella and escorted Pat to the shelter, located in what had once been the convent of the Carmelite nuns who taught at the Church of Martyrs elementary school, also long closed. He angled the umbrella against the rain and slowed his pace to allow the woman to keep up with his broader strides.

"How's the feet?" she asked. "Your friend told me they were cut pretty bad."

"They hurt like hell."

"You should get a tetanus shot."

Eddie was pleased that the woman seemed concerned. He didn't have a woman in his life. He had been too busy working with women to meet one.

"So I'm your first customer, huh?" said Pat.

"That you are. To be honest, I wasn't sure we'd ever get a client. This part of Cleveland is getting a little rough but it never occurred to me to open my shelter anywhere else. I was raised here. I love this neighborhood, even though some people thought it was a less than ideal place for a women's shelter."

"That's because they didn't have some violent bastard chasing them. This is a perfect location."

"Well, I'm glad you decided to stay. No suitcase?"

"I'm traveling light. I didn't think my ex would find me where I was staying. When he did, I left in a hurry. You have no idea how dangerous and persistent he is."

"They always are," said Eddie.

They reached the convent and carefully climbed the worn sandstone steps, made slick by the rain.

"Welcome to the Russo Hilton. No room service, valet parking or cable but cozy. Free tours of a haunted church included," Eddie said with a flourish. He opened the front door of the two-story building and led the woman down a highly-polished brown and white tiled hallway he had scrubbed for a week to resurrect after years of disuse. Eddie stopped at a thermostat and turned on the heat before taking Pat to her room.

"There's a high wall around three sides of this building and a stout front door. It's very secure. You're not afraid to stay here alone, are you?"

"I'll just have to hope those big bad statues like me as much as your little friend in the church claims they like you," Pat said teasingly.

"I can't think of any reason why the statues wouldn't like you." Eddie surprised himself by his uncharacteristic openness with a woman and quickly changed the subject. "You'll find all kinds of donated clothes and other things you might need in a room down the hall. There's even a brand-new Cleveland *Indians* sweatshirt in there if you happen to be a fan. And who isn't? Sweet dreams."

"Thank you, Eddie," she said.

"Don't mention it. I'll be leaving about nine a.m., if the cops are through by then. I have a funeral to attend. I should be back by early afternoon. There's some food in the kitchen at the end of the hall. I don't think you'll have to worry about Sergio bothering you. I have a feeling that he'll be gone by daylight at the latest."

"Tell me one thing before you go," Pat said.

"What's that?"

"Is your life always this exciting?"

Eddie took some comfort in the fact that the woman didn't know how dull and bungling his life had been before that evening.

"Sorry to disappoint you...Pat, but I've never even been to Disneyworld. The most excitement I've ever had, or ever hope to have, took place an hour ago in that old church."

FOUR

The first uncertain light of day entered the Church of Martyrs through a wall of broken and cracked stained-glass windows, one of which depicted pagan torturers yanking Saint Apollonia's teeth with horrifyingly large forceps preparatory to throwing her on a fire raging in the background. The doomed Apollonia, patron saint of toothache sufferers, did not resist. She clasped her hands in prayer, held her mouth open and accepted her persecution with eyes trained on heaven.

The morning light also fell on a more recent scene of painful death. The guilty parties had not fled but stood unrepentant on statue plinths no more than thirty feet from the corpses.

Yellow crime tape closed off the area around the confessional. A half-dozen police officers dodged vine-like silver strands of rainwater falling through the church roof. They collected evidence of everything on the scene. All took a few moments to study the unusual statues in the transepts.

Homicide detective Lieutenant Nick Piccione was in charge of the investigation. Like Eddie, Nick was a son of Briggs Hill; he grew up within sight of the Church of Martyrs bell tower. Nick had been baptized, made his first communion, was confirmed and married in the church. His grandparents and parents were buried in the adjacent cemetery. Nick hadn't moved his family to the suburbs like many of the other Italian residents of the neighborhood. He still lived in the small clapboard bungalow where the Picciones had lived since Nick's bricklayer grandfather immigrated to the United States in 1900.

Not a sentimental person normally, Nick made an exception when it came to the neighborhood. He took over the case when he learned that his friend Eddie was involved. Nick made the newspaper and television reporters, lured to the scene by the irresistible irony of two men killed in an abandoned church, stand outside in the cold rain. They waited and bitched.

Nick had stopped talking to reporters several years before, not because they misquoted him but because they quoted him all too accurately. He was a cop who said what he thought. He never hid behind the choppy, guarded semi-sentences of modern lawmen. Nick exempted himself from the constraints of all forms of political correctness. He considered himself grandfathered to the old police ways due to his long service on the force.

"Any reporters get inside this church, shoot 'em!" were the instructions from the engagingly flippant and always outrageous Lieutenant Piccione to his men.

At the first mention of killer statues, Nick stopped his questioning of Eddie and Sergio, who had not run away as Eddie had expected. The three moved to a rear corner of the church and settled in the last pew, as far out of eavesdrop range as possible. Eddie was glad Nick was handling the killings, even though it made for a much more difficult situation. With anyone else, Eddie would have made up a story, a real whopper. But he told Nick the truth.

Not that he expected Nick, or anyone else in the world, to believe it.

"Oookay, old buddy, ya had your little joke for today," Nick said, rubbing a hand through his thinning hair. "Now let's start over. This time leave out the statues."

Eddie, distracted by the Church of Martyrs interior as it came to life in the morning light, did not answer. He had not been in the church for many years before he entered it earlier that morning one step ahead of three killers. The church was darker inside than most, seemingly an atmosphere of planned melancholy. Murals honoring martyrs who had endured the stake, the rack, wild animals and worse—much worse!—for a faith Eddie no longer possessed lined the walls. A forest of marble columns drew Eddie's gaze upward to the partly-cloudy heaven painted in the dome above the main altar, the sublimity of the experience compromised by peeling paint and a leaky roof. In the center of the dome an artist had made a plucky attempt at painting God the Father seated on a throne among the clouds, his face as Italian as Nick's or Eddie's.

"Amazing how that artist knew God was Italian, ain't it?" said Nick, looking upward with Eddie.

"The Old Testament prophets may have broken the news to the world about God but he didn't have a face until we Italians gave him one," said Eddie.

"The statues, too, they look Italian. They even express themselves with their hands like we do," Nick said.

"I hate to trample your cherished beliefs Nick, but those men were from many different countries. You don't suppose their appearance could have something to do with the fact that they were carved by an Italian sculptor, do you?"

"You complicate things too much, Eddie. You always did. You'd make a lousy detective. The trick in this life is to keep things simple. It saves your brain."

"I'll work on it," Eddie said, giving in as he always did in discussions with Nick.

"Okay, you've stalled long enough, Eddie. Now back to those two dead sons o' bitches."

"Nick, with anyone else I would invent some wild story, something worthy of even you. And though I know you'll never believe me, I want to tell you exactly what happened. The statues came alive and killed those two men!"

Nick stared pityingly at his old friend.

"At least listen to the entire story before you call for a straight-jacket," Eddie said.

Nick agreed. He listened with eyebrows arched high in disbelief as Eddie matter-of-factly related the details of the killings, *La Mano di Cristo* and even Sergio's alleged papal *dispensa* tale that condoned murder for the good of Mother Church.

"Eddie, you haven't been using drugs have you?" Nick said. "You've been through some bad times lately, what with Donnie's death and all."

"No drugs, Nick. I've told you what happened just the way it happened. I don't lie, you know that."

"That's what scares me," Nick said. He scratched his sizable stomach, which he proudly called his "million dollar pasta and beer bank."

"We've known each other since we were kids, Nick. I know what I saw and I just told you." Eddie said. "For cryin' out loud, doesn't the evidence speak for itself?"

"I gotta' admit whoever iced those two dudes was original. But let's see if I understand what you've said so far: you fell asleep on the downstairs couch in the rectory." With a snicker, Nick changed the subject in mid-thought, one of his less endearing charms. "You weren't drinking, were you? You never were much of a drinker, Eddie. Remember that time at the Knights of Columbus picnic...?"

"Let's get this over with, Nick," Eddie said.

"Okay. Then you say these guys came into the rectory. One of them made a hell of a lot of noise and woke you up."

"My friend, Emile," Sergio said. "He got the big mouth."

"What? What'd you say," Nick asked Sergio sharply. Nick disliked being interrupted, except by himself.

"My friend, Emile, he make loud jokes, wake up *Signore* Eddie."

"I'll get to you next, Luigi. Meantime, keep your mouth shut!" Nick said. He turned to Eddie. "So anyway, since the killers figured you were in bed upstairs, it gave you a chance to run outside. You wound up in the church, which was bad enough, but then you hid in the confessional? And it never occurred to you that a confessional is a lousy place to hide? It ain't like you didn't spend a lot of Saturdays hearing confessions in there. Including mine. By the way, now that you ain't a priest anymore, are my sins still privileged information? You know, like a lawyer?"

"Don't worry, Nick. I could never hate the world enough to unleash your evildoing on it," Eddie said. "Getting back to the subject, no, I can't explain exactly why I entered the church *or* the confessional."

"The saints make you go into church and confessional, *Signore,*" Sergio offered.

Sergio's unsolicited analysis drew more disparaging attention from Nick. "Listen, you little dago, you better keep your mouth shut and start praying to those statues that I don't shoot you right now for trying to hurt my friend."

"Nick, lay off Sergio," Eddie said. "It was a very screwed-up night. Maybe the statues somehow *did* put me in that confessional."

"Okay, okay, we'll assume for the time being that the statues picked you up and stuck you in the confessional," Nick said. He checked over his shoulder and backed off an officer who had overheard them and tried to edge closer. "You should have taken the pistol I tried to give you that time. Then you wouldn't need any help from statues. I got plenty of clean heaters if you want one, including the one I picked up off the church floor when I walked in this morning. Belonged to your new buddy, Luigi."

"His name's Sergio. And keep your guns, Nick. You need them more than I do."

"Anyhow, while you hid in the confessional you heard a lot of noises and stuff and when you came out two guys were dead. One of them was shredded like Romano cheese by Saint Blaise and the other turned into a door knocker with arrows shot by Saint Sebastian. Is that right?"

Eddie smiled at his old friend's unfailing knack for making light of bad situations. "For the record, Sergio told me he saw Sebastian *throw* the arrows. The statue doesn't have a bow."

"Well, pardon me. At any rate, Saint Sebastian then came down from his pedestal and took his arrows back. I can understand that. A smart killer never leaves a weapon at the scene. Besides, arrows are expensive. I lost a dozen of the damned things last fall hunting in Michi..."

"Nick, can we please finish this? I've got a funeral to attend. Remember?"

"Okay, okay. Now, where were we?" Nick said. "Oh, by the way, did you know that the Mafia uses a picture of Saint Sebastian in their initiation? Yeah, no bullshit. They set it on fire and the guy being made has to hold it in his hand. Supposed to remind him how hot things will get for him if he screws the mob. Interesting, huh?"

"Have you ever had a complete thought in your life, Nick?"

"Can't remember one. Anyway, Saint Blaise climbed back on his pedestal after he tore up the other guy with...what did you call that? Some kind of hook?"

"A wool-combing hook, Nick," Eddie said in a tired voice. "It's what they used to execute Saint Blaise. They tore his body apart with it. Don't you remember the story?"

"That's right Eddie, *story,* they were just *stories.* You're the last person in the world I would think would believe them. Remember what you told me in the bar that night you decided to leave the priesthood? You said the whole religion thing was nothing more than a piss-poor magic trick because no one ever managed to pull anything out of the hat. Now you're telling me statues moved!"

"I remember that night well," said Eddie. "Near the end of my days as a priest I felt like a magician without any skills who had to rely on the audience's fear of hell to make it stay for the rest of the show."

"You shoulda' had the statues warm up the audience first with some tap-dancing or juggling," said Nick as he watched a forensic photographer snap pictures of the bodies. The Comedian appeared to float in a pool of rainwater and blood. The Wheezer remained planted in the splintered confessional door. A cop shooed away a hungry crop of early spring flies from the bodies.

"Geez, what a penance those guys got! And to think I used to get pissed at old Father Louis when he gave me thirty Hail Marys for chokin' my chicken," Nick said.

Eddie laughed dryly at his friend's irreverence. Nick was a few years older than he and had been his neighborhood hero when they were growing up. Nick was leader of the fabled *Dago Bombers,* the Briggs Hill gang of their youth that Eddie had never been tough enough to join.

Nick pointed to Sergio. "And why do you suppose the statues didn't kill this third little wop? They got some kind of union thing about only two killings on a shift? Or maybe their victims have to be a minimum height. You know, like you have to be to ride the coasters at Cedar Point."

Eddie saw that Sergio was about to speak and stopped him short with a look. He knew Sergio was anxious to relate the story of how his *own* hero, *Signore* Eddie, had called off Saint Stephen with just a few words.

"Exactly why they didn't kill Sergio is just one of many questions for which I don't have an answer," Eddie said, wanting to avoid the lecture he'd surely get from Nick for his intervention on Sergio's behalf.

"Eddie, I can't write any of this down. For Chris' sake, think of the field day those damned reporters would have with my report. Can't keep anything from those guys anymore. I can see the headline in the *Plain Dealer* already: 'STATUES TWO, BAD GUYS ZIP!' And then every religious nut within a thousand miles is going to want his picture taken with the statues. 'Course, maybe we could sell tee shirts and little wind-up saints. Maybe I could retire."

"It's really not all that funny, Nick."

Nick put a cigarette in his mouth. He struggled with the lighter. "I'd like to shoot the no good son-of-a-bitch that dreamed up these kid-proof lighters."

"Obviously the brainchild of a non-smoker," said Eddie, a dedicated and occasionally vocal tobacco hater.

"You think it's okay to smoke in here now that it ain't a real church anymore?" Nick had prevailed with the lighter. "How 'bout swearing? Maybe I shouldn't be swearing in here either, huh?"

"Smoke yourself to death. See if I care. And frankly, say anything you want in this church. Don't look to me for dispensation. Ask the new pope."

"He's too busy trying to give away all the Church's money. Wish he'd send some my way. Who deserves a handout more than a Cleveland cop?" Nick said. "Speaking of dispensation, you really believe your little friend's story about having an okay from some past pope to murder people? The sleaziest lawyer in Cleveland couldn't sell *that* to a jury. Not that he wouldn't try."

"The Catholic Church has had many enemies through the years," Eddie said. "I'm sure the need for professional services such as Sergio's would have come in handy from time to time. It's possible that an organization such as *La Mano di Cristo* exists. And if it does, is it any harder to believe that it was once given papal dispensation for murder? A lot of those old popes would be featured on post office walls if they were alive today."

"So you believe this guy?" Nick asked, pointing at Sergio with his cigarette, gruffly flicking an ash in his direction.

"The only thing I believe without a doubt is that Sergio would not lie about anything to me. Not today. Not in this church."

"Oh, sure, a killer would never lie."

"I not killer no more." Sergio defended himself. "And I no lie."

"Shut up, we ain't talking to you," Nick growled at Sergio out of the side of his mouth.

"Let up on Sergio, Nick. All he did was shoot at a statue. He'll never hurt anyone again."

"Yeah, right, and I'm gonna hit the lottery next week and tell the mayor to take this job and shove it in his rear end." Nick turned to Sergio. "Hey, Luigi, you got any idea who the head banana of this *La Nutso*...whatever organization is?"

"My name Sergio, Sergio Beneviaggio. I no understand head... banana?"

"Yeah, banana, the head banana, the boss."

"Only once do I hear something about the boss of *La Mano di Cristo*. Very dangerous man. Much money and power. He known as *morte domina*. That mean 'death boss.' I never see him."

"That's it? That's all you know?"

"He have a nickname, too."

"What would that be?" Nick asked, acting bored and making no effort to write down any of the information.

"When *morte domina* not around, he called *'Santo Cane.'* Funny, no?"

Nick wrestled with the nickname. His Italian was a little rusty.

"Saint Dog!" Eddie said.

"Huh?"

"*Santo Cane*! It means 'Saint Dog,'" Eddie repeated. "Must be a real peach of a guy."

"Saint This! Saint That! Next thing you know my palms will start bleeding and there'll be a weeping Virgin on my cop car window. Please, no more saints! I don't want to hear about no more saints today." Nick looked at Sergio. "Well, Luigi, this is your lucky day. Get your ass out of here."

"My name Sergio, not Luigi. I stay here. I no go."

"You here legally? You have a passport?" Threateningly.

"I have many passports."

"I'll bet. Not that you'd be the first killer our hospitable immigrations department welcomed into this country. Well, stay out of sight. *My* sight!"

Eddie didn't mention it to his blustery detective friend but he knew that the statues were the only things Sergio feared. Besides, Sergio had probably dealt with much tougher cops in his day than Nick Piccione.

Dismissed from the questioning, Sergio walked to the front of the church for a closer examination of the three statues in the south transept: Saint Bartholomew, Saint Lawrence and Saint Elmo.

Sergio stopped in front of Saint Bartholomew. Exposed ribbons of raw muscle and cartilage crisscrossed the martyr's body, covered minimally with a bloody death shroud. Enraged, baited-animal eyes bulged from a skinless face. Bartholomew's teeth were clenched to keep from screaming the disavowal of his faith that would have saved him from torture and death. The saint held out a butcher knife in his right hand. The knife represented the one with which the martyr had been skinned alive for the crime of being a Christian in the second century. The curved two-edged blade, sculpted from stone and painted seven hundred years before, appeared razor sharp. Saint Bartholomew seemed to challenge any and all to take the knife from his hand and match his manifest love of Jesus Christ.

Bartholomew's skin, olive-toned on one side, pinkish on the other, was draped over his left forearm like a raincoat. Discernible within the folds of the skin were a grieving mouth and tangled, blood-encrusted beard. Two elongated, expressive openings enabled the martyr to stare back at Sergio from *two* sets of eyes, both silently screaming the true zealot's indifference to consequence.

Diverting his stare to the floor, Sergio backed away from the statue. He bumped into Saint Lawrence's plinth, turned around and looked up.

Lawrence wore a black Passionist's robe engulfed in orange flames. A fiery red scapular hung from his neck. Peaked hood and sharp ascetic facial features made Lawrence appear more sorcerer than saint. Fanatical eyes set in a scorched face bore the fatal audacity he took to his death, remarking to executioners even as he roasted to "turn me over, this side is done." The saint's robe was gathered at the elbows, seared and blistered flesh on outstretched arms impossible to ignore.

Sergio touched Lawrence's symbolic flaming gridiron, placed at the martyr's feet. He took his hand away quickly as if he feared the painted stone flames might consume him.

Nick nudged Eddie and laughed out loud at Sergio's devout trepidation.

"That guy don't act like much of a killer," Nick jeered. "More like a rabbit. Whoever heard of anyone being scared of statues?"

"You had to be there, Nick," Eddie said. "You'd feel a lot differently. For the first time in your life, you'd have more questions than answers."

Sergio approached the statue of Saint Elmo. A bluish corona wreathed the martyr's tonsured head and face. The corona was meant to depict Saint Elmo's fire, the name early Christian sailors gave to the static electricity that trailed from masts, sails and lines during storms at sea. The sailors believed the blue lights to be torches from Elmo to guide them. It was a stretch. In fact, landlubber Elmo had only earned his arguable connection with the sea by having his intestines drawn out of his body and wound on a ship's capstan.

With his left hand, Elmo fed his intestines to the capstan which he held in the palm of his right. The saint, his eyes driven past sanity, bowed forward slightly at the waist, conceding to the agony. His lips were parted in what could just as easily have been a curse as an absolution, the last words of a vindictive mortal grappling with those of a forgiving saint.

Sergio backed away a few steps, directly under a waterfall of rain that poured through a hole in the roof. He paid no attention to the soaking as he rubbed his stomach.

"Your new friend is sure goofy," Nick said, slanting a look at Eddie and laughing.

Eddie didn't comment; nor was he amused. He had always considered the statues of the south transept more intimidating and their countenances far more representative of the grim realities of martyrdom than those of the three statues in the north transept that had come to his aid. Stephen, Blaise and Sebastian had always seemed to Eddie like the *nice* guys of the Church of Martyrs. He preferred not to dwell on what Bartholomew, Lawrence and Elmo and their disquieting instruments of martyrdom, their so-called "holy attributes," might have added to the show.

"Why don't you tell Luigi to peek into the chapel," Nick said. "Let him get a load of...what's his name?...the one holding his melon in his hand?"

"Saint Dionysius," Eddie answered. "I think Sergio has been scared enough."

Since Sergio didn't look in the small domed chapel located in the front corner of the church, he spared himself the spectacle of Saint Dionysius cradling his head in his left hand. In his right hand, the martyr clutched a red-stained broadsword. Known in legend as a *cephalophore,* or "head carrier," Dionysius was among a number of beheaded early Christian martyrs said to have carried their heads around after execution.

While the sculptor had used blood-red paint liberally on all the statues, he outdid himself on Dionysius. A frothy bloody geyser bubbled from the martyr's neck and ran down his nude body. Saint Dionysius' death had been mercifully swift and not prefaced by torture. His face, therefore, was not contorted like those of the others. The severed head, with eyes closed, seemed to be sleeping peacefully in the saint's hand, all the more chilling for its perceived serenity. Dionysius was deemed the most disturbing of the statues and had long ago been exiled to the seldom-used corner chapel, well out of sight of nervous parishioners.

The road to sainthood had been a rough one in the early days of the Church. The sculptor, whatever his reasons, had captured the dreadful reality with his seven creations. If the statues never moved again, it would be too soon for Eddie. He especially hoped he would never get the chance to see Saint Dionysius in action.

Eddie remembered how the French-American Gypsies once made annual pilgrimages to the Church of Martyrs to honor Dionysius, patron saint of France, on his feast day in October. They would crowd into the small chapel and kneel on the terrazzo floor for hours, praying and chanting in the quirky Romani language of the Gypsy.

Father Louis, pastor of the Church of Martyrs at the time, hated the Gypsies and dreaded their yearly visits. Father Louis had been born and raised in Italy. He brought to America the native Italian's mistrust of Gypsies, or *zingari*. Eddie smiled when he thought of how Father Louis would patrol the church while the gate-crashing *zingari* prayed to Saint Dionysius. Despite the pastor's best security measures, many items left with the Gypsy pilgrims each year. Votive candles, little red glass holders and all, were favorite souvenirs. One particularly fruitful year the Gypsies made off with the spare baptismal font.

Eddie also remembered, without a smile, a story Father Louis told many times about how the Gypsy women reached up with silk cloth and wiped tears from Dionysius' closed eyes. Father Louis always finished the story the same way: "Gypsy tricks! If Saint Dionysius cry, it only because he see how the evil *zingari* rob my church!"

There were the alleged healings, always children, never adults. According to the stories, the Gypsy women dabbed the tear-dampened cloth to the afflicted part of the body. Children who had entered the Church of Martyrs on the backs of their fathers walked out under their own power. Blind children left the church marveling and shrilling at their first sight of the world.

Eddie recalled how he had laughed at the stories, which he and everyone else in Briggs Hill chalked up to Gypsy chicanery. But hadn't fools always laughed at miracles? After all, miracles were something that only happened to pious farm girls at the site of future grand cathedrals in France, not in a poor parish in Cleveland, Ohio that could hardly pay the light bill. And certainly not to Gypsies inclined to loot the temple on the way out.

During his priest days Eddie had often preached the power of faith to accomplish miracles, yet he doubted miracles said to have occurred within sight of the pulpit.

"I'll kiss your ass on Public Square every time the light changes if that half-pint Luigi's still around by the end of the day," Nick said.

Nick's comment snapped Eddie back to the present. "You've been saying that since we were kids, Nick. Did you ever stop to think who'd want to collect on that stupid bet in the unlikely event you were ever wrong about anything? Who the hell would want you to kiss their ass on Public Square every time the light changed? Or even once in private, for that matter?"

"Hard to tell in these screwed-up times. Lots of real cute guys out there," said Nick, who took a close look at the old statues for the first time that day. "Ya know something? These statues could pass for a lot of the perps I deal with. Which one ya think is the scariest?"

"I don't know. None of them ever exactly put me at ease."

"Personally," said Nick, "Saint Bartholomew over there always spooked me the most, what with that big salami slicer and holding his hide and everything. Whew! Once, when we were kids, I came into the church to steal a quarter out of the Poor Box. After all, who was poorer than me? I had my hand on the two bits when I looked up and caught Bartholomew staring at me with those bulging eyes of his stuck on high-beam. I almost pissed my pants."

"Did you drop the quarter?"

"Bet your ass I did! But that doesn't mean I believe your story. Besides, I found out later that no matter where I stood in the church it looked like *all* the statues were staring at me. I never quite figured out how they did that."

"Be thankful that's all they ever did is stare at you," Eddie said.

A young detective, who had been collecting evidence from the crime scene, approached.

"I need to talk to you, lieutenant," he said. He motioned that he wanted to talk to Nick alone.

"Go ahead, I was raised with this guy," Nick said, pointing to Eddie with an approving jerk of his head. "He's got enough on me to have me punching out license plates with my big dago nose for the rest of my life. You sure you can't tell about my confessions, Eddie?"

"Oh, brother," Eddie sighed, rolling his eyes. He had long since put his priesthood behind him. Would anyone else ever forget it?

"Whaddaya' want, Lemoyne?" Nick said, turning to the detective. "We're kind of busy here. Make it quick." Ignoring years' worth of memos and sensitivity training urging Cleveland Police Department superiors to treat underlings with respect, Nick wrenched his face into an expression of feigned interest in the detective's information.

Detective Lemoyne stalled for a moment. He seemed to build his nerve for the reaction his evaluation of the crime might elicit from his irascible boss.

"Of course we won't know for certain until forensics gets finished," Lemoyne began, "but from what I can determine by the way the flesh is damaged, it appears that the one stuck in the confessional door may have been killed with some kind of pointed weapons. Maybe, uh, spears or even arrows."

"You pretty good cop, I think," said Sergio, who had finished his tour of the statues and returned to the back of the church.

In unison, Nick and Eddie ordered Sergio to keep his mouth shut.

Nick then sprayed sarcasm all over the young detective. "Spears? Arrows? Hear that Eddie? Sherlock Lemoyne here thinks that dude was killed with spears or arrows." Nick stepped close to the detective. "So, who do you suspect, some Watusi warrior or maybe Sitting Bull? Or maybe that statue of Saint Sebastian over there. He's got plenty of arrows sticking out of him."

"Since you've brought up the statues, lieutenant, there's a trail of blood between the corpse on the floor and that statue with the hook in his hand," Lemoyne said. "There's blood on the hook."

"Well, you've solved the crime then. Great! Want me to file for an arrest on that statue?"

"...not exactly."

"Listen Lemoyne," Nick said, becoming serious. "I looked at those bodies myself and I didn't see any evidence of, what did you say? Arrows? Spears? Hooks, for Chris' sake! I'm gonna' be going through all these reports today. Nowhere do I want to see any mention of arrows or spears or hooks. *Nient*! Understand? Personally, I think those guys both got it point blank with a shotgun."

Detective Lemoyne bravely stood his ground. "Shotgun? There's no powder burns on the bodies, lieutenant. And we didn't find any empty shells."

"So what?" Nick said in a loud voice. "There's a shotgun in my car. Go get it and shoot the bastards. You can't hurt 'em. Spread shotgun shells all over this church. Would that make you feel any better? Did those guys have any ID or cash on them?"

"They each had a *bunch* of passports, all with different names, and a ton of cash."

"That settles it! Where there's bogus passports and a lot of cash these days, there's drugs involved," Nick said. "Drug guys kill each other all the time. They both no doubt needed killing! Are you starting to get the picture, Lemoyne? You cabeesh?"

"I think I understand, lieutenant," Lemoyne said. He retreated.

"That kid's got potential," said Nick, when the young detective was out of earshot. "Mind you, he'll never be as good as me, but then he's not Italian. He doesn't have that way of, well, you know..."

"...of bullshitting himself?" Eddie said.

"Yeah, something like that."

As Nick improvised an acceptable explanation, he rubbed his face, prematurely lined by irregular hours, beer, cigarettes, bad diet and five sons every bit as wild as he himself had been as a youth. "Eddie, here's how I'm gonna' handle this. I know you didn't do it and you seem to think that this Luigi guy didn't either.

I believe the strain of Donnie's death and the shock of being chased by three bad asses made you imagine you saw things you really didn't. I've seen situations like this before."

"Have it your way, Nick," Eddie said.

"Just leave it to me. I can make up stories even better than those *Plain Dealer* clowns."

Eddie resented Nick's patronizing tone but didn't try to dissuade him. When Nick Piccione made up his mind, there wasn't much use in trying to change it. Besides, no one who didn't see the statues in action was ever going to believe what happened. A faked account was the only alternative. If anyone could come up with a workable story, it was Nick.

"Eddie, my big concern in this case is protecting *you*. I don't give a shit who killed those guys. Just go along with me."

"Whatever works for you, Nick," said Eddie.

"Good. Meantime, I'll do some checking on this *La Nutso*...?"

"*La Mano di Cristo,* Nick," Eddie said. "The Hand of Christ."

"Yeah, right. Keep in mind that if there is such a group, which I doubt, they might not be finished with you yet. Killers arrogant enough to name themselves after Jesus Christ are gonna be hard to discourage."

"I appreciate you playing this down," Eddie said. "Right now I have to worry about getting Donnie buried. You going to make the funeral?"

"You have to ask? I'll be there, you know that." Nick's eyes clouded and he turned his head away. He pretended to scan the interior of the church. "God, I'm sorry about Donnie. And I'm sorry about what happened to you and that it happened in here. You *and* this church deserve better."

"Actually, I'm kind of thankful it did happen here," Eddie said.

"This place brings back a lot of good memories," Nick said, ignoring Eddie's comment. "Hey, remember when me and you were altar boys and we got into the wine that time?"

"I sure do." Eddie said. "You drank most of it and I was the one who got caught. You remember what my punishment was?"

"No, not really."

"Father Louis made me get a ladder and dust the statues. Took all day. They're even scarier up close, I might add."

"You never were very good at gettin' away with stuff," said Nick. "You're too damned honest."

"I don't think I was ever very good at anything."

"You're wrong about that. You were a good priest, Eddie. You weren't a priest for a real long time but you were a *helluva* good priest while you were!"

"How would you know? Rarely saw your fat ass in this church."

"Easter and sometimes Christmas. That ain't bad. Besides, listening to you preach wasn't what impressed me. That's just window dressing, a lot of talk that don't mean much. Priests are like cops, it's what they do on the street that counts. You were good on the street. You helped anyone who needed help. And God only knows how many times you bought food and stuff for people with your own money. All priests should be as good as you were."

"Thanks," Eddie said. He was grateful for the recognition from Nick, who was not known for handing out praise.

"Don't mention it. As long as I've known you, you've been trying to save the world. Still are! You and your women's shelter! You're a good-looking guy. You should be out chasing babes, not trying to shelter them. Know what I mean?"

"Women don't seem to want to have anything to do with an ex-priest, even a good-looking one," Eddie laughed. "I guess they think it'll land them in hell."

"Where those guys who tried to kill you are burning now, I hope," Nick said. He slapped the top of a brass pew finial shaped like the head of a lethargic, yawning lion. "Damn, I'd sure like to know how those sons o' bitches were killed. Maybe you weren't seeing things. Maybe I oughta give the TV stations and the *Plain Dealer* a real story and throw some cuffs on the statues. Haul their asses in!"

"Take it from me, Nick, there aren't enough cops in the city of Cleveland."

As he left the church, Eddie resisted looking at the statues that had saved his life. But he was involuntarily drawn to them, especially their eyes, so penetrating, so impenetrable. He felt compromised by and mortgaged to the martyrs. He wondered when the first payment might be due.

FIVE

Eddie took his place in the front pew at Saint Rocco's Catholic Church for his brother's funeral mass. He sat next to two Vatican clergy. One of them, Salvatore Cardinal Viviano, president of the Vatican Bank, had been Donnie's boss. The other, Eddie learned after the mass, was Bishop Lorenzo Sacchi, a friend of Cardinal Viviano. Eddie thought it odd that Vatican big shots would travel so far for the funeral of a priest but was grateful that they had come.

Viviano nodded at Eddie when he entered the pew but Sacchi stiffened and his jaw dropped. Eddie's arrival obviously startled the bishop. Eddie wrote it off as the reaction of someone seeing a duplicate of the person who had died.

Cardinal Viviano, by far the most famous ex-patriot of the Briggs Hill neighborhood, had begun his career as a parish priest at the Church of Martyrs. Young Father Viviano showed a talent for earning large returns on parish funds, a talent which caused the Cleveland diocese to recruit him. For thirty years Viviano advanced patiently through dozens of dreary Church banking posts on his way to becoming president of the Vatican Bank and, ultimately, a cardinal. The one-time parish priest from Cleveland was now keeper of the storied wealth of the Catholic Church.

It was no secret that the cardinal also desired to become the first American-born pontiff. According to information leaked after the Conclave of Cardinals, Viviano had been a finalist, losing in a close vote to Gilberto Cardinal Lorini, who was now Celestine the Sixth.

Bishop Barnard McIlvaine, head of the Cleveland diocese, said the Mass of the Dead for Father Donald Russo. Donnie had once worked for McIlvaine, who enlisted him away from the Church of Martyrs when he learned of the priest's investment skills, just as an earlier bishop had once enlisted Father Viviano. Bishop McIlvaine later tried without success to keep his young discovery from going to the New York diocese. No one could keep Donnie from Rome when the Vatican Bank learned of the young priest's investment talents.

The fact that two Church of Martyrs' priests, separated by twenty-five years, possessed such extraordinary investment skills had been a source of amusement among parishioners. Perhaps, people joked, there was something in the Holy Water that turned its priests into financial geniuses.

Not all of them, however. Eddie, by his own admission, could not read a bank statement.

Inspired by the Vatican VIPs, Bishop McIlvaine put on the show of his life. He spoke interminably about death and judgment, stretching for analogies and quoting extraneous Bible verses with the abandon of a television evangelist.

Eddie fidgeted on the hard pew during the hour and a half service. He had taken the advice of his first women's shelter client and stopped at a hospital emergency room for a tetanus shot and to have his feet re-bandaged. He couldn't decide which hurt most: his swollen feet throbbing inside his shoes, his sore rear end where he got the shot, the eighty dear dollars he paid for the emergency room visit or, most agonizing of all, the bishop's droning. Eddie hadn't slept much in the past twenty-four hours and fought to keep from passing out. He fought even harder to sweep events from the night before from his mind.

After the mass, Eddie declined a ride to the cemetery in Bishop McIlvaine's limousine. He didn't care for the grumbly old bishop, who had tried to block his efforts to turn the vacant Church of Martyrs property into a women's shelter, even though it was supported by the county and private donations and not the diocese.

Eddie drove his own car, a road-weary, temperamental Dodge of indeterminate color and vintage. He held up the funeral motorcade several long minutes trying to start it, harshly coaxing the car under his breath in front of Saint Rocco's.

"Start, you son-of-a-bitch!" did the trick.

The storm, in its second relentless day, peaked as the motorcade entered Holy Cross Catholic Cemetery. Blackened skies dropped improbable amounts of rain. Water flowed down the cemetery's hills like a thousand small rivers, channeling around monuments and large headstones and drowning grave markers flush with the ground.

A throng of about fifty mourners, mostly Briggs Hill residents who had known Donnie all his life, braved the storm to attend the graveside service. A flimsy canopy over the gravesite accommodated only about a dozen people. Most huddled in the rain; the more prudent among them folded their umbrellas in deference to the lightning.

Eddie wondered how many people would attend if *he* was being buried rather than his twin. He guessed the number at about a half-dozen, but only if it was a nice day and free lunch and beer were provided. He and Donnie had been equally popular with parishioners when they served as young priests at the Church of Martyrs but Eddie knew many in the neighborhood held it against him that he had quit the priesthood.

Eddie walked to the gravesite under a faulty umbrella he had grabbed from the collection in the rectory. He closed the umbrella and took his place at the head of Donnie's casket. Displays of cut flowers, most of them courtesy of the Vatican legation, lent a cloying essence of death to the cold, airless environment. Along with the others, Eddie waited for the obese Bishop McIlvaine, in full brocade, to work his way, one equivocal demi-step at a time, up the hill to deliver the eulogy. The bishop's doting entourage kept his bulk dry with a battery of umbrellas.

Someone put an arm around Eddie's shoulder and whispered into his ear. "What wouldn't you give to see that fat mick trip and roll back down the hill like a bowling ball, maybe take out a dozen headstones?"

It was Nick Piccione, of course. Eddie acknowledged the comment with an unkind smile. Nick never failed to make Eddie laugh, even in the worst situations. The two men watched the spherical bishop negotiate the hill. McIlvaine paused at the top of the climb to catch his breath before moving to the casket. He began the eulogy, making almost no reference to the dead priest as a person. It was a lazy cop-out that infuriated Eddie.

Say something nice about him! He wasn't just a priest. He was a great guy, a lovable human being. Go ahead, tell everybody how we're burying the wrong Russo twin. We're putting the brighter one, the more worthy one, into the ground. Say it!

Eddie blocked out the remainder of the eulogy. He tried to concentrate on Donnie's life and the good times they had shared but the statues denied him that pleasure; they tugged his thoughts to their anguished faces, murderous hands and unknown motives. The moral horror of the slaughter in the church distressed Eddie, but he also could not suppress a certain euphoria as the benefactor of such an intervention. There were so many unanswered questions. Eddie feared he would never learn the answers almost as much as he feared he would.

On whose payroll were the statues? Who was the wizard behind the screen? Had the statues invented themselves, just for the hell of it, for something to do? Or, maybe Nick was right. Perhaps distress over Donnie's death and fright induced a strong autosuggestion that caused Eddie to only imagine that statues brutally killed two men. Maybe the two men *had* killed each other. How much easier that would make things.

Get your mind off it. You've got to bury Donnie. Don't cheat your brother's memory. Those statues will wait. They've been around for centuries. They seem good at waiting. They seem good at a lot of things.

Cardinal Viviano and Bishop Sacchi were among the privileged enjoying the protection of the canopy. Tall and unashamedly handsome, Viviano wore a scarlet cassock and red-trimmed shoulder cape. A weighty gold chain and jeweled pectoral cross projected a picture of royalty. Viviano was a Church power broker and seemed to want everyone to know it. The seventy-year-old cardinal prince was without his scarlet *biretta*. The better, thought Eddie, to show off a full head of silver hair.

Bishop Sacchi, on the other hand, did not present as well. His eyes hid behind a reptilian squint, fleshy hoods and red-tinted glasses. Thick black eyebrows met at the bridge of the bishop's nose like a jack-o'-lantern. Heavy lips, fixed in a downward curl, framed pearly capped teeth. Loose, depthless skin hung like bunting from his facial bones. Sacchi looked to be powerfully-built, as round, stout and bald as a section of concrete sewer pipe.

Bishop McIlvaine droned on, as monotonous as the falling rain, which he worked into his close. "...the rain must certainly be great tears of joy from Almighty God as he receives Father Donald Russo to his house," McIlvaine said, his heavenward glance blocked by the canopy. "Let us pray..."

The bishop dismissed the drenched mourners with a peremptory, godly flick of his ruby-encrusted gold staff, thus concluding the ceremony. McIlvaine's retinue resumed efforts to protect him from the rain as he waddled down the hill to a waiting limousine.

As the mourners left, Cardinal Viviano unexpectedly broke down over Donnie's coffin; he wept quietly but openly. Eddie thought it odd and out of character for someone of Viviano's station and bearing to shed tears over Donnie who was, after all, merely an underling at the Vatican Bank. Then the cardinal did something even more baffling. He walked up to Eddie, embraced him tightly for a moment and left without saying a word.

Sacchi showed no emotion. He wore the look of disinterested arrogance that is the face of the Vatican where it meets the public, a kind of shield against unwanted encroachment. He and Viviano walked at a fast pace under large black umbrellas to their own limousine parked away from the others. Eddie had questions he wanted to ask of them. They would have been among the last persons to see his brother alive. Eddie dropped his own uncooperative umbrella and ran to catch up. He ignored the downpour and the pain in his feet, which pulsated nonstop as they tried to break free of his shoes.

"'Scuse me, Bishop Sacchi," Eddie said, touching the bishop lightly on the shoulder from behind. Sacchi stopped and turned around; the hem of his cassock twirled imperiously above the wet grass. Icy eyes and pursed lips told Eddie the bishop wasn't a man accustomed to being summoned so casually or touched by *anyone*. Sacchi stood slightly uphill and looked down at a soaked Eddie from under his umbrella. The cylindrical bishop's bald head was slightly pointed. Eddie thought Sacchi resembled an enormous artillery shell.

"Yes?" The bishop's voice, flat and aloof, had an edge to it that cut through the sound of the rain. Sacchi looked at his gold wristwatch. Eddie sensed the bishop was setting a timer on the conversation. He had encountered self-important clergy many times in his career as a priest and knew from experience he would be allowed only a few seconds of Sacchi's precious time.

"I'm Eddie Russo, Donnie's brother. I just wanted to ask you if you know anything more about how my brother died."

Sacchi studied Eddie for a few moments before speaking, in perfect English. "It's very sad what happened to your brother. I'm sorry. No one can predict God's plan, can they?"

"Do you know any more of the details?" said Eddie.

"I really don't know too much about it," Sacchi said. "I understand your brother ate alone in a seafood restaurant, though we're not sure of the name of the restaurant. He was saying mass the next morning when he collapsed. He died later that day of acute food poisoning. We did everything we could for him. That's all I know. I am in charge of Vatican security. We are conducting a complete investigation."

Without offering Eddie a chance for cross-examination, Sacchi gave a curt nod of his head, obviously meant as a period to end the conversation. He turned and walked toward the waiting limousine. Cardinal Viviano sat inside, staring straight ahead.

Fast rewinding Sacchi's words in his head, Eddie stopped abruptly on "seafood restaurant."

Seafood? Donnie? Just the thought of seafood made Donnie ill. He became so sick from fish when he was a kid he almost died. Donnie wouldn't have gone into a seafood restaurant for any reason, not even to have lunch with Jesus Christ!

Eddie struggled to think of something else to say to Sacchi as the bishop put distance between them. The seafood comment might just be a case of bad information. No one would have had a reason to harm Donnie. What else could he say to the bishop before he got away? Sacchi was about ten yards from the limousine when a thought came to Eddie.

"Santo Cane!" Eddie screamed the ridiculous nickname he had gotten from Sergio, the nickname of the supposed boss of *La Mano di Cristo*. Eddie didn't know why he said it. He felt stupid and embarrassed. He almost followed the comment with an apology until he noticed the hesitation, a detectable balk in Sacchi's haughty stride, as if he had started to stop, maybe even started to turn around but didn't.

An innocent man *would* have turned around, would have been puzzled or irritated that a stranger had called him "Saint Dog." Eddie read the faltering in Sacchi's walk as acknowledgement of the nickname and, perhaps, everything that it represented.

Did the prick recognize the nickname? And why the hell had the head of Vatican security come to a priest's funeral in Cleveland? So now what?

Sacchi never looked back at Eddie. He joined Cardinal Viviano in the limousine. They drove off.

"Santo Cane!" Eddie repeated to himself. Tears of futility ran down his face. He knew he would never again have the chance to question Bishop Sacchi. As the limo faded from view on the cemetery road, Eddie shouted out, not caring who might hear. "Seafood restaurant, my ass!"

Pushed along by a strong wind at his back, Eddie walked to his brother's deserted gravesite. He fell to his knees and rested his head on the casket, which he noticed for the first time was made of bronze.

"The Vatican always did know how to bury its dead," said Eddie. *"Arrivederci, mio fratello."*

The wind moved an undulating silver sheet of water horizontally across the cemetery. It ripped the gravesite canopy away and threatened to take Eddie with it. He held on to Donnie's casket.

SIX

After the funeral, many of those in attendance stopped at the Epicurean Restaurant in Briggs Hill for the post-funeral meal that is Italian custom. Eddie learned that Cardinal Viviano had picked up the tab, though he would not be able to attend. Eddie, only halfway dry, also wanted to skip the occasion and return to the women's shelter but decided to put in an appearance.

Outside the restaurant, Nick Piccione hid from the rain in his unmarked police car, smoking a cigarette and reading the morning newspaper. He motioned for Eddie to join him.

"Does the police chief know you're smoking in one of his vehicles?" Eddie said, getting into the car.

"Screw him," said Nick. "Here's the story on the fun in the church last night if you care to read it."

The late-edition *Plain Dealer* story read like an idea soundly rejected by *True Detective Magazine*. The newspaper reported that an argument over drugs between two men in the church had apparently escalated into a fight that resulted in the men somehow managing to kill each other. The story, quoting Nick throughout, was rich in phony yet remarkably plausible details. Neither Eddie's nor Sergio's names were mentioned.

"I thought you didn't talk to reporters anymore," said Eddie.

"The only reason I did was to control the story," said Nick. "To protect *you*, I might add."

"I appreciate it," said Eddie. "Must admit, you've got a pretty good imagination."

"I've got a pretty good imagination? Is this coming from someone who claims he saw statues kill two guys? Truth is, reporters will print any damned thing you tell them just so they can finish their stories and hit the nearest bar. It's the only thing cops and reporters have in common."

Eddie glanced at a Page One story on Pope Celestine the Sixth, the recently-elected controversial pontiff who had challenged the Vatican clergy and Roman Curia bureaucrats to "return the Catholic Church to the gospel of the humble and the poor intended by Jesus Christ." To that end, the pope had created the Office for the Distribution of Christ's Wealth.

According to the newspaper, Pope Celestine would reveal details of his plan and the new Vatican department in two days in a speech in a Mexico City shantytown. Typical of the new pontiff, the trip was spur of the moment. It had only been announced to the world the night before. Eddie recalled Sergio telling him that he and his comrades were to proceed to Mexico City after killing him. He added this latest tidbit to the equation that turned on a spit in his mind.

"By the way, Eddie, did you happen to notice the look on the face of that Vatican honcho when he saw you at Saint Rocco's this morning?"

"The cardinal?"

"No, not Viviano. The other one, the bald homely guy. What's his name?"

"Sacchi!" Eddie said. "His Loftiness Bishop Sacchi. He told me he was head of Vatican security when I tried to talk to him after the funeral. He's one tough customer, let me tell you. And, yes, he did act a little shocked when he saw me."

"A *little* shocked? He about shit his pants! Maybe he wasn't expecting to see *either* of the Russo twins alive today. After the mass, he couldn't get outside fast enough to use his phone."

"I wonder if he was the one who objected to sending Donnie's body back to Cleveland for burial," Eddie said. "I had to make twenty calls through the Vatican bureaucracy and create a big stink before they agreed to ship the body. And you say the other one, Viviano, didn't act surprised when he saw me?"

"Not a bit," Nick said. "The only time I saw Viviano notice you was when he hugged you at the gravesite. What the hell was that about?"

"I have no idea, never met the man before," Eddie said. "But as long as you've brought up Bishop Sacchi, I've got something to tell you. Fact is, I did a little detective work of my own."

"This I can't wait to hear, Dick Tracy."

"After the funeral I ran after Sacchi and Viviano and tried to ask for more details about Donnie's death."

"And? How'd that go?"

"Not great. Viviano walked away from me and Sacchi brushed me off by saying something about how Donnie died from food poisoning he got in a seafood restaurant in Rome, something they didn't tell me initially. They just said the cause of death was food poisoning."

"And?"

"Donnie couldn't even *smell* seafood without becoming sick. When we were kids the old man caught about a million perch at the lake one day. He put on a neighborhood fish fry. Donnie ate so many he was sick for a week, almost died. There's no way he would ever have been in a seafood restaurant."

"I remember that. I ate about five hundred of those perch myself. Anything else happen?"

"Well, Sacchi's explanation and the way he treated me made me suspicious. He started to walk away from me and, without knowing what else to try, I called out that nickname Sergio told us about in the church this morning."

"Nickname? What nickname?"

"Could never accuse you of not paying attention, Nick."

"Cops only hear what they want to. It's an acquired skill, takes years. Simplifies things greatly. Works good with the wife, too."

"In the church this morning Sergio told us that very few members of *La Mano di Cristo* know the name of the boss but they all know he's known as *'Santo Cane,'* Saint Dog, because he's so damned mean and ugly. Remember?"

"Yeah, kind of. So?"

"I hollered it out as Sacchi walked away. I called him *'Santo Cane!'"*

"A hunch," said Nick. "Lots of bad people doing time because of a cop's hunch. Did he react?"

"I think so. I could swear he recognized the nickname, like it struck a nerve or something. He didn't quite turn around when I yelled it but he sure as hell started to."

"That's not real convincing evidence. But it probably would have made me suspicious, too."

"Do you think if you had a nickname like 'Saint Dog,' you'd know it?" Eddie said.

"Everybody knows if they've got a nickname. The new detectives call me 'Banjo Ass' behind my back."

"Banjo Ass?" Eddie repeated, amused at the accuracy of the nickname. "A perfect fit! That big butt of yours really is kind of round and flat."

"Very funny. Any ideas why this Sacchi would want you dead? Or Donnie, for that matter?"

"I really don't. I can't believe anyone outside of Briggs Hill even knows I exist. Far as I know, neither Donnie nor I ever did anything to anyone."

"First thing I learned as a cop is that you don't have to do anything special to get your ass killed. Murders tend to fall into two categories, either very random or very well-planned. I'd say someone went to a lot of trouble to plan yours. Those two scumbags who got whacked in the church weren't there by accident."

"Any possible way we can pursue this, Nick?"

"We're kinda screwed. Even if we had something to go on, which we don't, they live in their own private little world in the Vatican. It's a sovereign state, can't get near 'em. Just one big safe house called Saint Peter's, a perfect setup for someone who wants to commit a crime, including murder. Remember that pope twenty, thirty years ago that only lived a month or so? I seem to remember that there were a lot of unanswered questions about his death. What was his name? John Ringo George or something, wasn't it?"

"John Paul...John Paul the First," Eddie said. "I read a book, an investigation into his death. John Paul was in perfect health but died mysteriously of a reported heart attack after he had reigned only thirty-three days in 1978. The author claims it was murder."

"Who'd he piss off? Did it say in the book?"

"He died a week or so after making inquiries into..." Eddie paused, mentally adding another factor to the building equation.

"Into what?"

"...into Vatican finances, among other things. Viviano is head of the bank and he and Sacchi seem to be buddies. Too bad we didn't get a picture of Sacchi and make Sergio stick around so we could show it to him."

Nick had a cocky grin that Eddie recognized all too well from their pinochle games, his I-got-a-trump-card-your-ass-is-grass-look. He dug a phone out of his pocket, fussed with it a few seconds, and showed a picture to Eddie.

"I take it from the less than delighted look on the esteemed Bishop Sacchi's mug that he didn't exactly pose for you."

"He acted real pissed. I took it at the cemetery when he got out of his limo. I was suspicious of everyone at that funeral. Like I said, I didn't like the way this guy reacted when he saw you at Saint Rocco's. I figured a picture couldn't hurt. Didn't even tell him who I was. Walked right up to that chrome dome and snapped it. Figured I'd give him something to think about while he spun his linguini on the flight back to the Old Country."

"Not much emphasis placed on subtlety at the police academy, was there?" Eddie said.

"Good cops, like good priests, ain't subtle. As for your new buddy Luigi, or whatever his name is, I had him tailed. He's been at your shelter all day. A couple of women showed up and he cooked for them. He spotted the tail right away, invited him in for lunch."

"And?"

"My man had lunch! What else? This Luigi makes a terrific *verde fagioli,* I'm told. Crook to cook! I'm starting to believe that little guy really did see Jesus last night."

"Sergio's his name and we saw the *statues* move, Nick. The jury's still out on Jesus."

"You're not the kid I knew who went to mass every day and wanted to be a priest," said Nick.

"Yeah, and I once knew an idealistic young cop with a skinny waist, polished shoes and a shiny badge who was going to change the world."

"Whatever! Show Luigi the picture. I sent it to your phone."

"I'm on my way to the shelter now," Eddie said, encouraged to hear that the women's shelter had acquired some new clients, even if an assassin one day removed from the job was doing the cooking. Not to mention watching after the women.

"Your girlfriend was helping him," Nick said, with a lewd grin.

"My what?"

"Your girlfriend. Pat. Isn't that her name?" Nick tossed his head back and squinted at a note on his phone to verify the information. "Pat Adams. My man says she's got a nice shape, not bad lookin' either."

"What makes you think she's my girlfriend?"

"Because she kept asking every cop that came by if they had seen you. She wanted to know how you were doing. When a babe's that worried about a guy, there's usually something going on."

"Anything you say, Nick."

"Hey, Eddie, this might be your last chance to enjoy wedded bliss like the rest of us. You ain't gettin' any younger."

"Thank you for the vote of confidence," said Eddie, who was pleased that Pat had expressed concern about him. But he scoffed at the idea of a girlfriend, something both he and Nick knew was about as unlikely as...well, statues of saints turning assassins into Italian sausage. After his laicization, Eddie met several women in whom he was interested but remained clueless how to approach the situation. The truth was that Eddie, who as a priest had earned a reputation as an innovative and effective marriage counselor, didn't know how to ask for a date. His one sexual experience, Nick's nymphomaniac, thrice-divorced cousin Chastity, visiting from Pittsburgh, almost made him return to the priesthood. Nick's speculation seemed even more ludicrous since Eddie had only been around Pat a total of about thirty minutes, maybe a few seconds longer if he included the time it took to tackle her to the ground.

Not that he was about to tell any of this to The Great Piccione. Besides, Pat was a client of the shelter and off limits. Gutsy, intelligent, attractive, she would eventually shake the monster chasing her and get back on her feet. She'd move on. What could she possibly see in a forty-four-year-old jaded ex-priest-turned-social worker on the county payroll at three hundred bucks a week? For that matter, very few women would have any interest in a loser who counted a reformed killer and testy statues among his few friends and had the *La Mano di Cristo* after his ass.

"Eddie, why don't you go underground for a while, give me a chance to figure out what's going on? I know a bunch of places you could hide."

"I finally get some women at the shelter and you want to get me out of sight. Thanks anyway, Nick. These *La Mano di Cristo* goons aren't coming back right away. Their losses were too heavy. Besides, according to Sergio, they're all in Mexico City."

"I'm not even gonna ask what *that's* supposed to mean," Nick said, shaking his head. He produced a deeply-blued semiautomatic pistol from somewhere inside his sports jacket and tried to hand it to Eddie, who refused it.

"C'mon, take it. It's a dago pistol, a Beretta. It belonged to your friend Luigi."

"His name's Sergio."

"Oh, yeah. I'm sure...Sergio could teach you how to use it. Just don't give it back to him."

"Keep your gun, Nick."

"Don't think of it as a gun, think of it as Saint Ninemillimeter, patron saint of the well-protected Cleveland citizen. Holds a whopping sixteen bullets, much better than old rusty arrows. I took the silencer off it. It's loaded. Give them assholes something to think about if they should come back. One funeral this week is enough, keemosabe. C'mon, take it."

"I don't like guns, Nick."

"Ya know, Eddie, when we were kids and we'd get in fights and I'd always kick your butt, I thought you weren't tough. But for what it's worth, you might have the biggest balls of any guy who ever lived in Briggs Hill."

"It's worth a lot, especially from a former leader of the *Dago Bombers*. But don't forget, I have some pretty mean friends on retainer in the church."

"On second thought, maybe I shouldn't trust a nut like you with a pistol." Nick replaced the weapon in his coat. "Oh, see if this Sergio guy can make a good cannoli. Tell him to leave out the chocolate chips. Chocolate chips are the only fattening thing I hate!"

Eddie laughed. He opened the car door and started to step out. "See ya Nick. Thanks for coming to the cemetery. It helped more than you know."

"Hang on a minute, Eddie, I've got something I'd like to run by you." Nick lit a cigarette before he continued, stalling as much as he could. "Give me the okay and we'll exhume Donnie's body. We might learn a lot."

"Not just now," Eddie said. "Like you say, you can't prosecute those Vatican pricks anyway."

"But you'll at least know the real cause of Donnie's death."

"Nick, I want to believe that Donnie's death was an accident. I *need* to believe it. If it turned out to be anything else, I'm not sure what I might do. You'd be arresting *me*."

"If it turned out that this Sacchi or anyone else had something to do with Donnie's death," said Nick, "you wouldn't have to worry about it. I'd go to Rome and kill them myself!"

SEVEN

The rain had stopped by the time Eddie left the restaurant. A strong wind off Lake Erie dispersed the clouds into a ragged patchwork over Briggs Hill. Maybe Bishop McIlvaine was right, Eddie thought, maybe the rain *had* been tears from God. No one believed in God more than Donnie. Except, perhaps, his brother Eddie. Once upon a time.

On his way to the women's shelter, Eddie followed the route of the Procession, held annually when the Church of Martyrs was still active. The tradition started in fourteenth- century Italy during the Black Plague. Dying victims could not make it to the church to pray, so the church came to them. Literally. Everything that could be moved, including statues, was taken out of the church and paraded through the streets.

Each August, during the Church of Martyrs' *Festa,* men of the parish lifted the seven statues off their plinths, placed them on pallets and carried them on their shoulders through Briggs Hill. Streets were washed and rose petals spread. The weather was usually warm, the statues heavy and there were hilly streets to climb but the men never complained. It was considered a great honor to carry the statues. Long ribbons trailed from each martyr. Spectators pinned money on the ribbons to help with church expenses. The entire neighborhood turned out, an act of group worship as fervent and moving as any on Earth.

The statues seemed worlds removed as they bobbed along on the pallets. The sunlight, the cash-covered ribbons and brassy tunes from Balardo's Band mingled awkwardly with the martyrs' mutilated bodies and sullen faces. Watching them paraded through the streets, one got the feeling the statues were anxious to return to the salving dimness of their home in the church. Eddie thought the saints pretty good sports to have gone along with the Procession gig for so many years, since he now knew they had a choice in the matter and could have staged a boycott no one would have soon forgotten.

Maybe the martyrs were even better sports than he thought. Eddie recalled the year one of the men carrying Saint Elmo tripped, causing the statue to wobble on its pallet. If Elmo had fallen to the ground a number of persons walking alongside would have been injured, maybe killed. But the statue of Saint Elmo did not fall, even after it tilted well past any reasonable hope of recovery. Somehow the statue settled back on the pallet.

A woman spectator fell to the pavement on her knees and wailed that a miracle had occurred. Eddie, at the time a young altar boy marching in the Procession, turned away and bit his lip to keep from laughing out loud at the woman's foolishness.

Indelible memories and spectral faces beamed from everywhere along the narrow streets of the Procession route. Eddie passed his boyhood home. He could almost see his stepfather, the gentle and sage Frank Russo, sitting on the front porch smoking an Italian stogie and drinking red wine he made himself. Though a simple laborer all his life, just being Italian was more than enough happiness and fulfillment for Frank Russo. He enjoyed an equilibrium of work and pleasure unknown to later generations. Only since the neighborhood began to break up did Eddie understand what his stepfather had meant when he warned—daily!—that the penalty for people who forget their past is that they are doomed to live in the present.

His stepfather had good-naturedly lectured the parish women who walked by the porch on their way to services at the Church of Martyrs on summer evenings. *"Dia un riposo alle statue. Li porterà fuori,"* he would joke, warning the women that if they didn't give the statues a rest they would wear them out.

"Pop, take it from me, they didn't wear them out," Eddie whispered to the empty porch.

Was his stepmother's statue of the Virgin Mary still in the garden in the side yard, hiding in the weeds? The Virgin of the Weeds! The garden butted up against a small house rented in Eddie's youth by the Lanes, a family of what Eddie's father called *"Americanos,"* which Eddie as a young boy thought meant anyone not Italian or Jewish.

Mr. Lane was already close to death when he and his family moved into the house in the middle of that distant summer, one of the hottest in Cleveland history. No one ever lingered longer at death's door or suffered more publicly while waiting in line than Mr. Lane. Throughout each sweltering night, diminished lungs broadcast his fight for breath and life from his opened bedroom window. Long bouts of raw, spontaneous coughing followed each attempt to gasp a mouthful of priceless air. One night Eddie begged God to make the coughing and gasping stop.

Mr. Lane was dead before dawn.

It wasn't exactly what young Eddie had in mind. As a child, Eddie never doubted for a second that God not only heard, but also responded to all his pleas and prayers. He felt the death had been his fault, another layer added to the strata of guilt that is the requisite Italian baggage.

Eddie had walked these same streets each Halloween with his buddies, some dressed like the statues in the Church of Martyrs. The statues' gruesome appearance made perfect costumes for haunting the streets of Briggs Hill. Which one had he been? Oh, yeah, Saint Dionysius. A little catsup on top of a pulled-up sweatshirt made him appear decapitated. A wood broadsword and paper head that he carried in his hand completed the costume.

His stepfather obligingly feigned fright. His stepmother thought the getup sacrilegious.

His mind full of the past, Eddie turned his old Dodge onto Brewer Avenue and headed for the Church of Martyrs. The sight of the bell tower brought him back to the present. And the future. For the first time in many years, Eddie tried to speak to the unknown, though it was more inquiry than prayer. Uncertain to whom or to what he was directing his plea, Eddie asked, with all the sarcasm he dared, for a little less protection and a little more clarification.

EIGHT

Eddie arrived at the Church of Martyrs about four in the afternoon, much later than he had intended. The smell of home-cooked Italian food, with all its subtle distinctions meaningful only to those raised in Italian homes, wafted across the courtyard from the convent kitchen. The place hadn't smelled so inviting in years, not since the days when Sister Virginae, master chef and tyrant, ruled supreme. True to Nick's billing, Sergio seemed to make a better cook than assassin, if perhaps a bit too aggressive with the garlic.

Two women, neither of them Pat, laughed with Sergio outside the shelter. Eddie nodded and moved on, not wanting to get involved in conversation for the moment. He hoped Sergio hadn't told the new clients about the statues but would not have bet against it. He had half-expected to find Sergio giving an interview to CNN with the statues in the background waving at the camera.

The small, century-old cemetery adjacent to the church summoned Eddie. He had to tell his story to his dead friend Father Louis, the last pastor of the Church of Martyrs as well as the last person buried in its cemetery. Father Louis had taken charge of Eddie and Donnie when they were four years old, after their unwed mother committed suicide. Their father was unknown. Father Louis convinced Frank and Mary Russo, an older, childless couple in the neighborhood, to adopt the twins. He even shared some of his meager priest's stipend with them.

When the Church of Martyrs closed, the diocese had tried to place Father Louis in a retirement home for priests but he refused, protesting that he didn't want to live out his days surrounded by *"preti matti vecchi,"* crazy old priests. Father Louis continued to live in the rectory, defying the diocese to evict him. He died seven years later and was buried next to the church to which he had devoted his life.

Standing at his friend's grave, Eddie flashed back to the day Donnie and he had been ordained as priests and how Father Louis had sat in the front row of the downtown cathedral, crying with joy. And how, years later, Father Louis had not condemned him for his decision to leave the priesthood.

There was also that day when Eddie, like his mother, turned to suicide. Father Louis happened by Eddie's rented room to visit and found him overdosed on sleeping pills and near death. After Eddie was released from the hospital, Father Louis moved him back into the rectory. He found Eddie professional help and didn't let him out of his sight for three months. The only place to which Father Louis hadn't followed him was the bathroom, though he stood outside the door and talked and read the newspaper to him.

One of Eddie's favorite memories of Father Louis was the night the pastor had been invited to a downtown shindig to honor a visiting archbishop. Father Louis, who believed that Church assets were best spent for the benefit of those in need, was appalled by the gold place-settings, the fine wine and the lavish six-course dinner menu. He excused himself and left.

Eddie, still a priest at the time, inquired about the dinner when Father Louis returned to the rectory. "You're home kind of early, aren't you? How was the dinner?"

"I could not eat from gold dishes. I come home," Father Louis said.

This is stupid but I know you'll haunt me if I don't tell you what you missed last night, you old fart. The statues that only you loved!

In a very soft Italian, the bootlegged fusion of numerous regional dialects Eddie learned growing up in Briggs Hill, he talked to Father Louis through the dead priest's headstone. He told in great detail about the killings, how the saints Father Louis had prayed to every day for almost sixty years had come to his aid.

"E ringrazia i santi per me." Eddie asked the dead priest to thank the saints, a gesture that was a tribute to Father Louis' faith, not his own.

After saying it, Eddie hoped no one heard him, at least no one who understood Italian. He sensed another person's presence and turned around. It was Sergio, who grinned broadly, as if gladdened to hear Eddie concede his debt to the statues.

"Sergio, do you always sneak up on people?"

"I sorry, *Signore*. Is old habit." Sergio was smoking a cigarette.

"Smoking's bad for you."

"Everyone in Italy smoke. I quit right now if you want, *Signore*."

"That's not necessary. You've given up enough vices for one day."

"Who you talk to, *Signore*?"

"Father Louis."

"Who he?"

"An old dear friend of mine who was once pastor of this church. He's buried here. He was a crazy little Italian from the Old Country, just like you. You two would have gotten along fine."

"You call me crazy but you the one talk to the grave. You think he hear you?"

"If anyone could, it'd be Father Louis. Never mind that, I need to ask you something."

"Anything, *Signore*!"

"Sergio, didn't you tell me that you and your two friends were going to Mexico after you killed me?"

"*Si,* to Mexico City, *Signore*. But I not go there now. I wonder today how I get stuck in...Cleveland?...Ohio? Too cold here! Why you live here? Why anyone live here?"

"It ain't sunny *Napoli,* that's for sure. Just think of it as banking a little time for the future. Every day spent in a Cleveland winter should cancel out at least a thousand years in Purgatory."

"I not be here next winter, *Signore.*"

"Where're you going to be?" Eddie said, puzzled that Sergio seemed to know the future.

"I find out pretty soon, I think."

"Well, make sure you send me a postcard," Eddie said, preferring not to pursue the riddle of Sergio's forwarding address.

"Why you ask about Mexico City, *Signore?*"

"I don't want you to make a big deal out of this, but I read in the newspaper today that Pope Celestine is going to speak in Mexico City in two days. The trip was only made public last night."

As Sergio put the clues together, Eddie was certain he heard gears turning in the little guy's brain.

"And you think because my friend Emile know to go to Mexico City that he sent by someone who know *Il Papa* go there?"

"It's possible. Someone very close to...*Il Papa,* or at least close to someone who does his scheduling. Oh, while we're on the subject of suspicious bastards with access to the pope, I have something to show you. Eddie pulled out his phone and retrieved the photo of Bishop Sacchi.

"Have you ever seen this person before?"

"This a priest? He pretty ugly."

"He's a bishop. His name is Sacchi. He's a bigwig at the Vatican, in charge of security. Sacchi seems to be good friends with Cardinal Viviano, the head of the Vatican Bank. Sacchi lied to me today about how my brother died. I'm certain of that. My brother also worked at the Vatican Bank."

Eddie recounted for Sergio the dubious seafood story and how he had later called out the nickname *"Santo Cane"* and the effect, however minimal, it had on Bishop Sacchi.

Sergio nodded and rubbed his chin, the gears in his brain picking up speed. "Vatican? Security? How he act when he see you? He surprised?"

"As a matter of fact he did act surprised, very much so. But Sacchi may have just been shocked at seeing me because my brother and I were identical."

"Look at that face, like mean snake, *Signore.* You no shock this man too easy, not if he see *six* people who look the same. Maybe this bishop expect you dead, like you brother, and then see you at you brother's funeral. That shock him good, eh?" Sergio studied the picture. He laughed.

"What's so funny?"

"Maybe this my old boss, maybe this man *morte domina* for *La Mano di Cristo.* Maybe this *Santo Cane.* He look mean enough to be Saint Dog, you no think? Bow wow!"

"If you ever met this character, you wouldn't think he was so damned funny. Take my word for it."

"This bishop is friend of cardinal who run the Church bank, huh? I bet they not like new pope who give away all the money."

"Would your *La Mano di Cristo* goons do it, would they kill the pope?"

"As quick as we kill you...or try to. *La Mano di Cristo* never question orders. If *La Mano di Cristo* in Mexico City waiting on *Il Papa,* then he good as dead already."

"I'm afraid there's not much we can do about that," said Eddie.

"Is too bad. *Il Papa* a good man. Before him, no pope ever give away much Church money to the poor. Church give you lots prayers, all you want, but just a little money."

"That's how the statues got here in the first place," Eddie said.

"Eh?"

"In 1902, when this church opened, the pastor asked Rome for a donation. Instead of money, he got the statues. Some Vatican wiseass at the time described them as 'treasures of the Vatican.'"

"Some treasures, eh *Signore*?"

"That they are!"

"You think maybe the statues spare us so we can help Holy Father?"

"What could we do for him? If the statues want to save the pope, I'm sure they'll find a way."

"I no think you understand, *Signore*."

"What don't I understand?"

Sergio didn't reply. His silence irritated Eddie.

"Somehow I knew I shouldn't have mentioned this to you."

More silence from Sergio.

"Okay, suppose we Fed-Ex the statues to Mexico City. Would that make you happy?" Eddie said.

The look in Sergio's eyes told Eddie that the statues were one subject about which his new friend didn't care to make jokes.

"Sergio, let's just say I don't have your faith in the statues. Okay?"

"I not have faith in statues, *Signore*."

"You don't?"

"Faith for people who no see the statues move. You know that. You, me, we see the statues move. That give us power that come from knowing."

"Knowing *what*?"

"It not matter *what*!" Sergio snapped. "It is enough to know there is something *else*!"

"That almost makes sense, Sergio," Eddie said. "You wasted a lot of time being an assassin. You should have been a salesman. You could have sold Edsels."

"What is this...Edsels?"

"An Edsel was an automobile before my time that I identify with closely. It never found a place in this world."

"We waste time with you bad jokes, *Signore*. This thing you read in the paper about *Il Papa* visit to Mexico City a sign."

"Religion's in even worse trouble than I thought if God needs the Cleveland *Plain Dealer* to deliver his messages."

"You joke now, but when time is right, you understand," Sergio said.

"Understand *what*!?"

"You find out," Sergio said. "When time is right, you understand."

"Okay, whatever you say," said Eddie, too tired to continue the discussion. "Where did you get those clothes, Sergio? That shirt looks familiar."

"In the priests' house." Sergio seemed ill at ease and uncertain how Eddie might take the next bit of news. "That where I live now. Is okay?"

"Those were Father Louis' clothes, Sergio. He wore them to work in his garden," Eddie said. "But I don't guess he would mind you wearing his stuff or sleeping in his bed...for a little while."

"Thank you, *Signore.* Remember, Holy Father be in Mexico City in two days. I think already *La Mano di Cristo* wait for him."

"Oh, sure," Eddie said, disinterestedly, "but I've got to get some sleep. I'll probably still be in bed two days from now."

"*Signora* Pat and me, we take care of things while you sleep."

"Pat's still here?"

"Sure she is. She in the priest house."

"The rectory? What's she doing in there?"

"She say you make the convent nice and clean for the women, now she do the same where we live. I offer to help but she told me to cook. And she clean."

Caruso's *O Sole Mio,* its magnificence undiminished by scratches and a tired, antiquated turntable that dragged the tempo by a sixteenth note, met Eddie as he entered the rectory. He had not heard the recording since the day of Father Louis' funeral. After the funeral Eddie sat in the rectory all day, more alone than he had ever been in his life. He played the dead pastor's cherished Caruso collection well into the night. Then never again. Caruso's voice was the last thing in the world he expected, or wanted, to hear that day.

Pat came down the steps from the second story of the rectory. She carried two bulging trash bags and hummed along with The Great Caruso. She smiled at Eddie with the merest movement of her lips. Without a word, Eddie took the trash bags from her. Together they walked out to the battered garbage cans huddled together in the alley that ran alongside the rectory.

"You really didn't have to do this," Eddie said. "Not that I don't appreciate it. Where'd you find the Caruso records?"

"Where *didn't* I find them? There must be a hundred scattered around in the rectory. They were my only choice. And who still owns a turntable?"

"In case you haven't noticed, this whole place is kind of a museum," Eddie said.

"So, you like Caruso?" Pat said.

"Actually, if I never heard Caruso again, it'd be too soon. The records belonged to Father Louis, the former pastor of the church. He was a dear friend. He played those records night and day. The old guy loved the freakin' things so much I can't bear to throw them away."

"I think I understand," said Pat. She paused before continuing. "Eddie, Sergio told me you lost your twin brother. I'm very sorry."

"It's been a rough day," he said. "Thanks for your concern."

Fading sunlight pushed through the scattered clouds, casting shadows on Pat's dark-blonde hair and soft facial features. Her eyes, an uncommon shade of blue-green, radiated the sun's rays like a prism. Eddie guessed Pat to be in her early forties. Except for a hint of weariness, her face was not careworn; it didn't mirror the bruised emotions and irretrievably depleted passions that marked so many of the abused women with whom he had worked. Nor did Pat seem to burden herself with the humiliation other battered women often brought with them to shelters.

Eddie could not avoid glancing at the faint traces of a bruise under Pat's left eye. She caught him looking at it.

"Sorry you had to see that," Pat said.

"No, I'm sorry it happened. And I'm sorry I noticed."

"Forget it," she said. "Had dinner yet? Your sidekick Sergio made some excellent pasta today and a soup with nothing but cabbage and white beans that was the best thing I've had in a long while."

"Verde fagioli."

"How's that?"

"That's what it's called in Italian," Eddie said, *"verde fagioli.* Greens and beans. By the smell, Sergio may have gone a little overboard with the garlic."

"Do I detect a trace of professional jealousy?"

"Probably. We Italians are all partial to our own cooking. We only eat other people's cooking as a courtesy."

"From what I could see by the trash in the rectory, your own cooking consists chiefly of Frankie's Pizza and donuts from someplace called Mazone's."

"It's just a few blocks from here. The biggest cream donut on the planet! Guaranteed low calorie and good for you."

"I'll bet!"

"Gourmet cook or not, I'm not sure I want Sergio for a roommate," said Eddie.

"If I were you, I'd be happy to have someone else living in that rectory. It's creepier than the church and that's saying something. Did anyone who lived there ever get rid of anything?"

"I keep meaning to. I'll find the time one of these days." Eddie knew he never would.

"Eddie, tell me, if you want to, who is Sergio, really?" Pat said. "There's something I don't know about him, isn't there?"

"A *lot* you don't know," said Eddie. "I probably shouldn't tell you this but, since we seem stuck with Sergio, you should know that, until last night, he was an assassin, as were the two men who were killed."

"Assassin? I was with Sergio most of the day. He seems so gentle and harmless."

"Yeah, statues can do that to a guy," said Eddie.

"Those statues! Again, if you want to, tell me what it is I don't know about *them*."

"Pat, let's just say that the television and newspaper stories about the killings in the church are a fabrication dreamed up by a cop friend of mine who is doing the investigation."

"Why? What...*really* happened?"

Eddie thought, what the hell, she would never believe him and telling the story to a thoughtful listener like Pat might even help him deal with the experience. "Pat, what if I told you the statues, the same ones that seemed to fascinate you so much when you arrived, killed those men? Would you believe me?"

"I'm not sure," she said. "You come across as an honest person and I just can't help thinking that something very unusual happened in that church."

Eddie was totally unprepared for Pat's answer. He had anticipated a solid "Hell no!" response.

"If Sergio was one of the assassins, why didn't the statues kill him too?" Pat said.

"Okay, it gets better. The statues saved my life and then I intervened with them on Sergio's behalf. Now, *that* should convince you I'm lying."

"Why did you intervene?"

"I could tell you that it was because I'm such a good and forgiving person, but that's not why I did it," said Eddie. "I simply could not bear to watch another brutal murder."

"So that's why Sergio worships you."

"Worships me? You think he worships me?"

"He sure as hell does!" said Pat. "So, Sergio and the others were here...to kill you?"

"Yes, they came here, at great expense, all the way to Briggs Hill, just to kill me. But I have no idea why," said Eddie. "Please tell me now that you don't believe me. It'll make me feel a lot better."

"I don't know. Who would make up such a story? Who *could* make up such a story? And why?"

"When you figure that out, please let me be the first to know," said Eddie. "I've said way too much. Maybe we should change the subject. I see we have some new clients. As much as I hate the reason they're here, it's a good thing they had a safe place to come to. Looks like we're going to have a women's shelter after all, despite my unorthodox welcoming policy of tackling the arrivals, the first one at least, in my underwear."

"Blue-striped underwear at that! The ladies have no idea what they're missing!" Pat said, causing Eddie to beam like a baby. "Did you get that tetanus shot?"

"Sure did," said Eddie. "Eighty bucks!"

"Well worth it. I've seen many cases of trismus...lockjaw to you."

"Sounds like you might have a medical background."

"I'm a nurse when I work. I've had to quit two jobs recently to stay one step ahead of my ex-husband."

"A nurse? Is that why those two dead bodies in the church didn't frighten you?"

"No. I should have been scared to death, but I wasn't," she said. "I really don't know why."

"I can't say the same for myself," said Eddie. "To tell the truth, I thought you'd be gone."

"I kind of like it here."

"Sergio's cooking? The Caruso records?"

"That's part of it," Pat said, causing Eddie to beam again. "You'd better get some sleep. We'll talk later. Okay?" She turned and began to walk away.

"It's a deal," Eddie yelled, clumsily. "We'll talk later." He watched Pat from behind for longer than what might have been considered polite.

NINE

Before going to bed, Eddie fixed himself a bowl of Sergio's *verde fagioli* and turned on his computer in the rectory to catch up on the day's news.

Pope Celestine the Sixth's ongoing war with Vatican conservatives dominated the headlines, as it had almost from the day the pope was elected a few months before. While Eddie's interest in the Catholic Church had, to put it mildly, waned in the years since he left the priesthood, it was difficult to ignore the energetic sixty-six-year-old pope's efforts to rid the Church of its pomp and arrogance and distribute its wealth, *all* its wealth, to the needy of the world. Celestine the Sixth saw himself not just as a spiritual leader but as the head of a large, rich company with the simple goal of, in his own words, "significantly reducing its inventory of money."

The College of Cardinals, the Roman Curia and Catholic dioceses around the world bristled and complained publicly about the unprecedented order from Celestine: keep what you need for day-to-day operations and improve the lives of the poor with the rest. The complaints came not only from within the Catholic Church but from leaders of other Christian denominations and other religions, who carped that the pope was making them look bad for hesitating to likewise empty *their* coffers to solve the problem that Celestine preached was responsible for every woe of man: poverty.

The pope believed poverty was not a natural human condition but that it was man-made. Any condition created by man, he insisted, could be corrected by man. Celestine blamed greed for keeping millions in want and the world in turmoil. He openly attacked the politics of Third World countries for, in effect, endorsing deprivation among their people. He criticized the United States, calling its low minimum wage laws "the greatest government gift to moneyed interests since slavery!" Celestine even broke a sacred rule and lashed out at previous popes, whom he faulted for "standing idly by and allowing poverty and hunger to grow and fester for two millennia."

"Some of my predecessors washed the feet of the poor, but then forgot to feed them! Nor did they teach the hungry to grow food!" the pope roared in a recent blistering speech from a street corner in a South African slum.

Nothing would be overlooked or spared. Celestine had ordered the Vatican Bank to call in its loans and liquidate its stock, land and business holdings. He called for auctions to sell the Church's treasures, some one million pieces of paintings, sculptures, artifacts and books. Vatican curators protested, saying that the works were priceless and that it would be impossible to set a value. Celestine was quick with his reply: "Nothing is priceless except Christ's love for us."

Only museums would be allowed to bid on the art and artifacts. Museum directors from around the world bowed their heads, said a prayer of thanks, made pleas for contributions and readied their checkbooks.

Hey, Mr. Pope, I've got a few ex-Vatican treasures here in Cleveland that I would gladly donate to the auction. No reserve. They could deliver themselves!

Even Saint Peter's Basilica, centerpiece of the Catholic Church, was not exempt from Celestine's sweeping measures or his outspokenness.

"Our great basilica will of course remain, but only as a museum, a magnificent and historical work of art but also, sadly, a monument to centuries of wasted resources that could have been better spent helping mankind," said Celestine in a speech broadcast worldwide. "Symbolic of my resolve to bring Christianity back to its real meaning, I will not celebrate mass at Saint Peter's. Grand basilicas and cathedrals do not honor Christ's Gospel of the humble and the poor. They *mock* it! If we would heed our Lord's blessed words, we would build many more hospitals, houses and schools for the less fortunate."

A sidebar story told how Celestine resisted saying mass in "grand basilicas and cathedrals" when he traveled; he preferred to say mass outside, the weather be damned, so that thousands could be present. Shortly after becoming pope, he gave a Sunday service in the middle of an Irish soccer field. A rare heavy snow, which had not been forecast, began to fall. Most of the fifty thousand in attendance stayed till the end of the mass to see if the new pope would stick it out. Which he did! Pope Celestine the Sixth and his "Sermon in the Snow" owned the social media for months.

Some Catholic Church hierarchy championed the pope as "saint-like," but even they joined forces with those who warned Celestine's "liberal immoderations on behalf of the poor" would bankrupt the Church.

The pope's answer to such dire predictions of insolvency could hardly have been reassuring. "Good," Celestine replied, "then our dear Church will be free, for the first time in many centuries, of the paralyzing encumbrance of wealth."

Others branded Celestine a dreamer and unrealistic. His reply to the charges was equally troubling to his detractors. "I can't guarantee my plan will work," the pope admitted. "I know that even the vast means of the Catholic Church may not end poverty and hunger. I desire simply to set an example and chart a course, which was also the intent of the man who died on the Cross! Jesus Christ certainly had no guarantee that his sacrifice would someday result in millions of followers around the world. He gave his life. All I ask is that we give our wealth."

The Italian media had dubbed Celestine the "bluffer pope" because of his success at keeping his reformer spirit and progressive inclinations secret from the one hundred and thirty cardinals who elected him. Celestine won the papacy on a compromise vote when the cardinals, locked up in the Sistine Chapel and arguing for two months, wearied and settled on the quiet and unassuming Cardinal Lorini from northern Italy, who now called himself Celestine the Sixth.

Many in the College of Cardinals huffed later that they had been betrayed or, at the very least, deceived. After conclave they admitted, off the record, that they thought they were electing a pope who could be trusted to lead the Church without making waves. Nothing could have prepared them for the loose cannon that was Celestine. Several cardinals, talking among themselves, characterized the pope as a "false prophet," an Old Testament crime punishable by death. They entertained the notion that Celestine's election was the Devil's work. The conversation was overheard and found its way to the media, which served it up to ridicule around the globe.

When asked to comment, Celestine shrugged and said, "I am sorry to hear of this. My cardinals don't seem to understand that I am *undoing* the Devil's work of the last two thousand years. They accuse me of giving away money that is not mine to give. They are correct, it is *not* mine, nor is it *theirs*. It is Jesus Christ's money! I would ask my cardinals and members of the Roman Curia who object to my plans how they will explain to Christ someday why they greedily hoarded his money instead of doing what he would surely have done with it: help others!"

The Roman Curia and the College of Cardinals tried to block Celestine's every move. They justified the obstructionism by claiming the pope "was operating outside the bounds of his papacy" and "overstepping his role as spiritual leader." As usual, Celestine had a ready and quotable reply.

"I ask my opponents to rethink Jesus Christ's expectations of them. Christ was a spiritual leader but he also practiced charity toward the poor. He cared for people as best he could in his short time on Earth. Did Christ 'overstep his role' or 'operate outside his bounds' as I am accused of doing?"

Eddie knew that, except for some governments, the Catholic Church was already the largest provider of social services in the world. But it wasn't enough for Celestine. "It is wonderful that we give so much," the pope said, "but until all the excess wealth of our Church is gone, we are stealing from the poor—and from Christ!"

Celestine's benevolence had the unforeseen but welcome effect of moving the hearts of people. Catholic Church attendance was up as were donations, including many from those who had never dreamed of giving money to the Catholic, or any other, religion.

The unexpected generosity proved something of a dilemma for Celestine. "We have a problem, but a nice problem," he told a reporter. "I sometimes worry that we will never become a poor Church at this rate. The more we give away the fish and the loaves, the more fish and loaves there are! God is listening! And, just as important, the good people of this world are listening!"

There were many stories and pictures of the pope's new living quarters and Church administration offices. Celestine had famously ordered everything relocated from Vatican City to five large vacant buildings in a blighted Rome neighborhood, a warren of twisting streets that was home to some of Rome's poorest citizens as well as every variety of criminal. He instructed his bishops and cardinals around the world to do the same.

"Live with the poor and the rejected," the pope told his clergy. "When Christ returns to Earth, it is where he will expect to find you!"

Church big shots squirmed under the directive but found little sympathy. When a French cardinal complained that there was no one wealthy enough in his province to buy or even rent the mansion he was being ordered to leave, the pragmatic Celestine said, according to one account that made the news, *"Scottatura loro,"* burn it to the ground.

About time, Eddie thought.

Celestine was a man of many surprises, not the least of which was his daily schedule. Each day at four a.m. the pope, who came from a family of bakers, joined the bakers charged with feeding the papal staff and the poor who lived around the new papal headquarters. Celestine enjoyed sharing recipes with the other bakers, including his mother's long-guarded secret recipe for *biscotti di pepe*, Italian pepper biscuits.

As he worked, the pope invariably launched into short impromptu sermons that were cherished in the kitchen. "Spiritual sustenance from the Host means nothing without a little bread in one's belly. Bread is the most vital of foods. It would serve the world well if all my bishops and cardinals, the troublesome Roman Curia and every politician on Earth learned to bake bread. To see bread rise is to see proof of God. Ghandi had the yarn from his spinning wheel. We have the bread from our ovens."

It amused Celestine when his quotes, spoken so offhandedly in the kitchen, appeared on television, the internet and Page One of the afternoon newspapers, misquoted, out of context and the subject of endless analysis and review.

"POPE TO WORLD LEADERS: BAKE BREAD, DO SOME HONEST WORK!"

And, "PONTIFF COMPARES CHRISTIANITY TO HINDUISM!"

Also, on Page One of almost every newspaper and computer screen in the world, his mother's long-guarded secret recipe for *biscotti di pepe*. In no less than twenty-two languages!

At six a.m., after his baking duties, Celestine said mass on a wooden makeshift altar in a musty warehouse adjacent to his new digs. A well-meaning aide had hung a valuable painting of the Crucifixion above the altar. Celestine removed it himself and handed it to the aide. The painting, like everything else of value in the Vatican, was to be auctioned.

Eddie read that the new pope was only five feet, five inches tall, although he seemed to more than make up for it with an oversized sense of purpose. Within a week of becoming pope, he had abolished all papal ceremonial roles as a "complete waste of time." A reporter noted that "His Holiness Pope Celestine the Sixth thrives on only four hours of sleep a night. He walks bull-like, head down, striking sparks with his heels, each day brushing aside ever more Vatican traditions he sees as too costly, too extraneous or just plain silly."

The new pontiff also chose not to dress the part. Celestine had donned the white garments of the papacy for only one day, the day he became pope. After that, he wore a simple black cassock and hat with no markings to signify he was anything but a priest. When reporters asked about his plain garb, he said, "I prefer a working man's clothes. There is much to be done. If I need a costume to prove that I am pope, then I should not be pope! Let my cardinals and bishops strut like peacocks if they like."

Page One of an Italian newspaper several hours later: "POPE CALLS CARDINALS AND BISHOPS DANDIES!"

Quiet hysteria spread among Catholic clergy and laypersons responsible for running the Church on a day-to-day basis, especially those who felt they alone possessed the long view. What other possibilities beyond the pope's gravely misguided philanthropy might be in store? If Celestine could end the Church's time-honored roles as landowner, banker, art collector and librarian, then surely the issues of birth control, abortion, celibacy for priests, the prohibition of women priests—all part of the same grand tradition—might be on the table.

Not that the pope had time to indulge himself in re-writing Church doctrine. When asked about it, he replied, characteristically, "When all the bellies in the world are full, maybe then I will have time for doctrine. Doctrine means *nothing* to the hungry!"

"FOOD FIRST, HOLD THE DOCTRINE!" read one headline.

Eddie read with interest several stories of the pope's trip to Mexico City to reveal details of his new Office for the Distribution of Christ's Wealth in a speech he would give in the neediest section of the city. Those responsible for Celestine's welfare expressed serious security concerns about his insistence to travel so far with such short notice and to speak in what they referred to as a "slum." Instead of the usual months of painstaking preparations, the security staff was having to make everything ready in just two days. Without a Popemobile! Celestine had ordered it sold.

Eddie turned off the computer. This pope was indeed a very good man, he thought. Was it possible, as Sergio said, that they had been spared to help him? The idea was too stupid to even think about. Wasn't it? The statues could take care of matters themselves, if that's what they wanted. Couldn't they? Eddie's brief encounter with Bishop Sacchi at the cemetery convinced him that the bishop, for one, was not the type to rejoice over the pope's eagerness to give away money, certainly not to the poor. Celestine's death would put a quick end to such nonsense. It would also give Cardinal Viviano another shot at the papacy. Men with the power and access of Viviano and Sacchi would not have much trouble killing the new pope.

Even less trouble killing an insignificant young priest named Donnie Russo and an ex-priest named Eddie Russo, who would already be dead were it not for the aid of some amazing statues previously thought to be good only for scaring people.

TEN

Eddie climbed the narrow flight of stairs to his room. The room begged to be painted, offering as argument a grimy outline of the Crucifix that once hung over Eddie's bed. Stacks of books and a welter of magazines towered among Eddie's few other possessions. These included several boxes of what Eddie called his "priest crap," which he kept meaning to throw out. Eddie often wondered if he would ever escape the confines of the Church of Martyrs Home for Wayward Ex-Priests.

Eddie turned on an electric heater, which arced and hissed before settling into an irregular hum. He stripped to his underwear, washed and climbed into bed, delighted to find that Pat had changed the sheets. For a while he fought sleep, unlike Sergio whom he heard snoring in Father Louis' room. Eddie fell asleep even as he worried that he couldn't or shouldn't. He awoke with a start several times within the first hour certain someone was in the room. He fought an impulse to check under the bed.

Fatigue overcame apprehension and Eddie closed his eyes, muttering drowsily to the imaginary co-occupant or occupants of the room, "Go ahead and kill me. I could use the relief."

Eddie's dreams began with a few unrelated details and scattered memories of his life whizzing by in rapid slide-show fashion, passing too quickly for Eddie to identify any one event.

The slide show stopped at an all-too-familiar scene inside the darkened Church of Martyrs. Eddie guessed where things were headed and tried to change direction of the dream but to no avail. He ran out of the church only to find himself in another church, then another. He ran into a confessional.

Oh, no! Not the confessional again!

This time Eddie didn't cower in the confessional. Without a moment's hesitation, he stepped out, raging obscenities at the attackers he knew were on the other side of the door. But there was no Comedian, no Wheezer and no Sergio. Eddie was alone in the Church of Martyrs. Even the statues were missing. The scene frightened Eddie far more than if there had been a hundred statues and a thousand *La Mano di Cristo* killers reloading their Berettas and honing their stilettoes.

On impervious bare dream feet Eddie retraced his earlier, glass-strewn path to the altar. He sat down on the altar steps, put his head between his hands and waited.

C'mon, get it over with!

He heard the statues before he saw them. Stone feet slapped purposefully on the Church floor. Clearly, stealth was not among their demonstrated abilities. One by one, six saints appeared out of the darkness, led by Stephen, Blaise and Sebastian. The trio from the south transept trailed behind. Lawrence's flames and Elmo's blue flashes provided lighting. The skinless Bartholomew walked at the end of the line. Eddie studied the darkness behind the six saints, dreading the arrival of the headless Saint Dionysius but the seventh martyr never showed.

The parade of living statues, at best a tricky balance of flesh and stone, halted in front of Eddie. The martyrs' chests did not swell and contract; the statues lived but did not breathe. Their eyes remained perpetually open in a shark-like stare. The saints' faces bore the expressions carved into them but lacked human nuance. The scent of their mutilated bodies was that of raw meat and oil paint. Eddie stood and backed away, uncertain and fearful of what might follow.

A swirl of wind began to blow around the gathered statues, lightly at first but soon building to a howling whirlwind that stirred up a collection of debris to the ceiling. The hungry vortex drew in everything not fastened down. Yanked from their roosts, choir-loft pigeons attempted to fly away but became suspended in air, their forward flight barely equaling the pull. As they tired, the whirlwind sucked them in tail first, along with rats and any other creatures caught out in the open.

Eddie, dressed in only a pair of boxer shorts, his customary, preferred year-round sleeping attire, crouched close to the floor. He used his hands and forearms to protect himself from a churning barrage of discarded automobile tires, broken glass and frenzied vermin. At the very least, he expected to be cut by flying glass. But he sustained no injuries.

Of course not. It really is a dream this time. If I learned anything the last time out in the Church of Martyrs' Fun House, it's that no pain means no reality.

The terrazzo floor in front of the altar quaked as if something beneath struggled to be free. The floor buckled and raised upward; it cracked open and peeled back like an emerging flower bloom, leaving a gaping hole several yards in diameter. The air filled with the smell of fresh dirt. The statues descended into the opening. All except Bartholomew, who stood at the edge and stared at Eddie with a look that was far more command than invitation.

The vortex tugged at Eddie, who resisted as best he could but the pull was too powerful and dragged him to the opening. The skinless Saint Bartholomew held out his bloodied death shroud, which Eddie took hold of but only because he dared not. Bartholomew, anxious hitchhiker in tow, descended into the void.

Six statues and one trembling human advanced through the dirt, which opened ahead of the procession as it moved. Eddie clutched Bartholomew's shroud with both hands, fearful that if he lost his grip he would be left behind. Elmo's blue-arcing wreath and Lawrence's burning body illuminated disturbed worms and insects writhing along the walls of the exposed earthen corridor.

Eddie shuddered. Not fond of bugs, he picked small creatures of every description off his body.

It wasn't an easy dream. Moving and breathing became difficult in the closeness of the tunnel. Unlike the saints, who plowed ahead with unflagging energy along sharp rocks and snarled roots, Eddie fought for each step. He tripped once and fell against Bartholomew's skinless back and exposed spine. Eddie did his best to follow, half-fearing that Bartholomew, knife in hand, might turn around and tell him to keep up the pace. Or else!

Eddie's knee struck an object protruding from the side of the tunnel. He reached down; the object seemed to be man-made, a box of some kind. As he moved forward, a passenger on Bartholomew's death shroud, he felt more of the boxes. Coffins? Eddie assumed they were in the Church of Martyrs cemetery, surrounded by dead generations of parishioners.

The procession formed a circle around a rotting coffin. Saint Lawrence unceremoniously lifted the lid. A Roman collar, Crucifix and red Rosary in skeletonized hands told Eddie that the corpse was that of a priest. A leather-bound journal, which seemed to have escaped decay, lay at the corpse's side. Father Louis' journal! The former pastor, who had asked to be buried *un povero*, a poor man, in a wooden box, requested that his journal be buried with him. Eddie had personally placed it in the coffin seven years before.

Lawrence lifted the journal from the casket and pushed it into Eddie's hand when he refused to take it. The statues departed. Eddie tried to follow but could not. Calling in a drooling sleep gibberish to the statues, Eddie rocketed from graveyard back into the Church of Martyrs, to the narrow catwalk in the bell tower. Holding Father Louis' journal to his chest with both hands, Eddie lost his balance and fell. With his eyes tightly closed, he waited to land on the church floor below. He fell faster and faster and forever!

Eddie awoke. He lay in his bed, out of breath and covered in sweat. He adjusted his eyes to the wavy redness of the heater elements; his ears picked up its wandering hum. At least this time it *had* been a dream.

"Damn, that was some lethal *verde fagioli*! Must keep Sergio away from the garlic," Eddie said. He sighed in relief and slapped his hands down at his side. A brown beetle with orange pinstripes looked at him from a muddy knee cap. The confused stowaway turned a slow pirouette on its hind legs, surveying its new surroundings. Eddie's hands and face were covered with blood. Saint Bartholomew's blood? He felt Father Louis' journal resting against his leg.

"Shit!" Eddie brushed the beetle off his knee and threw the journal across the room, furious at being the patsy of the statues' practical joke. "Do you guys have to make such a big production out of everything? Couldn't you have just mailed it?" He glanced at the luminous dials on his alarm clock: three a.m.

Eddie knew he could not go back to sleep. He showered, got dressed, retrieved Father Louis' journal and sat at his small desk. The journal's incredible delivery confirmed Eddie's worst apprehensions: what had started in the Church of Martyrs was far from finished. He began to accept that he was a reluctant participant in whatever plans his stony buddies had in mind. He was a puppet manipulated by strings that reached into another dimension, a lab animal with nothing to look forward to each day except more exotic, painful tests.

Far more anxious than curious, Eddie opened the dog-eared journal. The familiar sight of Father Louis' smallish, eccentric Italian handwriting calmed and beckoned him.

ELEVEN

The first entry in Father Louis' journal was dated October 21, 1938, the day he arrived at the Church of Martyrs following his ordination as a priest in Italy. At the time there existed a great demand for Italian priests in America. Immigrant communities were slow to accept *Americano* priests in their parishes. They desired a genuine priest from the Old Country.

The first hundred or so pages in the journal contained nothing more than the predictable highs and lows of Father Louis' first years as a parish priest in an Italian neighborhood in a new land. He inventoried every facet of life in Briggs Hill, including detailed descriptions of *bocce* ball throwing techniques employed by neighborhood champions. The priest devoted a full page to the unique and highly effective sidearm delivery of Eddie's stepfather.

Frank Russo's ball seems to be guided by divine hands to its mark, seldom failing to inflict doom on his opponent.

A few secrets of Briggs Hill that Eddie assumed lost forever surfaced in the journal. Father Louis made lengthy notes on the wine-making methods of John Morabito, who produced some of the best wine in the neighborhood. The priest, however, did not approve of some of John's customers.

Powerful men who live outside the law buy John Morabito's wine each year. They will drink no other! These are men who can afford anything. While I condemn how they choose to make their living, I agree with their choice in wine.

Father Louis devoted a half-page to the secret ingredient in the lemon ice made in a neighborhood candy and ice cream store. The priest had been in the store on a summer day in the 1950s when the owner was making his lemon delicacy. Father Louis observed the maestro folding beaten egg whites into the frozen mixture. The priest could not have been more excited if he had witnessed the creation of life itself.

The egg whites must surely be the secret to the exquisite texture!

Eddie was aware that many people had asked the owner of the store the secret of his lemon ice and other delicacies, only to be rebuffed. Eddie acknowledged that true masters have always been loath to entrust their genius to dilettantes. Taking secrets great and small to the grave was very Italian.

At the start of World War Two, Father Louis wrote how the Italian immigrants of Briggs Hill publicly burned their Old Country Fascist black shirts as proof of their hatred of the *schifoso,* Italian low life, Mussolini after Italy joined the Axis. Few native-born Americans were as patriotic and protective of their adopted country as were the immigrants in Briggs Hill, wrote the priest. He listed every man from the neighborhood killed in the war and admitted that accompanying the agents of the armed forces to the homes of the dead or missing servicemen had been the most difficult task he ever performed as a priest.

Today, I must accompany the man from the army to see Mrs. Rizzio. I pray as I write this for a way to explain to her why God Almighty took her dear son. How will I explain to her what I don't understand myself? I fear it will be a severe test of faith for both of us.

The meandering journal was poignant and interesting, but nothing to murder—or to die—for. Eddie raced over the next fifty or so pages and was about to give up and go back to sleep when he found the first mention of the statues, the only subject that could have kept him reading.

The year was 1950. Father Louis, by then the pastor of the Church of Martyrs, traveled to Italy, the only vacation he ever took. While visiting Rome, he wanted to learn as much as possible about the statues.

I know only that a minor sculptor of the thirteenth century—Cuccio he was called—made the statues that so disturb my parishioners. Beyond that, I know nothing of the history of the statues, except that they were shipped from Rome to the Church of Martyrs in 1902. In Rome I hope to find someone who dealt with the statues when they were still the property of the Vatican. For a week I searched and asked. I was ready to give up when someone offered the address of an old man he thought had once worked as a Vatican laborer in the early part of the century. His name is Giuseppe Coreno. Even though it is unlikely that this man ever had any contact with the statues, tomorrow I will call on him.

Father Louis wrote that he hired a cab to take him to Coreno's humble two-room ancestral home in the craggy hills outside Rome. The cab dropped Father Louis off at the base of a long path that led to the home. As the priest walked the path, a lean, shoeless, sunbaked old man smoking a cigarette and straddling a rickety wooden chair backward in front of the house eyed him guardedly. Father Louis wrote that the old man jolted him with an enigmatic greeting.

"You took a long time to come, priest. How long did you think I could wait? I am almost dead!"

I asked the old man how he knew to expect me but he would not answer. I learned he was indeed the Giuseppe Coreno I sought. He was a bullheaded, puzzling man with a great distrust of others, especially, I am sorry to say, priests. He studied me for a long while through black eyes set deep in his thin face before he asked, "You are here because of the statues, are you not?" The man would not tell me how he knew why I had come but admitted that he was indeed one of the laborers who had carried the statues out of the catacombs beneath Saint Peter's Basilica and shipped them to America a half-century before.

Father Louis wrote that the retired Vatican laborer would at first volunteer nothing of the statues. The priest noted, however, that Coreno's reluctance did not appear sincere and that the man seemed anxious to tell his story. He noted an inquisitiveness on the old man's part about the history of the martyrs after they left Italy. Father Louis coaxed him, explaining that he served as pastor of the church where the statues were kept. He told Coreno how their damning faces distressed his congregation.

"That is all the statues do, priest? Nothing else?"

Of course I related to Coreno the miracle said to have occurred when the statues first arrived at the Church of Martyrs.

Eddie knew the story well and, up until about twenty-four hours before, had always thought it merely neighborhood myth. According to the story, Father Zitiello, the first pastor of the Church of Martyrs, helped several parish men uncrate the statues when they arrived from Italy a few days before the newly-completed church opened in 1902. When Father Zitiello saw the statues' torn bodies and scornful faces with eyes that seemed to reflect the very fires of hell, he vowed to never allow them to defile his beautiful new church.

After saying a quick prayer that the Vatican would not learn of his ingratitude, Father Zitiello and the men worked quickly to dispose of the statues. They nailed the lids back on the crates and loaded them on a horse-drawn wagon, which hauled them to the Cleveland docks. The crates were transferred to a hired barge. Father Zitiello, according to the story, instructed the captain to steam several miles offshore. The pastor rode along and helped dump the statues, still in their crates, into a deep and anonymous watery grave in Lake Erie. Good riddance!

The story did not end there, of course. Father Zitiello entered the Church of Martyrs early the next morning to prepare for the inaugural mass, sans statues, the following Sunday. What he saw chilled his spine. The statues, which he had personally drowned in Lake Erie the day before, stood on the polished marble plinths that had been prepared for them.

Oh, how accusingly the spurned martyrs glared at Father Zitiello! Did their molested flesh so offend him? How could they not be welcome in a church named to honor martyrs? Were their suffering faces and bloodied torsos so unworthy of representing a religion that had been founded on torture and christened with blood? The first pastor of the new Church of Martyrs dropped to the floor, where he wept and prayed for forgiveness until his knees bled.

Father Louis wrote that Coreno expressed no emotion upon hearing the story. To the contrary, he acted unimpressed and laughed like it meant nothing.

This odd Coreno fellow looked at me and said, with a great deal of mockery in his voice, "So, your statues swim like fish, do they priest? Ha! That is nothing. Listen while I tell you what it is to be frightened by statues."

After swearing Father Louis to secrecy, Coreno related the strange events that took place in a secret room beneath Saint Peter's fifty years before. Coreno said someone in the Vatican knew of statues of martyrs stored in the necropolis that is the basement of Saint Peter's and suggested they would be an excellent gift for a new church in America fittingly named the Church of Martyrs.

Equipped with kerosene lamps and centuries-old maps of the labyrinthine passages, Coreno and four other workmen began their search for the statues in an obscure and seldom-visited section of zigzagged tunnels and catacombs known as the "Constantine Maze." The section contained many crypts of long-forgotten popes, who in life had been neither saintly nor wicked enough to warrant internment in the basilica above. Sketchy information available to the men showed the statues had been stored somewhere in the maze six hundred years before, almost from the day the sculptor completed them.

After searching without success through smothering dust and thick cobwebs for an entire morning, Coreno said he and the others were about to give up when they heard sounds like the rattling of large pieces of wood. The workmen traced the sounds, which led them to a passage they would never have otherwise found. The passage ended at a room secured by a heavy iron door with a primitive but sturdy padlock. Coreno said they hesitated at the entrance to the room, even as the sounds within grew louder. Curiosity won out; the workmen broke the lock and entered the room.

Once inside the room, Coreno told me they were nearly knocked over by a suffocating stench of death, both ancient and perhaps not so ancient. Holding handkerchiefs over their mouths and noses, the men surveyed the contents of the room by the light of their lamps. Coreno said the scene was unlike anything he had ever known in the catacombs. Red flames and demons had been painted on all four walls, a portrait of hell! Many cloth bags were tossed about. The workmen cut into one of the bags. What they found troubled Coreno so much that he was unable to talk about it for several minutes.

Father Louis, his interest piqued to bursting, wrote that he begged the reluctant man to continue. Coreno at last obliged and the priest recorded.

The workmen found a corpse within the bag, although that in itself did not mean much. Finding corpses beneath Saint Peter's was routine since an untold number of bodies, Christian and pagan, had been interred there over the centuries. But this corpse was different than anything they had ever seen. The limbs had been bound and the mouth gagged, evidence that the poor devil might have been alive when placed in the bag. Bones distended at askew angles under blackened skin suggested a severe beating had been administered. Coreno said the corpse had not turned to a skeleton. Thin, dry air in the room had mummified the body, which was intact except for what vermin had eaten. Shrinkage around the mouth and eyes left them opened in an expression of anguish and despair. In death the victim had been denied even the visage of serenity.

The workmen cut into other bags and found more of the same. Most of the corpses had obviously been in the room for a very long time but others appeared to have been placed there much more recently, perhaps only a few years before. Clothing on some of the victims identified them as clerics, including bishops and cardinals! Nor were all the bodies those of men. Coreno spoke of females among the dead.

Father Louis wrote that the old laborer trembled as he recalled what he and the others had found that day.

I did my best to calm Coreno. He still had not explained the sounds he and the other workmen heard, the sounds that led them to the chamber. Where did they come from? What of my statues? But the man was not ready to explain any of this. Oh, how this Coreno fellow tried my patience. If he had not been such an old man, I might have shaken the story out of him!

Eddie smiled. Patience had never been one of Father Louis' priestly virtues.

Holding Father Louis in suspense, Coreno digressed in his story. He related that for years there had been rumors among Vatican workers of a dungeon below Saint Peter's known as the *"Stanza di Castigo,"* the "Room of Retribution" used by assassins as a secret dumping ground for their victims.

Eddie's imagination ran wild. He envisioned the victims in the Room of Retribution as reformers and papal critics who would not be quiet about corruption and excesses. They must have been exceptional men and women, stout souls who stood their moral ground in the face of death. The victims would surely have vanished swiftly, one moment playing their power cards in the high-level politics of the Vatican and in the next moment dying a slow, painful death, alone and dispossessed.

All, no doubt, neatly prefaced by excommunication, that most papal of papal tortures that condemns the soul to hell. There are no appeals to higher courts. A person simply goes to hell! Eddie tried to imagine what it was like for the excommunicates. Neither fully dead nor fully alive, their suffering would have been magnified many times by the thought of everlasting flames. Eddie took a moment to savor the irony: everything noble and beautiful and everything evil and ugly about the Catholic Church converged in that room. He returned to Father Louis' journal.

I pressed Coreno for more information. Where, in the sweet name of Jesus Christ Almighty, did the statues in my church fit into all this? What of those sounds, those cursed sounds? God held my hand! Coreno stared at me in silence for a few minutes, as if trying to determine if he could trust me with the rest of his tale. The old man took a deep breath and continued.

Coreno told Father Louis that a thorough search of the room produced no statues, nor clues as to the source of the sounds of wood against wood, which continued. They saw nothing in the room that could have produced the sounds. Coreno said that as he and the others started to leave, the air grew scant; they struggled to breath. Without air, their lanterns flickered and died, leaving the jittery workmen engulfed by an ominous darkness and choking for breath.

In the far corner of the room, a bluish light seeped through what appeared to be the outline of yet another door, as if someone had lit a lantern behind it. The rattling sounds became louder and insistent. The room refilled with air. The journal continued.

After relighting their lanterns, Coreno told me they cautiously opened the newly-discovered door that had revealed itself so mysteriously. The source of the bluish light that had guided them was not visible. They entered the room, which was much smaller than the main chamber. Inside were seven wooden crates the size and shape of very large coffins stacked haphazardly against the wall. The crates were moving. Moving! The noises they heard were produced by the crates bumping against each other, terrifyingly propelled by something inside. Coreno said that only burning curiosity bolstered by the shotgun that one of the workmen carried to dispatch rats they might encounter—rats that they so hoped caused the wooden crates to rattle—made them proceed further.

Coreno said they lifted a pulsating, monstrously heavy crate off the top of the stack and placed it on the floor. At that, all the crates stilled. The men pried the lid off the crate they had moved. Disturbed dust created a cloud which obscured the contents. When the dust settled, it revealed a stone giant, a statue of a man without skin, every muscle and cartilage visible. The statue held a knife in its right hand and a human hide over its left arm, the traditional representation of Saint Bartholomew. The workmen had found their martyrs.

Coreno told me he leaned into the crate and held his lantern near the face of the statue. Bartholomew's face, devoid of skin, stared back at him through eyes undimmed by six centuries. In those days, Coreno assured me, he feared nothing, not man nor beast. Yet he jerked away like a small child at the sight.

Father Louis wrote that Coreno paused to catch his breath before relating how the men proceeded to open the remaining six crates, the sight of each gruesome statue spurring them on to view the next. Behind the last crate they found a bag identical to those in the main chamber. The bag contained the body of a man who had managed to free a bound hand. He had scratched through the heavy fabric, a task which by itself must have cost him the last of his mortal strength. The mummified skin and bones of his right hand still reached from the bag.

Coreno held up his hand and with leathery, gnarled fingers mimicked the hand of the corpse. He said it appeared the victim had used his finger, and probably his blood, to scrawl a message on the wall. The men brushed away centuries of dust to reveal the dying man's last words: "Cuccio dorme suoi santi."

Eddie reread the words in the Italian: "*Cuccio dorme suoi santi.*" Then, his voice rising, he translated the long-dead sculptor's self-epitaph into English: "Cuccio sleeps with his saints."

The sculptor Cuccio had surely been murdered but why? Had Cuccio created his statues in condemnation of the papacy? The Church, uncompromising arbiter of art in those days, dictated that religious figures, beginning with Christ on the Cross, be portrayed as exonerating and redemptive, never menacing or denouncing. In Cuccio's day, the Church communicated with the unwashed masses through art that was meant to reassure, not frighten. Such an artistic protest as Cuccio's statues would have been a serious mistake in the thirteenth century, a time when even the kings and queens of Europe with their vast armies dared not displease the Vatican. Had Cuccio's statues earned him the ultimate censorship?

Coreno told Father Louis that he and the other workmen decided among themselves that the statues should remain in the chamber, hidden away from all eyes forever. After all, Coreno argued, who would pray to such statues? How could such hideous creations ever grace a church? Without taking time to replace the lids on the crates, they hastened to vacate the chamber.

Father Louis wrote that the old man broke down at this point in the story.

Poor Giuseppe Coreno began to cry the most tormented tears I ever hope to witness. He trembled so that I feared he might die before he finished his story. And, may Almighty God forgive me, I was myself ready to kill him if he didn't finish!

After much cajoling and soothing on my part, Coreno continued his tale. He told me that as he turned to leave, the statue of Saint Bartholomew reached out with its left hand and seized his wrist! Coreno said the statue moved with such speed that he never had a chance to elude the grip. He said the martyr squeezed his wrist so tightly that he feared it might snap. His eyes widened in recalled fright as he took my wrist in his hand and applied as much pressure as he could in an attempt to demonstrate Saint Bartholomew's strength. Coreno said his knees collapsed from fear and he fell to the dirt floor, his arm held in the air by the saint's vice-like hand. His face rubbed against Bartholomew's blood-drenched skin.

At first, Coreno said he tried to pull himself free. When that failed, he begged the statue to release him. When that, too, failed to earn him freedom, he began to pray. Coreno allowed that he was not the most religious man but said those prayers were the most earnest of his life.

The other workmen rushed to their comrade's aid but stopped short when Saint Bartholomew raised his right hand, the one that held the butcher knife, a knife no longer stone but steel! Stone to steel! The statue pulled its helpless victim up from the floor and into the crate until Coreno's neck met the blade. The statue drew the blade across Coreno's flesh several inches and deeply enough to draw blood! The old man showed me the scar that he bore the rest of his life. A wound inflicted by a statue!

Coreno told Father Louis that he continued to beg and pray for his life as best he could under the circumstances. One of the workmen shouted that perhaps the statue did not want Coreno's prayers but only wanted not to be left behind. Another of his comrades told him to promise the statue it would not be abandoned in the room. Maybe then Bartholomew might release him and they could all leave the damnable place.

Surely it was worth a try even though it sounded stupid, Coreno admitted. He promised the living statue that it would be carried out of the room. He vowed this on the lives of his children. Saint Bartholomew only tightened his grip and lengthened the knife cut, as if the statue wanted more of him. The desperate Coreno said that he guessed the martyr wanted a promise that all the statues would be taken out of the room. As his tears and blood dripped onto Bartholomew, Coreno told the saint again and again that he and the other statues would not be left behind. If Bartholomew would give him his freedom, he would do likewise for the statues. In the name of Christ on His Cross, he implored the martyr to let him live!

As quickly as Bartholomew had grabbed Coreno's wrist, he released it. The statue withdrew its arm back into the crate. Before the eyes of the assembled workmen, Bartholomew reverted to stone, blessedly harmless stone. Incredibly, the statue of Saint Bartholomew—and the others as well?—sought only to be liberated from their six-hundred-year incarceration. For whatever reason, the statues desired to be among the living. Madonna mia!

After telling his story, Coreno, so tough when I arrived, wept like a baby and begged me not to think him a lunatic. He swore to me on his mother's grave that what he related was the truth. I could only pray it wasn't.

Father Louis wrote that Coreno and the others, too afraid to do anything else, dragged the heavy crates out of the chamber. The old man said that his blood, oozing through a bandanna he had wrapped around his cut neck, reminded him and the others of his promise. Straining under their weight, the workmen carried the seven saints, one at a time, with great care through tight passages and up narrow, winding stairs to the world above.

Next day, in a small open work area, Coreno and the others cleaned and re-crated the seven statues, the first step in the long journey to the soon-to-be-opened Church of Martyrs in America. The men burned the old crates and swore among themselves to never reveal the strange events of that day. Not only would others think they had lost their minds but they also knew that the killers who might still use the Room of Retribution would not be pleased with those who spoke of its existence.

Of the Vatican laborers that day, Coreno was the only one still alive. Father Louis wrote that the old man broke his oath of silence only because he sought absolution. He confessed to a lifelong nagging guilt for turning the statues loose on an unsuspecting world and felt that freeing such aberrations was a sin, perhaps the worst he ever committed. Tearfully, he begged the priest's assurance that he had not been doomed to hell by his dealings with the statues. He asked that Father Louis hear his confession.

After hearing the man's confession, Father Louis wrote that Coreno turned away and motioned for him to leave. He would say no more. The priest returned the next day with many more questions for Coreno only to learn that the old man had died during the night, raving at the end about *"statue quello muove,"* statues that move! Father Louis blessed the old man's body, the house and all in it and returned to America.

Eddie exhaled deeply and dropped the journal to the desk. He wasn't certain whether what he had just read made him feel better or worse. Had the statues, forced by circumstances to be witnesses for centuries to the imponderable suffering of the victims in the Room of Retribution somehow absorbed—was that the right word, would *any* word be the right word?—the life energy and resolve of those murdered innocents?

Why hadn't the statues come to the aid of their creator Cuccio or, for that matter, the other victims? Eddie believed all of them were far more worthy of rescue than he. Why had the statues chosen to be guardians of death and dust for so long?

Reluctantly, Eddie began to accept that the statues may have rescued him because he was somehow paramount to their plans. But, more to the point, would they forsake him when he ceased to be of use? A life here or there didn't seem to make much difference to them. The seven men whose statues stood in the Church of Martyrs had gone to their deaths preaching the glories of everlasting life and the inconsequence of mortal existence.

Eddie was far from ready to concede the point.

In a note following the story of the startling discoveries in the cellars of Saint Peter's, Father Louis wrote that he never repeated what he had learned. For one thing, he had sworn to Coreno that he would not do so, but he also feared his parishioners would think him a fool or, worse yet, make him remove the statues. The pastor admitted to conflicted feelings about the martyrs. Despite his inexplicable fondness for them, he wrote that he was never comfortable in their presence, particularly when alone in the church at night.

"I couldn't agree more, dear old friend," Eddie said.

Eddie had an idea. He went into Father Louis' room, currently occupied by Sergio, who never heard Eddie searching for a book among the many jammed into the shelves.

Some assassin! Or maybe you just sleep better now.

Eddie came across the book he was looking for: *The Book of Popes.* The statues were believed to be about seven hundred years old. That meant they were made around the year 1300. Eddie wanted to know the name of the pope at the time, not really sure what good the information might be to him. With Sergio snoring in the background, Eddie turned on a lamp and thumbed through the pages until he found the reference he sought.

Pope Boniface the Eighth sat on the papal throne from 1294 to 1303. That bit of information meant nothing to Eddie until he read that Boniface had tricked the sitting pope in 1294 into resigning. According to the book, the scheming Boniface, a Vatican lawyer, ran a tube into the pope's sleeping quarters and spoke to him at night, pretending to be the Holy Ghost. Over and over, Boniface told the pope to leave his throne.

Popes have gotten a little smarter since then but you lawyers haven't changed much.

After the pope resigned under orders from the "Holy Ghost," the lawyer declared himself Boniface the Eight. He imprisoned the duped ex-pope and starved him to death, apparently all in a day's work for the cunning Boniface. Nothing too surprising about that. What surprised Eddie was the name of the gulled pope.

The pope tricked into resigning and who was later murdered was Celestine the Fifth. Was this the crime, the *sin*, Cuccio protested with his statues and paid for with his life?

According to the book, Celestine the Fifth was a hermit, an extraordinarily humble man who lived in a cave near Rome. The locals considered him a living saint. Drafted to the papacy against his will when the Conclave of Cardinals could not elect a pope, Celestine showed a complete disdain for the wealth of the Church, much like the *new* Pope Celestine. Popes take their name from a past pontiff they admire and whom they wish to emulate. It appeared to Eddie that Cardinal Lorini hadn't chosen the name of Celestine by coincidence. Though separated by seven centuries, the two Celestines seemed to be men cut from the same cloth. And maybe doomed to the same fate.

Two hours had passed since Eddie began reading. He gave up on the idea of sleep. He returned to his room and again read from Father Louis' journal. He skimmed the pages until he spotted a mention of Father Salvatore Viviano, who in 1958 was a new priest assigned to the Church of Martyrs parish. Eddie knew that Father Louis had disliked Viviano, even as he respected his gift for finances.

Regarding his talent with money, I have nothing but the highest praise for Fr. Viviano. Given the chance, he soon gains great returns on any amount of money given to him. Receipts from this year's church festival doubled in his hands within a few months! But my new assistant has great ambitions for himself and, sadly, little regard for the everyday duties of a parish priest. At the first opportunity I will mention his name and abilities to the diocese.

On the same page Eddie found Father Louis' most serious complaint about his assistant: the handsome Father Viviano had become involved with a number of young girls in Briggs Hill. The name Anna Roshelli, Eddie's mother, blared out from the page.

Little sweet Anna came to me to confess she has been physically involved with my assistant, Fr. Viviano. She is expecting a child and says he is the father. With her permission, I summoned Fr. Viviano into our meeting. He reacted with unexpected vehemence at the sight of the girl. He is a large and strong man and I feared for Anna's safety! As well as my own! I pray daily for a resolution.

The seismic revelation dizzied Eddie. Father Viviano, now *Cardinal* Viviano, the man almost elected the first American-born pope, was his father! His father was a cardinal, a prince of the Catholic Church and president of the Vatican Bank! Father Louis, as was his style, maddeningly digressed to other matters for the next ten pages or so.

Eddie thumbed through the journal, searching for further mention of his mother or his...father? The next mention of Viviano was a scathing condemnation of the priest for having turned his back on Anna Roshelli after she gave birth to twin boys. Eddie's mother committed suicide when Donnie and he were four years old. Father Louis fought off county child welfare efforts to take custody of the boys while he scurried to find a couple in Briggs

Hill who would adopt them. Frank and Mary Russo, who had no children of their own, agreed to take the boys.

About a year after Anna's suicide, as if in answer to Father Louis' prayers, the Cleveland diocese recruited Viviano as a financial advisor. Father Louis was greatly relieved.

We will get along nicely without the errant Fr. Viviano. I will force myself to pray for his soul.

Father Louis wrote that Anna, a few months before her suicide, asked him to keep the identity of the boys' father a secret. He, too, thought it a good idea.

I agree with Anna that it would serve no purpose to tell the boys that Fr. Viviano is their father. I will take the secret to my grave.

Eddie understood why Father Louis had not told his superiors about Viviano. The clergy back then was expected to keep all instances of sexual abuse secret. Only quite recently had the Church, begrudgingly and under much outside pressure, begun to address the issue.

Father Louis wrote that the diocese would not at first allow him to say a Mass of the Dead for Eddie's mother nor allow her to be buried in the Church of Martyrs cemetery because she had committed suicide. The priest wrote that he broke his promise to Anna only once, when he told the diocese officials about Father Viviano. He threatened to scream the news from the church bell tower if the mass and burial were denied. The diocese folded under the pressure.

Ah, Eddie thought, Father Louis had used the extortion card. How Catholic! How Italian! Anna Roshelli had her funeral mass and was buried in the church cemetery. What's more, Father Louis let it be known in Briggs Hill that the church had better be filled with mourners, which it was.

Eddie already knew most of what he read in the journal about his mother's suicide, except the reason. Father Louis gave Eddie the answer in a dour postscript.

She is at rest now, an all too early rest. No more can Anna be taunted or hurt by Fr. Viviano.

Eddie sat with his mouth open, taking deep breaths, as he absorbed the sordid details of this unsolicited voyeuristic peek into his past. It was six-thirty a.m. Eddie went outside, holding Father Louis' disentombed journal.

TWELVE

A chilly morning breeze filled Briggs Hill with the elixir of nearby Lake Erie. Another smell, the promise of fresh-brewed coffee, drew Eddie to the kitchen in the shelter. He spotted Pat sitting on the shelter steps, shoulders hunched, her chin resting on her knees. She sipped from a coffee cup. Eddie sat down next to her.

"Up already? I figured you'd sleep at least until noon," Pat said, stretching dreamily. Her breasts pushed against the *Cleveland Indians* sweatshirt that had been donated to the shelter. Chief Wahoo, ageless long-suffering warrior mascot of the *Indians,* smiled, apparently unconcerned that his team lacked middle relief and that he was at the center of an ongoing controversy over political correctness.

"Couldn't sleep," Eddie lied. "You're kind of up early yourself."

"Actually, I've been waiting for you."

"Waiting for me? Why?"

"I have a funny feeling you've been off on another harrowing adventure with your pals in the church. Am I right?"

"Yes, I did have another 'harrowing adventure,' as you put it, with my pals. How did you know?"

"I was asleep when I heard a noise. I looked out my window and saw dust and debris swirling around in the church. There was a strange blue light. So what happened? Some kind of statue rally? Did you bring me a T-shirt?"

Eddie smiled cheerlessly at Pat's sense of humor. It was exactly the kind of flippant remark he would have made were the roles reversed.

"More scavenger hunt than rally. I went underground with the statues. Literally!"

"Underground? As in under-the-ground? With all the statues?" Pat's voice was lively, electrified.

"Just six. There's a seventh guy in the chapel, but I guess he's behind on his union dues or something. He and Elvis were the only ones not present."

"It's nice that you can make light of this," Pat said. "So where'd you go on this...underground excursion?"

"We walked among the coffins buried in the old cemetery next to the church. Believe it or not!"

"I believe it and I know how you got there," Pat said.

"You do?"

"When the noise ended and the dust settled, I got my nerve together and went to the church. The statue bases were empty and there was a large hole in front of the altar. Is that where you entered?"

Eddie jumped up and started for the church.

"Might as well sit back down, Eddie. I checked already. The hole's gone. There's no sign it was ever there. And the boys are back. Some trick!"

"I wish it were a trick," said Eddie.

"How did the statues do it?"

"That's one of the rules of the club: the members don't know anything. All I know is the statues kicked down the door that separates reality from...whatever is not reality. And we walked through, right into another world, a place where I wasn't quite human and the statues weren't quite statues. I was certain I was dreaming, until I awoke covered with mud, blood on my hands, a beetle on my knee and this journal in my bed."

Eddie held the journal up like he was going to auction it. "This was buried with Father Louis, the priest who used to run this church, the same person who loved those damned Caruso records. I personally placed this journal in his coffin as per his last wishes. He was always very secretive about it. The statues led me to the coffin, lifted the lid and handed it to me."

"Did the statues...say anything?"

"No, they didn't," said Eddie. "The statues are either unable or choose not to speak and I can't possibly tell you how thankful I am in either case."

"So what's in the book? Or shouldn't I ask?"

"I need a cup of that coffee first," said Eddie. "Can I get you a refill, Pat?"

"Let me get it," she said. "You've had a rough night."

Pat stood and walked to the shelter kitchen, returning with two cups of steaming coffee. "It's black. That okay? You look like you need black coffee."

"Just how I take it, thanks." *Actually, Pat, I add tons of cream and sugar. But suddenly black coffee is my newest favorite thing.*

"How 'bout a cigarette to go with it? Ultralights okay?" Pat removed a pack of cigarettes from her pocket and offered one to Eddie.

"No thanks, I don't smoke."

"You mind if I do? Does the smoke bother you?"

"No, not at all."

I can't believe you've just told someone you don't mind cigarette smoke, you hypocrite!

"I started smoking again about a year ago when things got really out of control with my ex," Pat explained with a smoker's practiced sigh of resignation. "Now I'm hooked again. Terrible habit."

"I understand." He didn't.

Together they watched the rising sun outline the decaying profile of the Church of Martyrs. Time had not been kind to the old girl. A century of fallout from nearby Cleveland factories and mills had darkened her red brick to a sullied black—a church in mourning for herself. The large stone corner blocks, which the Italian immigrants who built the Church of Martyrs must have thought indestructible, had begun to crumble. Rust from rotting gutters ran down the outside walls like dried blood.

"Was the church always this gloomy?" Pat said.

"On the inside for sure, mostly because of the hard-to-ignore statues," said Eddie, "but the outside was never very cheerful or inviting either. I guess the name says it all, the 'Church of Martyrs.'" He looked down at the journal in his hands.

"So what's in the book?" Pat said.

"I'll start with what I learned about the statues," Eddie said. "Seems the boys were stored for six centuries in a room, a dungeon really, under Saint Peter's Basilica. The dungeon contained many corpses, all of which had been bound, beaten and sown into heavy cloth bags."

"Who ran that charming operation?"

"Good question. Certainly people with access to Saint Peter's. The Vatican workmen who found the statues also found the body of the murdered sculptor in the same room. He apparently carved the statues to protest something, perhaps the murder of a thirteenth-century pope, a pope with the same name as the new pope, I might add. I hate to admit it, but what's going on around here might be part of a plan that goes back centuries. Not that I have any idea what that plan might be."

"And it worries you that you might be part of the plan?"

"Probably Sergio too. Why doesn't *that* make me feel better?" said Eddie.

"So what else was in the journal?"

"Pat, I never knew who my father was until I read this journal. He's a cardinal in Rome, a big deal, runs the Vatican Bank. His name is Viviano. He was once a parish priest at this church. He had a romance with a neighborhood girl and fathered my brother and me. He was at Donnie's funeral. Donnie worked for him at the bank. No one could understand why a cardinal came so far for a funeral. Guilt, I guess. He hugged me. Goddamn him!

“Father Louis wrote in this journal that Viviano turned his back on my mother and on my brother and me. He simply walked away from the situation. Went on to bigger and better things. Nice guy, huh?”

“Is your mother still alive?”

“She killed herself when Donnie and I were four years old.” Eddie waited for Pat to say something. She said nothing, but her expression sustained him.

“Father Louis implied in his journal that Viviano drove my mother to suicide with taunts. There may have been physical abuse as well.”

“Your father never owned up to any of it?”

“Just walked away and wound up a cardinal,” said Eddie. “Not that he set any precedent. Many times in the past, the Vatican was overrun with the illegitimate children of bishops, cardinals and even popes. When their fathers died, the kids and their mothers were thrown into the street.”

“Seems to me that women have always gotten the short end of religion,” Pat said.

“Not by accident either. In the Old Testament, it sure as hell wasn’t *Adam’s* idea to eat the apple. Did any *man* ever get turned into a pillar of salt? Biblical women are mostly portrayed as scheming and manipulative, the very same traits applauded in the Bible’s men.

“Then came Jesus Christ. He respected women, even broke Jewish law by including them in conversations. He desired that women be treated as equals but things got turned around after his crucifixion. The apostles were loyal to a fault, some of them died horrible deaths for Christ, but they were all simple men. I doubt if any of them fully understood what Christ wanted. He should have been a little more specific in his instructions.”

“All women know that when you want a man to do something, you have to write it down,” Pat said.

“How true!” said Eddie. “And it didn’t take long for Christianity to systemize female abuse. Early Church leaders had the paranoid mentality of heirs, not the confidence of initiators. The decision that priests should be celibate was a result of that paranoia and lack of confidence. Celibacy was a move by insecure men to put themselves above other men. The idea was that they would become more like Christ but the unfortunate and inevitable result was a lot of playing around by a lot of horny men. Worse, when priests became celibate every woman automatically became a temptress."

"And it wasn't much of a stretch from temptress to witch, was it?" Pat said.

"No stretch at all. Nothing so symbolizes the power men have had over women as the stake. There was a time when just being a woman was enough to get you killed."

"It still is," Pat said. "At some point in their lives all women understand that. Women unlucky enough to get involved with abusive men always suffer and die. One way or the other."

Eddie deferred to Pat's knowledge on the subject with a nod that was part acquiescence, part apology for his naiveté.

"Did your friend's journal help you make any sense out of what happened the other night in the church?"

"Not much. Except that it's common knowledge Cardinal Viviano would like to be the first American-born pope. Having me and my brother Donnie dead would certainly add to his peace of mind. Someone with a lot of power and money sent Sergio and his buddies to kill me. Cardinals have power and money. I learned a few things yesterday that make me suspect my brother's death may not have been accidental. He may have been murdered."

"By whom?"

"Another good question! Probably the same person or persons who wanted me dead. Sergio claims the gang of murderers he was part of are tied in with the Vatican."

"Can't trust anyone anymore, can you?"

"Religions aren't built on trust, they're built on faith, *blind* faith. The blind faith Catholics and members of other religions have in their leadership overlooks shortcomings. It allows pricks like Cardinal Viviano to rise to the top."

"But wouldn't this Viviano have to wait for the pope to die before he could be elected? Isn't that how it's done?" Pat said.

"That's where the story seems to come together. Sergio said he and the two men killed in the church were to meet some other assassins in Mexico City after they killed me. Mind you, these guys knew to go to Mexico City well before the pope announced his visit. Sergio has convinced himself that the statues saved our lives so that we could protect the pope."

"How?"

"You tell me. It'd be funny if it wasn't so ridiculous." Eddie picked up a small stone and heaved it across the courtyard at nothing in particular. "Celestine may be the first pope in history with the guts to do what's right. He's trying to set an example for the entire world, for all religions. Popes, including the last one, have always been big talkers. They profess to love the poor but have been slow to write the checks. Not this one! He's exactly the kind of man for whom those persons in that death chamber beneath Saint Peter's died."

"The same could be said for those men whose statues are standing in the church, am I right?" Pat said.

"I suppose," said Eddie. "Pat, you certainly catch on in a hurry."

"I don't think one has to be an ex-priest to understand it."

The comment stunned Eddie. Pat tossed his past into the conversation like she had known him all his life, the way a close friend might. Eddie wanted her to know that he was once a priest, but hadn't decided how he was going to tell her.

"So much for keeping secrets around here," Eddie groaned. "So who was it, a little ex-killer who makes a mean *verde fagioli*?"

"No, not Sergio. Actually, it was a cop named Nick, a decent enough guy, if maybe a bit pushy. He said he's a friend of yours from the neighborhood. He stopped by last night just after you went to bed. To check me out for himself, I suspect. He said you have trouble telling women about your past. I think he has the idea that we have a relationship. After just one day! Imagine that?"

"Imagine that," Eddie echoed. He was about to respond when Sergio happened by.

"Good morning *Signora, Signore,*" Sergio said, walking dutifully in the direction of the church. He carried a wooden toolbox.

"Well, look who's here," Eddie said. He was disappointed at losing the opportunity with Pat, but he was also grateful for Sergio's interruption since he hadn't the slightest idea how to follow Pat's comment.

"Sergio, where are you going with my tools? Planning on building an ark or something? Although that might not be such a bad idea. We get a helluva lot of rain in Cleveland. Watch that hammer, the head flies off."

"I go to the church, *Signore,*" Sergio said. "I going to see if the bell ring. If it do not, I fix it. Good idea, no?"

"No! You're going to break your neck climbing those bell tower stairs. That bell will never ring again. There's no gong in it! Besides, that isn't even a real church anymore."

Sergio looked at the Church of Martyrs and then at Eddie with something less than the unconcealed adoration he had shown since the moment Eddie saved his life. "This church more real than any church I ever in!"

"You would not like the sound of that bell, Sergio," said Eddie. "Then again, you might."

"Why? How it sound, *Signore*?"

"Forget it, you're never going to get it to ring anyway."

"You think more about Mexico City? We not have time to waste."

"I haven't thought about it at all," Eddie lied. "There's nothing we can do there. If the statues want to save the pope, they won't need us."

"You wrong, *Signore*. You no understand."

Eddie turned to Pat. "Okay, Sergio's right for once. I admit it. I *don't* understand."

"Didn't you tell me the night I arrived that your life's been short on excitement?" Pat teased.

"My idea of excitement would be a trip to Disneyworld, if I had the money," said Eddie. "The pope already has plenty of bodyguards, trained to shoot wiseasses like me on sight."

"I not tell you this before," Sergio said. "But I hear many times that *La Mano di Cristo* be part of *Il Papa's* bodyguard."

"Perfect! Then they wouldn't let anything happen to him, would they?"

"They do what they told, *Signore,*" Sergio said. He walked away in the direction of the church.

"I guess I shouldn't be so hard on the little guy, should I?"

"No, you shouldn't," Pat said.

"It's just that I'm afraid of what this could turn into. I'm not the hero type, Pat."

"There's no such thing as a hero type. As a nurse, I saw dozens of men and women who did heroic deeds. I treated burned, broken and half-drowned people carried into emergency rooms after saving someone's life, someone they didn't even know. The only thing they had in common was that they happened to be on hand when help was needed."

"That's my point. With enough time to stew about it, there'd be no heroes. Anyway, thanks for listening. Actually, my job here is to listen to *your* troubles."

"I'll be looking forward to my turn to lie on the couch, so to speak." Pat's face was animated, provocative.

The flames of Eddie's brief—and entirely imaginary—one-day relationship with Pat heated up a few hundred degrees. He didn't respond, knowing from past experience that anything he said would be witless. Some men knew how to talk to women and some didn't; the luckiest men had only to *look* at women to communicate their feelings. Eddie was content for the moment to savor his black coffee and enjoy the morning air tinged with the newfound intoxication of Pat's cigarette.

"Eddie, why did you tell Sergio he wouldn't like the sound of the bell?"

"I should never have said that."

"I want to know."

"The bell is engraved with the names of over a thousand Catholic martyrs. It's called the 'Martyrs' Bell.'"

"So?"

"Well, it didn't toll joyously like bells in other churches. The damned thing rang with a cheerless quality, depressing as fresh death. Some of the parishioners claimed they could hear human voices moaning in agony when it rang. They called the sounds '*canzone dei martiri,*' the 'martyrs' song.'"

"Did you hear the moans?"

"Not really. But then I never tried, either."

Sergio ran out of the church, straight to Eddie.

"Now what, Sergio?"

"*Signore,* come to the church! Please!"

"Forget it! I'm never going into that church again. And even if I did, I wouldn't climb those bell tower steps. My insurance doesn't cover stupidity."

"This no about bell!"

"What's wrong, Sergio?" Pat said.

Sergio looked at Pat and again at Eddie. He said nothing while he seemed to search for the right words.

"*Signore*, please!" Sergio implored, stepping closer to Eddie. "Come see what they write!"

THIRTEEN

Celestine had a problem: the Vatican Bank. More specifically: bank president Cardinal Viviano. When Celestine had requested an accounting early in his papacy, Viviano asked him to be patient and even sent a letter informing the pope that it was highly unusual, if not improper, for a pope to concern himself with such mundane matters as Church finances.

"Improper?" the pope said to his aide, Father Luca Villalobos. "What is 'improper' is holding a vast fortune while people suffer and starve in this world. It is not only improper, it is *sinful*!"

The day before he was to leave for Mexico City, the pope asked Villalobos to contact the bank and get "His Majesty Cardinal Viviano on the phone."

After his aide tried unsuccessfully for an hour to reach Viviano, Celestine took matters into his own hands and called the bank. A bank secretary, when she caught her breath at the idea of speaking with Celestine the Sixth, apologetically informed him that the cardinal was not available.

"You tell Cardinal Viviano to become available immediately or look for another job! Tell him I have several replacements in mind," said the pope, who then hung up.

Within minutes, the pope's secretary informed him that Cardinal Viviano was holding on the phone.

"Viviano, as you know, I will be leaving for Mexico City in the morning," Celestine said, without giving the cardinal a chance to speak. "I don't have the time to visit with you today but upon my return we will meet and you will tell me exactly what our Church is worth. You have lost my trust so expect independent auditors to verify everything! I want to know how much cash we have and I want to see a plan to divest all our holdings in a timely manner. Do you understand?"

"Yes, Your Holiness, I understand," Viviano said. "But I ask you to understand also that the Vatican Bank, like all banks, has many intricate, some might even say 'convoluted,' dealings. With all due respect, Your Holiness, is the subject of our ledgers really worth your time?"

"*Everything* connected to our Church is worth my time," bellowed Celestine. "I will not allow you or anyone else to interfere with my plans! I am not another confused, blinkered, octogenarian pontiff that you can push around. I have no strings attached to my hands, feet or mouth. If you can't do what I ask, I will find someone who can! Is that clear?"

"Yes, Your Holiness. Have a safe trip. And may God be with you."

"No, Viviano, may God be with *you* if you continue to obstruct me! One more thing: I do not intend to tell you again to move your offices and living quarters to the new location I have chosen for our Church. Working and living among the poor of this world will do wonders for your humility. When I return from Mexico, I will send the moving vans myself!"

The conversation with Cardinal Viviano, though brief, left the pope with an inexpressible foreboding. He realized Viviano was far more dedicated to preserving the wealth of the Church than in sharing it. Celestine was uncertain, however, how far the cardinal—or anyone else—would go to stop him. He knew, as did everyone, that Viviano wanted very much to be pope. Celestine also knew that popes were not immune from intrigue and murder. For the first time, Celestine felt a need to enlist the help of an old trusted friend that he had not wished to involve.

The pope told Father Villalobos to arrange a meeting later that day with representatives from the College of Cardinals and the Roman Curia. At the meeting Celestine would announce his choice for secretary of state, the second most important position in the Catholic Church.

Despite scheduling conflicts a good number of Vatican prelates and members of the Curia came to the hastily assembled meeting, each with his own list of suitable candidates, all of them cardinals or bishops and every name an entrenched and well-vetted member of the Vatican's cherished status quo.

"Holy Father, why have you decided to name a secretary of state now, after all these months and just before you leave for Mexico City?" a bishop in the room asked.

"I now feel there is a need," the pope said simply, without betraying his apprehensions. "And the man I have chosen is Gesa Danku! It is done!"

Each man present scanned his list, both long and short, for a name that matched Celestine's choice. They looked at one another, showing no emotion lest they offend the pontiff. Such a strange name and, worse yet, a name totally unfamiliar. All waited for someone else to ask the pope to repeat his selection.

"I beg your pardon, Holy Father," a cardinal in the room said. "Would you please repeat the name of the man you want as secretary of state? I don't believe any of us have heard of him."

"His name is Gesa Danku. What's important is *I* have heard of him. And God has heard of him! Gesa Danku will be my secretary of state!"

"Is he a bishop or perhaps someone you will name bishop, Your Holiness?" Villalobos asked.

"No, Gesa Danku is a priest, the most devout and hardest working priest on Earth!"

"He is only a priest, Your Holiness?" Villalobos said, stepping back as if he regretted the comment. He had been Celestine's aide for several months and knew how easy it was to upset the boss, normally a very agreeable person unless challenged. But

Villalobos was a Jesuit. His severe training, uncompromising and exhaustive, had taught him to involuntarily rail at anything opposed to the strictest traditions of the Catholic Church. The Vatican secretary of state was *always* at least a bishop.

"Only a priest!?" Celestine said, echoing Father Villalobos. The pope seemed astonished by the comment. "I would remind you that Jesus Christ was 'only a priest.' Priests do all the work in our Church. I offered many times when I was a cardinal to promote Gesa Danku but he always refused."

"Where can we find him, Your Holiness?" said Villalobos. "Is he here in Rome?"

"No, he is not. The last letter I received from Danku came from Africa, where he is doing Christ's work among the Hittabbe, a tribe of Congolese Pygmies. Africa is somewhat larger than Rome, but I'm sure he can be found. Father Villalobos, I should warn you that Danku can be very difficult, to say the least. You will need all of your Jesuit wiles."

"*My* Jesuit wiles, Your Holiness? *I* will have to find him?"

"Yes. Take someone along. It will be an arduous journey. I should also warn you that Father Danku is very happy in Africa. He will refuse to come to Rome. When he does, give him this." The pope handed Villalobos a sealed envelope.

"I will leave in the morning, Your Holiness."

A member of the Roman Curia, refusing to be browbeaten by the pope, spoke out. "With all due respect for your judgment, Your Holiness, what qualifications does this man possess? Vatican secretary of state is an extremely demanding position."

"I believe I have already answered that question," said the pope, his reserve of patience plainly running low. "Gesa Danku is the most devout and hardest working priest on Earth. What better qualification can a man possess?"

"The Curia may not place as much value on that qualification as you, Holy Father," the Curial official said. "We may try to block the appointment."

"Do not threaten me! Your Roman Curia has been telling popes what to do for a long time. Too long! That is not the way it will be from now on. You bureaucrats select men for all the wrong reasons. The Curia values circumspection; I value forthrightness. The Curia values wealth and prestige; I value callused hands. I know who is best for the position. I will not allow the Roman Curia, or any other worldly force, to interfere in my plans for the future of this Church! Shall I call a press conference and give my opinion of the meddlesome Roman Curia and how it is but a medieval vestige, an outdated, overpaid bureaucratic impediment to Christ's mandate? I could easily put the Curia on the defensive for many months, if you like."

The Curia official backed off. Celestine had been critical of the Curia even before he was elected pope. He was the darling of the world media and the Curia knew it. Celestine especially had the ear of the Italian media, always happy to enter any Church internal power struggle.

Father Villalobos allowed the air to settle, then continued his questions about the unknown priest with the unusual name.

"You have known this man for a long time, Your Holiness?" Villalobos asked.

"Since our seminary days," Celestine said. He smiled as if recalling a distant memory. "It may interest you to know that I once took a beating for Gesa Danku."

"Your Holiness took a beating for him?" said Villalobos.

"Yes. My friend Gesa Danku is a Gypsy. The other seminarians despised him because he has the odd, often dark ways of the Romani. They taunted him from the day he entered the seminary. He never fought back. He accepted the abuse and even the beatings with great dignity and piety. To my shame, I don't possess his tolerance. My family of bakers is not known for its Christian forbearance, I'm afraid. We fight at the merest provocation.

"Danku is a gifted violinist. I once attacked three seminarians who had broken Danku's violin, pushed him to the ground and were kicking him. Danku only fought back to protect *me*. We both took a good beating, although we managed to inflict our share of blows, I might add."

"I mean no impertinence, Your Holiness," said Villalobos. "But why do you expect Father...Danku to be of more use to you than one of the excellent men that have been recommended?"

"Father Villalobos," said the pope, "you will have the answer to that question the instant you meet Gesa Danku."

FOURTEEN

"So, what did they write, Sergio?" said Eddie. "And just who are *they*?

"They! The statues I think. They write something on the altar. Come look," said Sergio.

"What does it say?"

"I not sure what it say. Maybe it is Latin. Please come, *Signore*." Sergio looked at Pat for help.

Pat intervened. "Eddie, at least go into the church and see what Sergio's talking about. C'mon, you know you're dying to see. So am I." She stood and nudged Eddie's elbow.

"Dying! Now there's a curious choice of words," Eddie said.

"Thank you, *Signora*."

"This better be good," Eddie said, swigging down his coffee.

As Eddie walked toward the side door of the church, it occurred to him for the first time that the massive door had been swollen shut for years. Yet it opened easily the night Sergio and the other two assassins chased him into the church.

They say little miracles are the best ones. Maybe I could get the statues to fix a few more things around this place. They've obviously got too much time on their hands.

The three of them entered the Church of Martyrs. A morning sun ray shined through a missing window directly at the altar.

The shaft of sunlight reminded Eddie of those imaginary walkways to heaven the old-time Italian painters couldn't resist.

Sergio stood in front of the altar, his body mostly obscuring a word that appeared to have been roughly hewn into the wood.

"Can you tell what it say, *Signore*?"

"Not with you blocking it. Get out of the way!"

Sergio stepped aside.

"Sequemur...?" Eddie mouthed the single word cut into the altar. The large letters were not so much carved as hacked, deeply, the handwriting of a giant on the loose with a big knife. Eddie repeated the word in a loud voice that exposed his agitation: *"Sequemur!"*

"Follow? I, no, *we*...will...follow? We will follow!" Pat said in a halting voice almost too hushed to be heard.

"What you say, *Signora*?"

"I think it says 'we will follow,' or something like that. Eddie, you're the Latin expert here."

"Don't rub it in. But you're right, that's exactly what it says. You pass today's Latin quiz. How did you know?"

"You don't have to be an ex-priest to know Latin, just pay attention in high school."

"Sometimes I think I'd rather be an ex-convict than an ex-priest. People are easier on ex-convicts," Eddie said in a distracted voice. His eyes were glued on the inscription.

"Sorry," Pat said.

"If you really want to help, don't tell me what it *says*, tell me what it *means*."

"It mean the statues will follow, they will follow *you, Signore,*" Sergio offered. "I go with you. You need me. I good at these things."

"That's very comforting, Sergio. And just where in the hell do you think they're going to follow us *to*?"

"To Mexico City."

"Give it up, Sergio." Eddie walked to the altar and felt the letters, running his fingers along the cuts. He reached down, picked up a handful of wood fragments and let them cascade to the floor.

He looked at his chief suspect, Saint Bartholomew, the only statue with a knife. Eddie did a double take when he saw that the martyr's face had changed. Bartholomew's skinless lips were perceptibly more twisted, the teeth more protruding and canine, the lidless eyes more unyielding.

Eddie scanned the other five statues. Also changed. Also for the worse. He didn't think Sergio or Pat noticed the transformations and decided not to mention it. Pat didn't need to be drawn any further into whatever was happening and he certainly didn't want to give Sergio more ammunition.

"The saints will follow us...follow *you* to Mexico City, *Signore*."

"You and the statues can go anywhere you want, Sergio. I'm staying here."

"You really no understand, do you *Signore*?" Sergio said, raising his voice at Eddie for the first time. "Are you *stupido* or you just no want to understand?" Sergio's face burned with frustration; he clenched his fists.

Though a bit alarmed by Sergio's confrontational stance, Eddie did not back off. "You've said that before, Sergio, and it's starting to annoy me, really piss me off! What is it that I don't understand? If you know, then tell me. Right now! Tell me what it is that I don't get!"

Sergio shook his head, as if unable to believe that Eddie had not yet come to the same inescapable conclusion as he. "Okay, I tell you, *Signore Stupido*! What you no understand is you not need the statues, the statues need *you*. Statues get *life* from *you*, get *strength* from *you*! How come you no understand this?"

"Oooh, no. Don't lay that on me! This ex-priest already has all the guilt he can handle. I don't need any more, not from someone who used to go around killing people and sure as hell not from statues that oughta' be on the bottom of a landfill."

"Is the truth. I sorry if you not like it. Go 'head, you try put statues in this...landfill. I bet then they make you understand."

"I want no part of any of this. That's all I understand," Eddie said.

"Is not what you want, *Signore*," Sergio said with finality. "Is what the statues want. They will find a way to make you understand. Oh, how I would like to watch!"

"Pat, did I mention that this is not your average women's shelter?" Eddie said.

"A number of times," she said. "Was there anything about a message carved on an altar in the journal?"

"Journal? What is this journal?" Sergio asked, realizing that he had been left out of something.

"It doesn't concern you, Sergio," Eddie said.

"You wrong, *Signore*. I think it concern me, too. When it is time, you will tell me. You right about only one thing."

"That's good to hear. What would that be?" said Eddie.

"The bell, it no can be fixed. Someone steal the gong. I go make lunch for the ladies."

Sergio walked out of the church but stuck his head inside to proffer a last comment. "My Spanish pretty good, like my English. And remember, God work through simple, stupid people. You perfect."

Eddie turned to Pat. "No one should have to put up with scary statues *and* Sergio." He walked to a pew in the middle of the church. After checking for water puddles and vermin droppings, he sat down.

"Some great church the statues chose, huh?" said Eddie. "Just shows how smart they are." He said the words loudly enough to cause an echo, which retained the ridicule.

"They wouldn't be happy anywhere else," Pat said. She walked the aisle toward Eddie. "Other church statues I've seen looked like Greek gods or movie stars. These guys look like men you'd find in a tough neighborhood bar. I think they like it here."

"Truth is, these guys wouldn't have been allowed off the delivery truck at a high-rent church. Classy churches require their statues to look pleased about the suffering they endured for their faith. They want statues worshippers can feel comfortable around, light some candles in front of, write a nice check to, that sort of thing. Whatever it is these characters want, it isn't donations or worship. They repel familiarity."

Pat moved to the pew behind Eddie and leaned over his shoulder. "Eddie, what is it you're really afraid of? You don't have to answer me."

"No, I'll answer you. I *need* to," he said. "It's not just because I fear going to Mexico City and making a fool of myself. Or worse!"

"What, then?"

"Pat, I spent the first part of my life utterly devoted to God and the Catholic faith and every saint that ever lived, even these guys...*especially* these guys. I never doubted any of the Church dogma or hoopla or hocus pocus for a second. But after I'd been a priest for about eight years, I began to feel that I was devoting my energies, not to mention my life, to a belief that never seemed to make a difference. I was selling a product people bought readily enough but most of them never used it!

"One day I decided to stop banging my head into a wall and reclaim my life. Nothing very dramatic about it, kind of like I went to start my old Dodge that day and it wouldn't start. Just wouldn't start! I simply quit being a priest. I've been reasonably happy ever since, love-starved, miserably underpaid county employee that I am. The sad truth is that I don't have the capacity to believe anymore, not even in myself."

"The statues seem to believe in you," said Pat.

"You sound like Sergio."

"Maybe a little. Most people wouldn't need more than *one* walking statue to get their attention."

"Oh, they have my attention, no doubt about that," said Eddie. "And that's all they're going to get. How about we exit this church?"

Eddie looked again at the unsettling message left—for him?—on the altar. He also looked at the martyrs, all of whom stared at him with eyes capable of derailing a locomotive. "Hey, guys, I'll get back to you. Don't call me, I'll call you. And quit defacing that altar or I'll call the cops."

"As if you have any say in the matter. If they want you, they'll find you," Pat said. "Sergio's right about that!"

"Pat, you haven't seen these things move. All you saw was some swirling dust, a disappearing hole in front of the altar and some empty statue plinths. A rookie magician could have done those things. How come you sound so convinced?"

"Because I know you're telling the truth."

"How?" He gave Pat an askance look, trying to guess what she was about to say. He was not sure he wanted to hear it.

"Eddie, you couldn't lie if you wanted to. You don't have the face for it. I quit believing anything men told me long ago. But I believe you. You have eyes like those statues. They burn right through everyone you look at. Everything pours out of you with an honesty that's frightening. Frankly, Eddie Russo, you're easier to read than a comic book."

"I can only hope that's a compliment of some sort."

"The greatest compliment a woman can give to a man!"

Does that mean you know that, despite everything going on in my pathetic life at the moment, I can't stop thinking about you?

She nodded. "See what I mean?"

They laughed together as they left the church. Outside, they chatted in the courtyard while enjoying the few morning sun's rays powerful enough to punch through Cleveland's late winter armor. Pat spotted an abandoned greenhouse listing hard to port behind the rectory. Tangled weeds, tricked into life by the magnified heat, pushed against the glass like cornered inmates in a failed escape. A small, crude tombstone was visible inside the greenhouse.

"Who's buried in the greenhouse?" Pat asked, walking toward it. Eddie followed.

"Blackie."

"Another saint?"

"Trust me, Blackie was no saint. She was Father Louis' dog. She lived for nearly twenty years. That dog was a pain in the ass, crapped all over the place. If anything, *I* was the saint for putting up with her after Father Louis died."

"Why is she buried in the greenhouse?"

"Blackie loved the warmth. I think she had arthritis or something. She spent hours in there with Father Louis while he tended his herbs and tomato plants. After Father Louis died, Blackie spent every day walking between his grave and the greenhouse. I guess Blackie thought she could coax her friend back. She died in there, so that's where I buried her."

Pat squinted through the dirty glass. She read the grave marker: "BLACKIE. IF YOU LET HER INTO HEAVEN LORD, WATCH WHERE YOU STEP!"

That's terrible, kind of funny but terrible. Did you write that?"

"Who else?"

"I thought you didn't believe in things like heaven," Pat said.

"Father Louis did. I'm sure Blackie did. That's what counts."

"Speaking of heaven, I have a question. If there *is* such a place, would the saints in the church be there?"

"I suppose, though I've never seen a guest roster. Those martyrs certainly earned a free stay if anyone ever has."

"But they brutally murdered two men. Doesn't that go against everything heaven stands for?"

"Not the Christian heaven," said Eddie. "The rules for admission are all spelled out in the Bible, where killing is condoned and even encouraged in both the Old *and* New Testament. The Angel of the Lord in the Old Testament might be the best of many examples. It was not the cute little character on our Christmas cards. The Angel of the Lord was an assassin, perhaps the most deadly in history, slaughtering one hundred and eighty-five *thousand* Assyrian enemies of the Lord in one night.

"There're called prophets, but the Old Testament is really full of *politicians,* politician-generals to be exact. When something went against them or they lost the attention of their constituents, they turned to the Lord for divine air strikes. The Lord, on cue, would obligingly hurl catastrophes on the earth to get everyone's attention. We humans are cruel because our gods are cruel. We excel at killing each other because our gods taught us well. And they're always right there to encourage us in case we become squeamish: recite a prayer and reload.

"In the New Testament God seems at first to have changed his mind and softened a bit. Jesus Christ certainly preached forgiveness, turn the other cheek and that sort of thing but he also agreed with Old Testament Jewish law, including killing a son or daughter for cursing a parent. But all the evidence one really needs to make a case for murder comes at the end of the New Testament, the Book of Revelation."

"The spooky part, right?" Pat said.

"Yep, the spooky part. At the end of time, in Revelation, all scores are settled. No more tempering of justice with mercy. No more forgiveness. Don't even bother to apply. The bloodied martyrs, the very men in that church, demand from their graves that God avenge their deaths, murder thinly disguised as justified vengeance."

"I'll bet you gave some pretty good sermons in your priest days," said Pat. "Did you ever throw in any of this juicy stuff?"

"I pushed the limits now and again, especially toward the end of my run in the pulpit. I don't have to tell you that it didn't go over very well. Religion is like a favorite movie or play. The audience knows exactly what it likes and what it wants to see and hear. It hates when someone screws with the plot or shades a character. Priests should be given the most freedom of speech but they have the least. Suffice it to say that by the time I left the priesthood, most of the parishioners were more than ready to see me leave. There were a lot of candles lit in thanks that day. I'm sure of that."

"By the way, how is it that the statues are still in the church?" Pat said. "Surely someone would have wanted them, as old and unique as they are."

"The story just keeps getting weirder," said Eddie. "After the church closed, there was an auction. The statues of Jesus and the Virgin, both just ordinary statues, were sold right away to another church and went quietly. Not a kick or peep out of either. No other churches wanted the martyrs. Catholic churches have enough trouble trying to keep customers these days without putting Halloween statues on display. Art collectors passed on them, too. The boys aren't exactly great art."

"I'm not so sure of that," Pat said. "If the purpose of art is to command one's attention and get the mind pumping, these guys are hall of famers. Great art is about truth, no matter how messy."

"I suppose," said Eddie. "There *was* a buyer for the statues, a creep who ran a house of horrors museum or some such thing. He got all seven statues for a bargain price, next to nothing. But when the movers tried to lift the martyrs off their plinths, they began to crumble. The movers decided the statues were made from plaster or a similar material that had deteriorated too much to be moved. The creep's money was uncheerfully refunded and the statues stayed behind. They turned the Church of Martyrs into their own private house of horrors."

"They crumbled? Aren't they made of stone?"

"Yes, they are, they're made of stone. Unlike myself."

"Well, better gather up what courage you happen to possess because I'm going to re-bandage your feet. Let's go to the rectory."

"Thanks just the same. My feet are fine." Eddie's measured steps betrayed him.

"You may be making a trip soon, you're going to need those feet."

"I don't plan on going anywhere, except someday to Disneyworld. Though it probably wouldn't hurt to have a look at the feet, you being a nurse. I warn you, I'm kind of a baby when it comes to pain."

"All men are babies when it comes to pain."

In the rectory Eddie gathered what few medical supplies were available. He sat down on a chair in the study and removed his shoes and socks. His bruised, cut and still swollen feet hurt far more than he admitted.

"Ouch!" he cried as Pat yanked the bandages off with a nurse's clinical deftness. She cleansed the cuts thoroughly and re-bandaged them.

"The feet are in pretty good shape, considering. All in all, I think you'll live." Pat stood, leaned over and kissed Eddie on the cheek. "That's for being such a good patient."

The kiss pleased Eddie beyond anything it might have been meant to convey. It ignited fires within him he didn't know existed. He smoothed his cheek with his hand.

"Pat, how long do you intend to stay? I mean, you're free to leave when you want. And I wouldn't blame you for wanting to leave. It's just that...right now I need a friend, someone to talk to."

"Just a friend? Someone to talk to? Is that all you need?" Pat said. Her voice had the texture of cream.

Eddie tried to answer but could only manage a smile.

"I'll be here," Pat said. "Besides, how could I leave? I'd be afraid I'd miss something. I want to see those statues move."

"No, you don't," said Eddie. "You really don't! Nothing fun happens when they move!"

FIFTEEN

As evening neared, Eddie began to again dread sleep and the dreams that might await. A comet's tail of unpleasant surprises seemed to trail behind his friends in the church. He put off sleep until late afternoon, catching up with chores at the shelter. When the impossible burdens of the last two days finally overcame him, he gave into his body's need for rest and went to bed.

Screw it!

He dreamt of nothing. Not about popes nor statues nor confessional booths nor assassins, not so much as a single Church of Martyrs' rat. Eddie slept without interruption for almost seven hours before he awoke about four a.m. Very rested and very angry.

Angry at the statues, but mostly at himself for tolerating their intrusion. He wanted only to get on with his life. He had no time for statues, especially those who confused him with someone who cared about such matters as whether or not the new pope, or anyone else, got the Catholic Church on track.

The hell with the Catholic Church! *It has caused me nothing but pain. It ruined my life.*

Eddie decided to confront the statues, go to them before they came to him again. He got dressed and went to the church. Maybe there'd be another message on the altar, a more acceptable one this time, something like, "Sorry, asshole, there's been a mistake.

We had another loser in mind, another ex-priest who couldn't hack it. Our apologies for any inconvenience we may have caused you. Signed, the Boys."

Yeah, right.

Eddie entered the church and closed the door behind him. He planned to talk to the statues and didn't want to get caught at it. He wondered if talking to statues was in the same category as talking to oneself, which he did all the time. He didn't bring a flashlight because it might have alerted someone that he was in the church. As they had for a century, the Brewer Avenue streetlamps dimly lit the martyrs' faces on one side only, casting the other in darkness. No Hollywood lighting director could have made the boys scarier, Eddie thought. He again read the message—for him?—carved on the altar.

"Sequemur," Eddie muttered. He acted as if he was in control of the situation and even poked fun. "We will follow, huh? The only place I intend to go today is Mazone's Bakery for some Italian bread and cream donuts for the shelter. You guys gonna follow me there?"

As Eddie walked from statue to statue, his resentment grew in their hushed presence. He began a litany of indignation in a soft, measured voice, not entirely lacking in derision. "I guess I should thank you guys for the night's sleep. Appreciate it. But we need to talk. Actually, *I* need to talk; *you* need to listen. You guys leave me alone! Got it? I am of no use to you."

Eddie fought to remain calm, but his composure faded as he addressed the unresponsive audience. The more he spoke to the statues, the more he read their silence as mockery. The statues were laughing at him. In their own way, perhaps, but laughing at him nonetheless. Eddie's Italian temper, never very far away, bubbled to the surface and his voice rose.

"Go ahead, laugh at me all you want, but just leave me the hell alone. No more messages, no more dream visits. No more sneaking around. Go find someone who gives a shit!"

Eddie stood before Saint Stephen and pounded his fists on the pile of stones at the martyr's feet. His hands hurt like hell, instantly bringing his simmering temper to a rapid boil. He vented at the statue.

"Stephen! If you wanted something from me you should have asked me when I still believed. I would have done anything you wanted then. I would have gladly died for you. But not now! Not anymore! You waited too damned long." He studied Stephen's face for a reaction. Nothing. Taunts were obviously not the answer. Maybe a little diplomacy would help.

"Stephen, you were a brave man. You had faith well past anything I can imagine. They chained you like an animal and stoned you. I don't have your courage. Please let me out of this, whatever it is. You want to see me beg? Okay, I'm begging."

Still not so much as a blink of a glassy eye or a quiver of a stony lip. The statue's infuriating cosmic indifference brought Eddie back to taunts and anger.

"Leave me all the messages you want, damnit, the rats will read them. Go ahead and appear in my dreams. I'll wake up and laugh in your faces. You can't make me do anything I don't want to do!"

After his fury subsided, Eddie felt no better. He was certain he had not gotten through to the statues and even more certain he had not gotten the better of them. He had never felt so small or so foolish. The idea that these guys gained life and strength from him, as Sergio believed, now seemed more preposterous than ever.

Eddie began to walk away but stopped when he heard the clanking of iron chains behind him, the sound he heard the night Saint Stephen first moved.

SIXTEEN

Cardinal Viviano called a meeting with Bishop Sacchi to relate Celestine's ultimatum, which threatened to expose them. Viviano knew the pope would soon learn of the distressed and tangled state of Vatican Bank finances, including the many failed investments and risky loans to hundreds of Church officials and powerful people in return for various favors. Some of the loans had been so poorly researched and collateralized that they amounted to outright gifts.

Worst of all was the recent botched desperate transaction Bishop Sacchi had cooked up between the Vatican Bank and Italian counterfeiters in an effort to bolster the bank's cash. The counterfeiters had provided the bank with over two billion U.S. dollars' worth of "perfect and undetectable" fake Swiss bank notes and bonds in exchange for five hundred million U.S. dollars, just about all the cash the Vatican Bank had on hand at the time.

The phony paper at first sailed through as legitimate until a bank clerk in Switzerland sent samples to the U.S. Treasury Department for validation, a standard procedure. Treasury agents found the samples to be bogus and paid Cardinal Viviano a discreet visit. They offered the cardinal a deal he could hardly refuse: in the interests of maintaining the integrity of the Vatican Bank, avoiding a scandal and possible prison time for Viviano, the U.S. Treasury Department would keep quiet as long as the Vatican Bank ate the loss. Viviano agreed, thus leaving the bank short the five hundred million dollars it had "invested." Even Bishop Sacchi was not well-enough connected to force the counterfeiters to refund the money.

Celestine's benevolence soon absorbed the remainder of the Vatican Bank's ready cash and, for all practical purposes, left it broke. It was, of course, exactly what the pope had in mind for the bank. But the pope assumed, as did the world, that it would take years to spend the bank's wealth. After that, Celestine planned for the Vatican Bank to survive, but only as a mechanism to channel money, not to hoard it, loan it or invest it.

"His Holiness believes we have a fortune in the bank," Viviano told Sacchi when he arrived. "It will be inconvenient, to say the least, for me to have to explain the sad state of the bank's books to him at this time. The pope wants everything ready for an independent audit when he returns from Mexico City. We are going to be found out, Sacchi."

"Why allow the Holy Father to learn the bank's business?" said Sacchi.

"It is inevitable," said Viviano.

"Nothing is inevitable, cardinal. Only the weak believe in inevitability. Were it not for the pope's big spending plans, the bank would quietly persevere and survive this debacle with the counterfeiters, would it not?"

"Without a doubt," said Viviano. "The bank has survived much worse than this in the past. But under the pope's scrutiny, we will be discovered."

"And you won't become the next pope. And I won't become cardinal and president of this bank. All because of this reckless squanderer Celestine the Sixth."

"Becoming pope is the least of my worries right now," Viviano said. "I'm afraid our plans for the future are but wishful thinking, Sacchi. We could go to prison for our dealings with the counterfeiters."

"All hope is not lost," said Sacchi. "Who knows what might happen to our most Holy Father during his visit to Mexico tomorrow?"

"No matter what my future may be, I pray the pope is not harmed," Viviano said.

"Celestine has made enemies not only here but around the world," said Sacchi. "And Mexico City can be a dangerous place, a very dangerous place."

"Will you accompany the pope?" said Viviano.

"Yes, I will be there to make certain everything goes well."

"Sacchi, I have never asked for details of your special...services for the Church," said Viviano. "But I must ask you now. Are you going to harm the Holy Father?"

"I will only tell you this: a few days from now you will receive a ransom note from those who have abducted the pope. They will demand five hundred million US dollars, which, as you well know, is roughly the amount of the bank shortage. You will promptly pretend to pay the ransom and that will be your excuse for why the bank is overdrawn if outside auditors are ever allowed to look at the books, which of course they will not be!"

"Will the Holy Father be released?"

"If the Holy Father has an unfortunate accident during his ordeal, it can only help us," Sacchi said, skirting the question. "He will not be missed at the Vatican. The only people who will grieve for Celestine are the poor of the world, a most undeserving group at best. The poor will simply continue to be poor. The blame, with a little help from us, will fall on Mexico. After the spendthrift Celestine, the next conclave will be only too happy to elect a fiscally prudent person like yourself to the papacy. You will be elected in an afternoon!"

"Did my son also meet with an 'unfortunate accident,' Sacchi?"

"Your son was about to tell the world of the bank's malfeasance," Sacchi said, again without directly answering the question. "Besides, this is not the fourteenth century. If you are to be pope, a son was too much of a liability."

"I have another son," said Viviano.

"Yes, I know that," said Sacchi.

"Of course you know. It is the information you have used to blackmail me with for a long time."

"You may call it blackmail if you wish," said Sacchi. "I prefer to call what we have an 'arrangement,' an arrangement that has served us *both* well."

"Will my other son be killed?"

"All I can say is that he is still alive," said Sacchi. "Be strong, Viviano. You will need all your strength in the coming months. We are doing the right thing!"

"By killing the Holy Father? By killing my son? I have gone along with everything for a long time, but this is different. How do we justify this?"

"Justify?" said Sacchi. "We 'justify' it as necessary for the survival of our Church. As long as there has been a Church, there has been someone like me, someone hated and feared but someone not afraid to do what is required. I make no apologies. If all the Christian leaders who came after Jesus Christ had been as submissive and forgiving as he, there would be no Church today. Men have not turned the other cheek for many centuries, cardinal."

"But murder?" said Viviano.

"Yes, murder! You know as well as I that murder is nothing new for us. We simply never called it murder. When our Church was threatened in the early years, it didn't shrink from violence. If it had shown a lack of resolve, it would have soon disappeared. It couldn't afford to be weak. The Church rooted out and hunted down heretics, schemers and pretenders and burned them but never called it murder. We slaughtered Mohammed's followers in the untold thousands during the Crusades but never called it murder. In recent times Pius, thinking first of the future of this

Church, did not approve of, but chose to remain mostly silent on the treatment of the Jews and Gypsies and other enemies of the German Reich. He certainly helped some Jews but did not try to stop the wholesale killing of millions of others. Few called Pius a murderer, or even an accessory, then or now.

"The throne of Saint Peter has been brokered through murder many times. Those who might have called it murder kept silent because of people like myself, men who have always placed the future of the Church above everything else. Those indiscreet enough to object were not heard from again!

"As you know, the Catholic Church enjoyed a monopoly on Christianity in Europe for fifteen hundred years until Luther and Henry. The popes of the day would have murdered those two damned heretics without a second thought had they gotten the chance. Our Church had enough wealth and power at the time to survive and co-exist with the new Christian sects but not quite enough to prevent them or snuff them out, though we summarily killed every Protestant we caught for a long time. Needless to say, the Protestants eagerly returned the favor. No one on either side called it murder."

"Our Church has always had a great tolerance for bloodshed, I'm afraid," said Viviano.

"Tolerance?" said Sacchi. "No, cardinal, not just a *tolerance* for blood. The Catholic Church has always had a *taste* for blood. It has *thrived* on blood, as do most religions. Celestine's ideas are well-intentioned but the result will be a weaker Church. A weak Church is soon *no* Church. This is a pragmatic world. Pragmatism requires wealth. You are a money person, Viviano, you know it's true."

"Like you, I don't agree with the Holy Father's plan. It is too extreme," said Viviano, "but didn't Saint Peter say that charity covers a multitude of sins? Could Celestine be right and we wrong? Perhaps our Church *should* give everything it has to the poor."

"We give more than enough to the poor already!" said Sacchi. "We are in the right, cardinal! What Celestine wants is not charity, it is lunacy. If something happens to the pope during his visit to Mexico City, have no sympathy for him. Our first duty is to the Church, not to Celestine the Sixth! We will someday be judged by God, not by a pope!"

SEVENTEEN

Eddie's first thought when he heard Saint Stephen's chains rattle behind him was not to turn around but to run, full speed, out of the church. Somehow he resisted the urge. After all, hadn't he entered the church for a chat with the martyrs?

"We must be more careful what we wish for in the future," Eddie said to himself, his knees knocking. He turned around and faced Saint Stephen. He knew whatever followed would be difficult. Nothing was easy with these guys.

Stephen was not just alive but intensely alive, no part more so than his face. The martyr zeroed in on Eddie with the one eye that was not swollen shut. Stephen seemed angrier than usual, as if pushed to his limit. Eddie reevaluated his decision to stay. He took a short step backward and prepared to escape.

The statue had other plans. Before Eddie could react, Stephen leaned forward and clutched him by the neck. Eddie stiffened and almost wet himself. The feel of Stephen's hands added to Eddie's fright; the hands were warm but not human warm, cold but not stone cold. The martyr lifted Eddie until his toes just barely touched the church floor. Eddie grabbed the chain attached to Stephen's manacles and tried to pull the saint's hands off his neck. Stephen squeezed harder and drew Eddie closer until human face and statue face touched. The saint's beard rasped Eddie's chin. The beard was stiff like a wire brush but not wire nor hair nor stone. Eddie, who could hardly breathe, turned away from the martyr's seething, insistent eye. He imagined dying in the hands of a statue; he had a sudden fear not so much of death but of *this* death.

Thoughts, disconnected and confusing, began bombarding Eddie's mind. His head ached and pounded. He was unable to concentrate on any one thing for more than a second or two. Something was blocking his thoughts and substituting its own. The statue was attempting to communicate!

Oh shit!

Stephen relaxed his grip a bit to allow Eddie enough air to remain conscious. Eddie, knowing he had no choice, quit resisting. There was no beating these guys at their game, whatever it might be. While he awaited the saint's thoughts, he had an involuntary one of his own.

So it's come to this! *Intimidation*! *Big bad statue meets the skinny kid from Briggs Hill who wasn't tough enough to be a Dago Bomber or stick it out as a priest.*

Stephen retightened his grip on Eddie's neck. Eddie guessed that the saint was not in the mood for sarcasm. It was time to pay attention to the message Stephen had for him. Eddie concentrated hard in order to read the saint. He discerned only a short string of words, repeated over and over. But he couldn't make them out. Eddie mentally pleaded with the statue.

I can't understand you. What do you want? *Please tell me. Pleeease tell me*!

At that moment three words broke through and penetrated Eddie's brain like an ice pick: *dona nobis pacem*!

Dona nobis pacem? *My Latin's failing me at the moment but I think that means "give us peace." You want peace*? *What kind of peace*? *What kind of peace could I possibly give you guys*!?

In answer, Stephen lifted his audience higher; Eddie's toes left the floor and his vertebrae cracked as they realigned. Stephen shook Eddie as he might a stubborn child. The statue apparently expected Eddie to understand and was upset that he didn't. Eddie remained as still and attentive as possible. The last thing he wanted at the moment was to upset Saint Stephen any more than he already had.

I don't get it. I'm not as smart as you think I am. What do you mean by "give us peace?"

Again the telepathic message from Stephen, louder, more piercing than before: *dona nobis pacem*! The words stung Eddie's brain. He felt his head might burst. He closed his eyes tightly and tried to understand what the saint was demanding.

Okay, give us peace. Damnit, what kind of peace!?

A blurred mental picture gradually formed, soon focusing on an ancient scene of unutterable human agony, a scene of six men dying slow, calculated and all-too-recognizable deaths at the hands of master torturers. A seventh man carried his head in his hand as he walked to a shallow grave. They were the seven martyrs, not as statues, not as saints, but as men, vulnerable, terrified and defenseless mortals resolved to die rather than betray their faith.

Except that the men *didn't* die, even though they prayed for death, begged for death. Their combined voices rang in Eddie's head, all calling out: "*dona nobis pacem*!"

Tears began to fall from Stephen's battered eyes. He was weeping, the first human emotion other than anger the statue had ever exhibited. The bullying disappeared from Stephen's face; his lips quivered.

After a lifetime of being around them, Eddie finally deciphered the look on the statues' faces. It wasn't, as everyone had always thought, hatred of the living but rather envy of the dead. Their long-misunderstood expressions spoke not of condemnation but of desperation and helplessness. Saint Stephen was not demanding anything from Eddie. He was *pleading*!

Even as Eddie choked for breath, a series of unbearable pains racked his body head to foot. Was it a little sample, perhaps, of what the statues had endured for centuries? Were they still suffering their martyrdoms? Could that be? Is death the peace the statues wanted? Did they desire only to die?

The saints may have wanted death, but Eddie wanted only to live. He could think of nothing else besides life, sweet precious life. And Pat. And the innocent kiss on the cheek. And everything else he had missed.

The irony of the situation was not lost on Eddie. If it was true, as Sergio had said, that the statues got life, got strength, from *him*, from big deal *Signore* Eddie Russo, then all Eddie would have to do was refuse to go along with whatever the saints had in mind and he would kill himself through the statue. What a suicide! What a remarkable exit from such an unremarkable life! Eddie knew that Saint Stephen would not botch the job as he himself once had.

As Stephen squeezed his neck waiting for an answer, Eddie strung together the unlikely triangle of cooperation: goofy ex-assassin, cynical ex-priest and mean-as-hell statues. All involved in a mission, if Sergio was right, to save a pope from certain death. If one failed they all failed. The pope, Eddie and Sergio too would be dead and the statues would continue to suffer. For how long? Eternity? Till another headstrong priest dropout came along in another seven hundred years? Eddie's problems suddenly seemed like nothing compared to that of these rootless souls.

So you guys not only need me for life, you need me for death, too? When this is over you get to die and find peace. Okay, I want to live! And love! I'm going to do what you want, with or without knowing the rules. Screw the rules! But I'm going to do this for myself. For the first time in my life I'm going to do something for myself! Not for statues, not for the Catholic Church, not for Celestine the Sixth, not for God Almighty, but for Eddie Russo! I'm going to take the difficult way out of this: I'm going to allow myself to live.

Eddie opened his mind and acquiesced to the will of the statues.

With the deal cut, Saint Stephen loosened his grip and dropped Eddie unceremoniously to the church floor. By the time Eddie looked up at the saint, he had missed the transformation back to stone. He noticed a difference in the statue, however. Stephen's aspect had softened a bit. Not much to be sure, but the martyr's face had definitely changed for the better. His lips were not so curled, his good eye not nearly so indicting. Stephen seemed ready for anything.

Eddie wasn't. But he would try. Whatever lie ahead in the vague covenant he had made with Saint Stephen, he would try to keep his end of the bargain. He could only hope the statues would do likewise. For the first time, Eddie felt a bond with the statues. He also now felt like a voyeur in their presence, no better than the mobs that had gathered to watch their drawn-out ghastly martyrdoms. Eddie was overcome with pity for the statues' desperate neediness and the absurdity of their situation. And his own!

Eddie now had to tell Sergio, probably snoring peacefully in Father Louis' bed while he had been near-hanged by a statue. Eddie knew Sergio would be happy, his worship of *Signore* Eddie validated. He thought that he would rather have his teeth pulled out with forceps like poor Saint Apollonia than admit to Sergio that he now believed they should go to Mexico City.

As he left the Church of Martyrs, Eddie muttered to himself, "Okay, I'll lead and you guys follow. I just hope we're all going to the same place."

EIGHTEEN

After searching for hours through the records of Catholic missions in Africa, Father Villalobos found the file on Father Gesa Danku. He was, as the pope had said, working among the Hittabbe, a Pygmy tribe in Africa's Republic of the Congo. Villalobos chose another Jesuit priest to travel with him to bring back to Rome the Gypsy with the odd name who was Celestine's choice for papal secretary of state.

Following a long flight from Rome and a shorter but far more thrilling trip by bush plane, the two papal messengers, two native bearers and an interpreter/guide landed on a runway hacked out of the rainforest in Tanza. They hired a Land Rover with driver and lumbered for five hours along a muddy, pestilential road to the village of the Hittabbe on the Laina River.

Along the way, Villalobos and his Jesuit companion speculated as to how this priest they sought could possibly be of use in the Vatican. Secretary of state? A Gypsy, no less! They also discussed the pope and worried that Jesus Christ's most holy representative on Earth was, well, maybe a bit too *much* like Jesus Christ. Things had changed in two thousand years. How could the Holy Father not know this? Even though the two Jesuit priests had taken vows of poverty, they questioned how a religion could survive without a surplus of cash. What lie ahead for them and the Catholic Church?

Upon their arrival at the village of the Hittabbe, the messengers learned that Father Danku was away on a hunt deep in the rainforest. If the hunt was successful, he might be back as soon as the next day. The visitors were invited to wait. With no other options, they made the best of it, settling in among the villagers and, lest they offend, eating their simple fare of jungle game and wild sweet potatoes. Through his interpreter, Father Villalobos asked many questions of his Hittabbe hosts about Father Gesa Danku.

He learned the Gypsy priest was called "Hatti Hashi," Hittabbi for "he who sees nothing and sees all."

"Sees what?" Villalobos asked.

"All!" said the tribesman. "He sees trees and vines so that he may walk among them. He sees poisonous snakes so that he is never bitten. He sees game and kills it with a dart from a blowgun!"

"Is that so extraordinary?" Villalobos asked.

"It is a miracle!"

"A miracle?"

"You don't know that Hatti Hashi is blind? He has no eyes!"

Great! So Gesa Danku was a *blind* Gypsy priest.

Most noteworthy of all, they learned, was that Hatti Hashi negotiated with spirits, good and evil, that governed the fortunes of the village. Since the arrival of Hatti Hashi several years before, no woman had died giving birth. No young children had been stricken with disease. There was peace among the Hittabbe and the neighboring Woni. The blind priest had brought not only Christ's word but also prosperity to a tribe of people balanced on the brink of extinction before his arrival.

"He negotiates with spirits!?"

"Yes! And, what's more, he can see the future, as well."

How wonderful! A blind Gypsy priest handy with a blow gun who spoke with spirits and saw the future was to be their immediate boss in the Vatican. That night Villalobos and the other Jesuit messenger prayed for the future of the Church and, perhaps a bit reluctantly, the safe return of Hatti Hashi.

Early the next day a band of men approached from the south, laughing and joking in the uneven sing-song cadence of the Hittabbe. A white man was among the hunting party. Though not very tall, he towered over his Pygmy comrades. The Vatican messengers assumed he was Gesa Danku. Like the rest of the hunters, he had the carcasses of several monkeys yoked around his neck. Long black hair hung in ringlets to his waist. Like the Hittabbe men, a blue and red tattoo ringed his upper right arm and his chest bore the Hittabbe horizontal scars of manhood. The other hunters carried bow and arrow; the white man carried a blow gun. Father Villalobos half-expected to see shrunken heads hanging from the cord that held Gesa Danku's penis cone. Penis cone!? The future Vatican secretary of state, second in power to the pope, wore a penis cone!

And Gesa Danku was indeed blind. His eyes, devoid of iris and pupils, shone like polished ivory against the light olive skin of his face. Villalobos knew from Danku's records that he was in his sixties yet his skin stretched tautly over the muscles of a much younger man.

Gesa Danku put down his bounty and blow gun and walked straight to the visitors.

"Ah, how blessed we are. Tonight we will have monkey *and* Jesuits for dinner."

"How could you know we are Jesuits? How could you even know we are here?" said a perplexed Villalobos.

"You have the aura of Jesuits. I sense the presence of strong intellect, learning, discipline and perhaps a touch of arrogance. I detect the scent of beeswax and incense in your pores. Who could you be but Jesuits? There are two of you. You are from Rome, the Vatican!"

"And how could you know that?"

"That is only a guess," he said. "Am I correct?"

"Yes, you are correct," sighed Villalobos, who recalled the pope's prediction that Gesa Danku's extraordinary talents would be instantly recognizable. "We have come as representatives of His Holiness Celes..."

"Stop, please. In the village of the Hittabbe, no business is discussed until we know each other's names and feel comfortable that you have not brought evil spirits with you," said Danku. "So, on behalf of the Hittabbe and the benevolent God that watches this village and all villages, I welcome you."

Members of the expedition introduced themselves to Danku. He unerringly grasped the hands of both Vatican messengers and the others in the party, whose ancestral tribes he correctly identified from their scent and handshakes. At that point Danku, reasonably certain the two Jesuits and their party meant no harm, asked Father Villalobos to explain why they had come.

First, Villalobos raised the question the entire party was wanting to ask.

"Father Danku, how is it you seem to be able to see?"

"I can't see. Like all blind persons, my ears and my nose are my eyes. Twenty-twenty! What sounds like the rustle of a leaf to you is like a cannon shot to me. The flip of a monkey's tail high in the canopy dooms it to our dinner fire. By the way, monkey is a wonderful treat, as you may have already discovered. Not as tasty as freshly-killed hedgehog, but then there are no hedgehogs in the Congo."

"You talk as if your blindness gives you an advantage over those of us with sight," said Villalobos.

"Sight takes a heavy toll on the human mind and soul. My father taught me as a young boy that God made me blind because he wanted me to see things others could not. It is the thinking of the Gypsy that we are all born with gifts. We are taught to rejoice in our gifts, whatever they may be."

A blind Gypsy priest and philosopher! Who eats hedgehog!

"The villagers say you can negotiate with spirits?" It was the second question on their list.

"I cannot. The modern medicines we supply negotiate with the spirits. Birthing methods our doctors teach negotiate with the spirits. Full stomachs negotiate with the spirits. A soul filled with the love of God negotiates with the spirits. I've tried to explain this to the villagers, but they believe what they want to believe. The results are what count."

"They also say you can read the future. Is this true?" Villalobos asked. It was the most pressing question he had for the future Vatican secretary of state. The Jesuit was prepared to remind the Gypsy priest that the Church did not approve of reading the future, old friend of Celestine the Sixth or not.

"No, I can't read the future. What I have is a logic unknown to those with the burden of sight, who have too many visual distractions to ever develop workable logic. Logic allows me to predict most events with great accuracy. And now, please, why have you honored us with this visit?"

"Your friend Cardinal Lorini is now His Holiness Celestine the Sixth," said Villalobos. "Are you aware of this?"

"Yes."

"Did you deduce your friend was elected pope with your great logic?" said the other Jesuit, making no effort to hide his sarcasm.

"Absolutely not! I learned this from our mission hospital. It has radio, television and computers," Danku laughed. "No one could have *ever* deduced that the College of Cardinals would be logical or wise enough to elect such a worthy man! Who else but my friend Prala would attempt to raid the wealth of the Catholic Church to feed the hungry of this world?"

"Prala?" said Villalobos, "You mean His Holiness Celestine the Sixth?"

"Now one and the same it would seem."

"So you have heard of the Holy Father's plans?"

"Yes, I have," said Danku. "Now tell me why you have come."

"Prala...I mean His Holiness has named you Vatican secretary of state," said Villalobos.

"That is most flattering. And if I do not wish to leave here?"

"His Holiness predicted you would refuse. He sent you this letter. Would you like for me to read it to you?"

"It will be in Romani, which I taught to the Holy Father long ago. I would bet you my share of monkey you can't read it."

Danku took the envelope from Villalobos. He opened it and read the letter with his fingers. The villagers looked on in awe, as they always did when Hatti Hashi read from his sacred black book the same way. Was there no end to the magic and wonder of "he who sees nothing and sees all?"

Dear treasured old friend Gesa,

I have left you alone in paradise for as long as I dare. I am in great need of a pair of eyes as keen as yours. It is time to repay me for the beating I took for you. May God bless and speed your journey.

It was signed not "Celestine the Sixth" but simply "Prala," Romani for "brother."

"Can you share the information with us?" said Villalobos. "We will understand if don't wish to."

"I feared when I first heard of the Holy Father's ambitious plans that he had ventured into precarious waters," said Danku. "Our Church has always jealously guarded its wealth, the key to its self-aggrandizement, and will not surrender it willingly on the word of one man, even if he is the pope. My friend Prala feels threatened."

"The Holy Father has many sworn to his protection," said Villalobos. "May I ask why he needs you?"

"Our Holy Father needs my eyes."

"Your eyes?" said Villalobos. "But you have no eyes!"

"Then why can I see the poisonous spider that is crawling up the back of your shirt?"

Villalobos shuddered as he reached behind him. The other Jesuit swept the spider to the ground. Villalobos lifted his foot to step on it.

"Please do not kill the poor creature," Danku said. "The Hittabbe kill only to survive. They believe that the spider's unnecessary death would diminish all life in the village. Your so-called civilized world should be so civilized."

"Thank you," said Villalobos, moving away from the spider. "Will you come back to Rome with us?"

"We will leave in the morning," said Danku, who knew the pope was not a hysterical person and would not have sent for him without good reason. "I would leave now but can't. The hunt was successful. We must celebrate and offer thanks. Otherwise we will throw into disarray both the good and bad spirits. Let's begin with drink!"

Villalobos saw that the note from the pope was not in braille, but hand-written. He wanted badly to ask the Gypsy priest how he had read it, but decided not to, just as he had refrained from asking how Danku knew about the spider. The Jesuit sought to avoid another lecture about the onerous liability of sight.

Throughout the night, the villagers, Father Gesa Danku, the Vatican Jesuits and their party did indeed celebrate and give thanks with the Hittabbe. Danku played his violin for several hours. The strains of sad Gypsy songs, laments of a people disenfranchised from and shunned by the rest of the world for centuries, harmonized uneasily with the sounds of the jungle night. The unsentimental Father Villalobos, who had never been fond of such music, softened. He wiped watery eyes several times.

They were still celebrating when the sun, having once again battled successfully with the vile spirits of the darkness, climbed above the horizon. The rising sun was the Hittabbes' strongest proof that the good spirits outnumbered—and outgunned—evil.

Before he departed, Danku explained to the village that he was needed in a distant rainforest far more dangerous and with many more evil spirits and predators than the land of the Hittabbe. He assured them that Jesus Christ, greatest of all chiefs, would protect the village in his absence. He promised to return to them, one of the few places, along with the nomadic Gypsy camps of his youth, where he had known true happiness.

The Vatican messengers, unaccustomed to the potent Hittabbe honey brew, not to mention the hallucinogenic weed they had reluctantly smoked, were exhausted and sick from the night's celebration. For his part, Gesa Danku seemed invigorated and refreshed. He traded his Hittabbe penis cone for clothing brought for him and, in keeping with Hittabbe custom, he simply left. He did not look back or wave goodbye. The spirits would now be fooled into thinking Hatti Hashi might only be going to the river for water.

On the road back to Tanza, Villalobos asked Father Danku, "Were you truly happy living in that village, in those primitive and dangerous surroundings?"

"Since I am blind, all surroundings are alike to me," Danku said. "As for happiness, the Hittabbe are a very happy people and it spreads to those around them. There are few happy people in what you would call the 'civilized world,' fewer still, I suspect, in your Vatican world. In the village of the Hittabbe, I was accepted on my merits alone, a joy and advantage I have now lost. I expect not to be accepted at all where we are going because of what I am. As for danger, I was *far* safer in the rainforest."

Father Villalobos did not follow with another question. After all, this was Hatti Hashi, who sees nothing and sees all, can hear the sound of a spider's footsteps and make a stern Jesuit cry with his Gypsy violin.

NINETEEN

"Sergio, wake up, *svegliati*!" said Eddie, as he rushed into Sergio's bedroom following his chat with Saint Stephen.

Sergio awoke and sat bolt upright, swinging dreamy clenched fists.

"What is it, *Signore*?" Is *La Mano di Cristo*, huh? C*uelli Cornuti*! They come back! Is okay, I fight the *schifoso*. *Li mazzero quelli bastardi*! Too bad you fat friend the cop take my pistol. But I defend you with my hands, my teeth. I die for you, *Signore*!"

"Sergio, come on, quit screwing around. Wake up! I have something to tell you."

"Is not *La Mano di Cristo*?" Sergio said sleepily. He sounded disappointed. "What time it is, *Signore*?"

"Late, damned late, maybe *too* late," Eddie said. "It's four a.m. We gotta get going!"

"You always talk riddles, *Signore*."

"You'll understand this, Sergio. You and I are going to Mexico City. Whatever the hell the statues want us to do, we're going to do it. That ought to make you happy."

"It make me happy and it make me sad. Tell me, how they convince you? You head pretty hard."

Eddie decided not to tell Sergio about his near-death experience at the hands of Saint Stephen. The little guy would have enjoyed it too much. "Let's just say the statues hung it all out on a line for me, okay? I received a spiritual uplifting of sorts, a heightened moment."

"The statues, they talk to you?"

"With the eyes, my friend, with the eyes."

"I understand. So what we do, *Signore*? You have the plan?"

"Of course I don't have a plan, Sergio," Eddie said. "I don't have any idea what we're supposed to do."

"The saints no tell you?"

"Hell no! You don't think they're going to make this easy, do you?"

"All I know is the saints not fail us, *Signore*."

"How do you suppose the statues are going to get there?"

"If you there, they follow. Remember what they write on the altar? They say 'we follow!' We waste time talking, *Signore*. *Il Papa*, he there today. We not have much time. When we leave?"

"I'll call and book us on the first flight out this morning, if there're any seats left. Otherwise, I guess we'll have to ride on the saints."

Eddie called United Air Lines. He asked about two seats to Mexico City. There were no coach seats left, only first class. Hesitantly, Eddie inquired about the price. His credit card had very little remaining credit.

"Money no problem, *Signore*," Sergio interrupted, waving a wad of large bills. "First class only way to fly."

Eddie booked the first class seats one way, since he had no idea when—or if—he and Sergio would return. The flight departed at eight-twenty a.m. and, with a change of planes in Houston, would get them to Mexico City by one p.m.

"The pope will speak at three p.m., according to the internet," Eddie said. "If there's any action, we'll be there for it. With any luck, there won't be any action. We'll get a nice Mexican dinner and come home. Okay, let's get ready. I'm going to wake Pat and ask her to run the shelter while we're gone."

Eddie walked to the shelter in the former convent. He unlocked the front door, walked to Pat's room and knocked gently on her door. Unlike Sergio, Pat seemed to be a light sleeper and opened the door after making certain it was Eddie. She had been sleeping in the Cleveland *Indians* sweatshirt. Her legs were bare. Eddie thought it was the sexiest sight he had ever seen. As usual, he said something unblushingly stupid.

"Victoria's deepest secret?"

"Yeah, something like that," Pat said. She rubbed her eyes. "I haven't had a date in a long time, but most of the guys called first. Or is this a fire drill?"

"You could say that," Eddie said. "I'm sorry I had to wake you, Pat. I can't explain exactly why, but Sergio and I are leaving for Mexico City in a few hours. I need a big favor."

"Name it."

"I'd like you to look after the shelter while we're gone. There's plenty of food in the kitchen. Your cooking couldn't possibly be any worse than mine."

"Consider it done," Pat said.

"Thanks. Sergio and I will need a ride to the airport. Provided my car will start, of course. I'll come and get you in about an hour or so."

Pat nodded her head in agreement. Eddie started to leave.

"Hold on, cowboy. You don't think I'm going to let it go at that, do you? You're going to tell me more about this trip. Sit down."

Eddie was uneasy. He had never been inside a woman's bedroom in his life. Pat reached behind him and closed the door. Eddie sat in an overstuffed chair in the corner. Pat sat on the bed. He knew she sensed his nervousness.

"Now talk!"

"Pat, I really don't know how to explain because I have no idea what we're going to do when we get there."

"Then why go?"

"The statues made me an offer I can't quite refuse."

"The boys have been at it again, huh? Does this have something to do with the 'we will follow' message?"

"It has everything to do with it," Eddie said.

"Keep talking."

Eddie sighed and related the entire story of his experience in the church, including the revelation of the saints' endless suffering. When he finished, he looked at Pat and studied her face for a reaction. Not so much as a furrowed brow.

"If you believe any of this, I've got an old church, kind of a fixer-upper, I'd like to sell you."

"Quit talking like that! I do believe you. Besides, those marks on your neck are pretty convincing."

Eddie rushed to a mirror above a small dresser. A necklace of large fingerprints glowed red around his neck. He shuddered. The marks were probably meant as a little something to carry with him, a hint of things to come if he failed or tried to weasel out of the agreement. He tried to put it out of his mind.

Pat pointed at the chair and motioned for Eddie to sit down again. She walked over and sat on the arm of the chair. Her leg brushed against Eddie's hand. Not much, but it excited him. He let his hand remain on Pat's leg for a few seconds without realizing what he was doing. He caught himself and removed his hand. He started to get up. "I've got to go."

Pat stopped him. "Eddie, sit down please. I want to tell you something. I may not get another chance so I'm going to tell you now."

"Pat, why do I have the feeling that you're about to complicate my life even more than it already is? Can't you just drop me a line in care of the Mexico City morgue?"

"You're right, I am going to complicate your life and I'm going to do it right now!" She paused and seemed to collect her thoughts. "When I arrived here the other night I was a very cynical woman who had been badly abused by a man. I wanted to murder every man I saw."

"Go ahead and kill me, I could use the relief," Eddie said. It was one of his favorite lines.

"Eddie, we don't have time for your lame self-deprecation. Shut up and listen!"

"Yes, mam."

"What I'm trying to say is I don't feel that way any longer, not since that first night. I have changed more than you can imagine. Things seem to happen awfully fast around this place."

"Where are you going with this?" Eddie asked.

"Here's where I'm going: when Sergio told you yesterday that the statues get their strength from you, it hit me."

"Uh, what hit you?"

"So do I."

Eddie started to speak. Pat put two fingertips on his lips. "I know you don't want to hear any of this right now—God forbid I should shatter your treasured low self-esteem—but let me finish."

"Do I have a choice?"

"No!" Pat said. "You've made me feel like a woman again, very much like a woman."

"I don't think there was ever much doubt about your gender," Eddie said.

"There was with me. A real woman wants to love and be loved. I can't explain it completely, but all I know is that you've made me believe I can love a man again. And that, Eddie, is a far greater miracle than anything else that has happened around here, including your movable martyrs. Don't you see it when I look at you? I look at you the way Sergio looks at those statues."

"He looks at them with fear," Eddie said.

"No, he doesn't, *Signore Stupido*. You couldn't be more wrong. Sergio may have feared them at first but now he looks at them with respect for their power and gratitude for the way that power has changed him. That's not fear in his face, but love, maybe the purest I've ever witnessed. I feel the same toward you."

"No charge, all part of the service at the Church of Martyrs Women's Shelter and Lonely Hearts Center," Eddie said. Once again he tried to free himself of the chair and leave.

Pat pushed him back into the chair. "There's really not time for your bad jokes. I'd like to give you back some of the strength you've given me. You'll need it and we may not...get another chance."

"What did you have in mind?" Timidly. "A ride to the airport would be a big help." Eddie looked at his watch, anything rather than face the situation.

"Cut the act. You tell me how I can return the favor! Come on, I want to hear it from you." Pat moved closer.

Eddie might have fainted except for the adrenalin pumping full force in his veins. Pat's directness overwhelmed him. How very well he knew what Pat meant. Oh, how he wanted this. But he feared that in his present state of mind he might not live up to expectations. For one thing, he didn't know enough about it. Sex and love were just two more things to fail at in his ever-shrinking universe.

"Well, you're right about one thing," Eddie said.

"What's that?"

"Things certainly move fast around this place."

Pat smiled. "Maybe if you're talking about my feelings for you, but not about my wanting for you to make love to me. This is the new millennium and I've known you for almost three days. You're one great-looking ex-priest!"

Pat's humor helped put Eddie at ease.

"Pat, I want nothing more in this world right now than to... spend some time with you." Eddie stumbled on the words. "But you should know that I don't have a lot of experience in the sex department. The only time I ever did this kind of thing was with Nick Piccione's oversexed and drunken cousin Chastity."

"Chastity? Seriously?"

"Yeah, go figure! Anyway, it was pretty much against my better judgment."

"Why?"

"Mostly because it was on a back porch swing with a wedding reception going on inside the house."

Pat laughed. "Sex in strange places can be exciting. How does a former convent sound to you?"

"Make fun if you want, but the sad truth is that I kind of slept through my early years when I should have been doing what my friend Detective Nick calls "sport screwing."

"It's called 'sport *fucking*.' Get it right! And you're in luck because I *didn't* sleep through it."

Eddie felt the same powerlessness that he had while Saint Stephen suspended him by the neck. He searched through his vast repertoire of comebacks. He thought of a couple of good ones but nothing seemed to fit the occasion. Except one.

"Pat, I think I love you," he said, more than a little surprised at himself. "You should also know that I never thought I'd be able to say that to a woman."

"That's because you're too hard on yourself. But here's another little boost to your self-esteem. I love you, too. I love you more than you believe I do, probably more than you can comprehend right now."

"If I wasn't so afraid they'd lift me up in the air again I'd go light a few candles in front of the statues."

"What is it with Catholics and candles?" Pat said, moving closer to Eddie.

"They light up the way to heaven, I guess."

"Consider yourself there, Eddie."

They kissed. Politely at first, then eagerly, then passionately. Pat fell across Eddie's lap. He felt he could have kissed Pat for a year or two.

"Great kissing," Pat said, breathlessly. "I could have a climax kissing like that. You sure you didn't play around a little when you were a priest."

"No, not only did I not get any financial skills from my father, the esteemed Cardinal Viviano, but none of his promiscuousness rubbed off either," Eddie said before questioning Pat's comment. "Women can have a climax from kissing?"

"Yes, we can. But don't feel bad because most men don't know that either. Come on, you're stalling."

Eddie touched Pat's face lightly with his fingertips. He kissed her neck and then her mouth again.

"Keep going," she said, removing her sweatshirt.

Eddie fixated on Pat's breasts before touching them.

"It's only fair that you get undressed too," Pat said. "Tell you what, I'll do the honors. Stand up!"

Eddie popped out of the chair. His erection bulged the front of his pants like a pup tent. He looked down at it.

"Am I getting the idea?"

Pat squeezed the bulge playfully. "You've *got* the idea. And remember, this is supposed to be fun. The more you love someone, the more fun it is."

"Pat, I've never been more ready for fun in my life!"

Pat peeled Eddie out of his pants and shirt. She hesitated at the waistband of his shorts."

"You really like these silly striped boxer shorts?"

"They were on sale, but I had to buy a dozen."

"They were on sale for good reason," Pat said. She kneeled down and played with Eddie through his shorts for a few more excruciating minutes before pulling them down. She took Eddie's cock and put her lips around it. Eddie gasped involuntarily.

Pat let out a muffled giggle.

Eddie reached down and pulled Pat up to him. He kissed her again and wrapped his hands around her waist, bent over and kissed her breasts. He tried to be as gentle as possible.

"Suck them, suck them as hard as you like," Pat said. "The harder the better."

"Really?" Eddie leaned into the challenge.

"You're a quick learner," Pat said. "That's nice."

"Some things are a lot easier to learn than Latin," Eddie quipped.

"Put your hand inside my panties," Pat said. "If you don't, I'll strangle you worse than that statue did."

"Can't have that!" said Eddie, complying with the request.

"That's perfect," Pat said, swooning at Eddie's touch. "Let's get on the bed. And take these panties off me or leave."

"Five hundred mean-assed statues couldn't get me out of this room right now," Eddie said. He finished undressing himself before removing Pat's panties.

"Eddie, if you wanted to kiss my entire body, I wouldn't stop you."

"Where would you like me to start?"

"Anywhere you'd like. Just don't miss anything."

For nearly an hour Eddie was all over Pat, and she all over him. He unleashed a lifetime of sexual frustration and repressed love on a woman who couldn't seem to get enough of his efforts. Each sigh, each repeated affirmation of her pleasure inspired him. He forgot all about the pain in his neck, compliments of Saint Stephen. The fact that he was making love in a bedroom where nuns once slept added to his excitement, though he didn't try to understand why; he really didn't want to know. He wondered if the troublesome statues were watching. What the hell, they knew everything else about him.

Afterward, Eddie lay on his back, looking at the ceiling. "Damn, wouldn't those nuns just die if they could see me now?" he laughed.

"They might be proud of you," Pat said. "I am. Mind if I smoke? This whole sex thing is not complete without a cigarette."

"No smoking allowed in the women's shelter normally," Eddie said. "But, as the director, I can make exceptions. Light up a cigar if you like. Hell, light a bonfire!"

"You really don't like smoking, do you?" Pat said.

"No, I don't. Of course, it all depends on who's smoking," Eddie said. "I'd buy all the cigarettes my father the cardinal could smoke, that's for damned sure!"

Eddie jumped off the bed and found Pat's cigarettes and lighter. It delighted him that he was not bashful about his nakedness in front of her. He lit a cigarette and handed it to Pat, pretending to cough violently after he removed it from his mouth.

"You non-smokers never miss a chance to take a shot at us sinners, do you?" she said.

"I suppose not," said Eddie. "Sorry."

"I know I should quit," Pat said. "I'm sure I would live longer but life is far more enjoyable with a few vices."

Eddie wanted to remain with Pat and considered skipping the mission to Mexico City but remembered Saint Stephen's hands around his neck. No, he made a deal and he'd see it through. He'd go to Mexico City and do whatever was necessary to return to this woman.

Besides, nothing was likely to happen in Mexico City. He wanted very much to believe this.

TWENTY

"You gone long time, *Signore*," Sergio said when Eddie returned to the rectory. "You look different, better, not so, how you say?...the grumpy." He began to snicker lecherously. "You and *Signora* Pat, you do the...dance of love maybe?"

"Sergio, did it ever occur to you that what I do might not be any of your business?"

"No matter, *Signore,* you no have to tell me. I know."

"How?"

"Is you look, *Signore*. No one look like that except after dance of love. Is good thing. You need to, how you say?...loose up. You pain in the ass most of the time. *Signora* Pat good lady. She good for you."

"She is at that, Sergio. I just wish I could stick around and get to know her better instead of going to Mexico City and getting myself killed."

"You not get killed, *Signore*...until the saints no longer need you. And me. Then I not sure."

"As usual, you're very comforting," Eddie said. "You packed yet?"

"Wait here *Signore*. I have surprise for you."

"Oh boy, can't wait."

Sergio left the room and returned with two priest's cassocks, one long, and one short.

"Where'd you find those things, Sergio?" Eddie said.

"In you closet and closet of you dead friend the pastor."

Sergio slipped into the smaller cassock and buttoned the Roman collar. He looked at Eddie.

"I bless you, my son. Now you make the donation." Sergio held out his hand. "I make good priest, huh?"

"No, neither one of us makes a good priest," Eddie said. "Take that thing off."

"Oh no, is perfect cover. I see this in a movie. We go as priests, get good front row seat to see *Il Papa*. We need be close when something happen. Beside, you need to wear collar to cover marks on your neck. I not ask you where you get those marks because I know you no tell me. Right?"

"Right!"

"Get dressed like priest, *Signore*."

Eddie gave in and, with ten thousand misgivings, donned the cassock. "You know, Sergio, there'll be a million priests in Mexico City, all wanting to be close to the pope. What makes you think they're going to welcome us up front just because we're dressed like priests?"

"You leave that to me, *Signore*. You friend Sergio clever. Like I tell you before, I good at these things. I not let you down."

Eddie packed and went to get Pat.

She broke into a broad smile at the sight of her lover dressed as a priest. Father Eddie, in person.

"Go ahead, say something cute. Get it over with," Eddie said. "I sure as hell would."

"Does this mean our budding romance is over?" Pat said in a sad voice. "I thought it went pretty well."

"Ha, ha," said Eddie.

"Let me guess: Sergio's idea?"

"Who else?"

"Some kind of cover?"

"Let's just say that Sergio watches too many movies. This is like a big game to him. It sure isn't my idea of a game. I prefer Monopoly. I always lose but at least I know the rules."

"Maybe the statues think that if you knew the rules, you wouldn't play," Pat said.

"I don't want to think about it," said Eddie. "We're ready to leave for the airport anytime you are."

Pat and her two passengers fought their way through the early morning Cleveland traffic in Eddie's old Dodge, which started on the first try. Eddie thought it a miracle, perhaps compliments of the statues. They arrived at the airport with time to spare.

"No tip, necessary," Pat said. "But I do want something."

"One of those big sombreros?" Eddie said. "You'd look good in it."

"You know very well what I want," she said. "I want you guys to come back."

"We come back, *Signora*," Sergio said. "Then I show you how to cook good *Italiano*. The real stuff. I promise."

Eddie, much less optimistic about their return than Sergio, turned to Pat.

"Pat, this may sound nuts, but I'd like you to check in the church every now and then to see if you-know-who are still there. I'll call for a report when I get a chance."

"I understand. I'll make a bed check every couple hours on the boys."

At the departure area, Pat hugged Father Sergio and kissed Father Eddie long and passionately, oblivious to the small crowd of captivated spectators. She drove away without another word. Eddie saw she was crying; he fought the urge to chase after her.

At the United Airlines ticket counter, two priests without baggage paying cash in very large bills for one-way first class tickets to Mexico City raised no few eyebrows.

"Do you priests always travel in first class?" a passenger standing in line behind them asked. "Better pray the new pope doesn't hear about this. He doesn't want you guys living big."

"We from very rich parish," Sergio said. "Even the mayor one of our lambs."

"I happen to know the mayor," the passenger said. "He's not Catholic."

"See what I mean?" said Sergio. "Everyone come to our parish."

Eddie elbowed Sergio to shut him up. Bad enough Pat and he had almost made love at the passenger drop-off, but Eddie feared Sergio would draw too much attention before they ever boarded the airplane. Eddie was nervous. Not only did he fear he might be walking into a death trap but he also dreaded flying. He had only been on an airplane once, an unforgettable flight dodging thunderstorms for three hours. He swore he'd never fly again and rode home on a train. Saint Stephen's neck grip didn't seem so bad by comparison with the upcoming airplane ride. Walking down the jet way, he took short steps like those of a man on route to the electric chair.

"You no like to fly, *Signore*?" Sergio asked when they took their seats. His clue must have been Eddie's white knuckles clutching the arm rests of his seat. On the ground, no less. "No worry. Saints no let us crash."

"If you use the word 'crash' again, or 'saints' for that matter," Eddie said, "you'll be dead long before we arrive in Mexico City."

"You funny man, *Signore*."

A blond flight attendant working the first class cabin approached the two imposters.

"My name is Carol. I'll be serving you today. Can I get you gentlemen something to drink before we take off?"

"You have the nice Chianti?" Sergio asked.

"No Chianti but we have a Merlot," the flight attendant said. The look in her eyes told Eddie that she too thought it may have been a bit early to start drinking. Especially for a couple of priests.

"It's a little early for that, isn't it, Sergio?" Eddie said.

"Is never too early. Sure, you bring us plenty vino," Sergio said. "My friend afraid of the flying. He chicken. Bok, bok. He need the vino."

"Oh, but you look so brave," Carol said, touching Eddie's shoulder reassuringly.

"Vino make you brave!" Sergio said.

Carol delivered the drinks to Eddie and Sergio. "Now you boys let me know if there's anything I can do for you. Okay?"

"Anything?" Sergio said, lewdly.

She pretended not to hear him and turned away with the practiced unflappability of flight attendants. Sergio leaned over the arm rest and leered.

"Sergio, how about you act a little more like a priest," Eddie whispered.

"How they act, *Signore*?"

"Now that I've mentioned it, I'm not sure," said Eddie, leaning back and drinking his wine. "I'm really not sure."

"In Italy I have cousin who is priest. He know lots pretty girls, drink plenty vino."

"That doesn't surprise me," said Eddie.

A passenger across the aisle had been eavesdropping. He cast an askance look at the two priests.

"Sergio, let's speak in Italian, okay?" Eddie said.

Sergio agreed. "Now tell me everything that you have not already told me," he said, in perfect Italian.

"What makes you think I'm holding back information?" said Eddie

"It's just how you are. I need to know everything, *Signore*. You can start with those red marks on your neck."

Eddie adjusted his Roman collar in an effort to hide the bruises.

"I can still see them," said Sergio. "Someone with big hands left those marks. Which statue was it?"

As the aircraft taxied out, Eddie, loosened up by the wine, told Sergio everything, beginning with the red marks.

"I wish I was there to see that!" Sergio said. "I bet you didn't make your bad jokes when you were hanging."

"Actually, I did try out a few on Saint Stephen. He doesn't have much of a sense of humor. No one would if they'd been suffering a death like his for centuries."

"What do you mean?"

Eddie related how the statues had communicated to him that they continued to suffer the agony of their martyrdoms and Stephen's plea of "give us peace."

"My mother told me when I was a little boy that every sin makes the saints in heaven cry. Maybe she was right," Sergio said.

Eddie blocked out Sergio's observation. He was too busy anticipating his death during the take-off. In the air, having survived, he told of Father Louis' journal and its revelations. When he mentioned that the statues had been stored for six hundred years in the *Stanza di Castiga*, the "Room of Retribution" beneath Saint Peters Basilica, Sergio stopped him.

"I have heard of this room," Sergio said.

"Who told you about it?"

"Another *La Mano di Cristo* killer. I thought at the time it was just a story."

"It's real, at least according to the journal," Eddie said. "A lot of people died terrible deaths there. They were probably murdered by your *La Mano di Cristo* predecessors. It may be why the statues were so eager to kill your two friends."

"That makes as much sense as anything else about this, *Signore*," Sergio said.

Eddie saved the best part until last, the news that his father was Cardinal Viviano.

Sergio considered the information for a few seconds. He looked at Eddie. "This Viviano, you told me once that he runs the Vatican Bank, right?"

"Yes, he does. And he was almost elected pope at the last conclave, according to leaked information."

"This was your death sentence, I think," said Sergio. "Your brother, didn't you tell me that he worked at the bank?"

"Yes, he did."

Sergio did not comment but Eddie guessed from the look on his face that his friend also suspected Donnie's death may not have been accidental.

The smooth air, big breakfast and a few more glasses of wine induced Eddie into involuntary sleep, which he didn't resist.

Sergio, inspired by the wine, continued to charm the lovely Carol at every opportunity. He even offered to hear her confession in the galley. She declined.

When Eddie awoke, he stretched and learned there was only one-half hour remaining before landing in Houston, where they'd change planes for Mexico City.

"How you nap, *Signore*?" Sergio asked, speaking again in English.

"Better than I expected."

"When you sleep I think we like the Starsky and the Hutch."

"More like Don Quixote and Sancho Panza!" Eddie said.

"Who they?"

"Two characters in a book. Don Quixote was an impractical idealist, out to right the wrongs of the world. He had a weird little friend named Sancho Panza that had a peculiar kind of common sense. That would be you."

"What they do?"

"Not much, considering that the book was a million pages long. They were on a mission of sorts. Mostly, they had long talks. They learned from each other."

"What they learn?"

"About life."

"Sound boring."

"It is, Sergio, maybe the most boring book ever written."

"I like the Starsky and the Hutch. They kick the ass."

"Personally, I'd rather be bored," Eddie said. "I used to be very bored. I didn't know how good I had it."

The flight landed smoothly in Houston, where the two pretend priests changed planes and departed for Mexico City. Eddie's grim preoccupation with his future intensified the further south they flew. They landed about two hours later. Mexico City airport was packed with others who had traveled hoping for nothing more than a chance to see and hear Celestine the Sixth, a man who meant to change the course of the Roman Catholic Church and who sent shock waves rippling around the globe every time he spoke.

Eddie and Sergio cleared Mexican Customs using two of Sergio's passports, even though Eddie's was for a man about eight inches shorter than he. They worked their way through the crowds to a taxi stand in front of the airport and joined a line of hundreds of other people waiting for a cab. They learned from a Canadian priest also waiting in line that the pope would speak in about two hours, after a procession through Neza-Chalco-Itza, a Mexico City shantytown.

"Now what, Sergio?" Eddie said. "We're still going to be standing in line two *days* from now."

"You wait here, *Signore*. No move."

"Where are you going?

"Have faith in Sergio. Wait right here!"

Five minutes later a small bakery van pulled to the curbside. Sergio, chewing on a sugared roll, waved at Eddie from the passenger seat. Eddie wedged himself inside the van next to Sergio. The delighted driver, clutching three crisp U.S. one-hundred-dollar bills in his fist, welcomed Eddie aboard and offered him a roll.

"The money, she talk, the bullshit, she walk, no *Signore*?" Sergio said.

"You sound like Nick Piccione."

"Maybe you fat cop friend not as dumb as he look," Sergio said. "We no walk, *Signore*. Oh, I almost forget, here some money. Is no good how you broke all the time."

Sergio handed Eddie a wad of large bills. Without counting or commenting, Eddie transferred it to his wallet.

The bakery van driver dropped the two priests off as close as he was willing to get to the infamous shantytown, which he told Sergio housed four million and was as dangerous a place as existed in all of Mexico City. He warned them to be careful.

The area was alive with tourists and locals. Hundreds of peddlers were cashing in on the pope's visit, offering everything from Rosaries, which they swore had been blessed by Celestine the Sixth, to miniature plastic pontiffs that bore a closer resemblance to Poncho Villa than to the pope. Eddie and Sergio merged with the crowd and inched toward the start of the procession.

As Sergio watched in amusement, a pickpocket deftly lifted Eddie's wallet from his cassock pocket. Sergio grabbed the man's arm, punched him hard in the stomach and tripped him to the ground. The crowd backed away. Sergio retrieved Eddie's wallet and a few other wallets from the dazed thief, who stood and ran from the very un-priest-like priest.

"You say one hundred Rosaries or burn in hell," Sergio hollered in Spanish after the retreating crook. He turned to Eddie. "Is like I say, *Signore,* you need me."

"Well done, Hutch," Eddie said. "Did you learn that in *La Mano di Cristo* boot camp?"

"I pretty good with my hands. I also pretty good pickpocket, learn my trade as a boy in Rome stealing wallets and money belts from Americans. Okay, now you stay here, *Signore*. Right here! No move! I be gone a little while."

"Where you going now?"

"I need to get tickets," Sergio said. "How you say?...the 'box seat?' You stay here, *Signore* Starsky. Keep you wallet in you pocket. Let *Il Papa* give away money."

As Eddie watched Sergio disappear into the dense crowd, he tried to call Pat but his phone would not work in Mexico. He spotted a payphone nearby. It took about ten minutes to place the international collect call to Cleveland. He begged the operator to let the phone in the shelter ring for longer than normal. Finally, after twenty or so rings, Pat answered.

"Pat, we're here in Mexico City. I don't have much time. Please go look in the church and tell me if all the statues are still inside," Eddie said as he watched for Sergio to reappear.

A few minutes passed. Pat again picked up the phone. "Eddie, they're all still here, including the decapitated one in the chapel. I wish I could tell you otherwise. How are you guys doing down there?"

"So far so good," Eddie said. "Sergio already warmed up on a guy who picked my pocket. You should have seen it. I don't know what the hell he's up to now. He's getting us tickets or something. Here he comes now. I've gotta run, Pat. I'll talk to you later."

"I love you, Eddie," Pat said. "Get home soon or I'll come down there and find you."

Eddie hung up the phone without another word, then regretted not telling Pat he loved her. He was too distracted: the growing mass of spectators, deafening noise and, most of all, fear that something really might happen.

"So, where are the tickets, Sergio?" Eddie said, certain his sidekick was empty handed. "Are we on the first or third base side?"

"We at the, how you say?...the home plate," Sergio said. "You want to be bishop from Argentina or bishop from South Africa?"

"What?"

"We have both, *Signore*." Sergio reached inside his cassock and pulled out two Bishop *zuchettos,* sashes and laminated credentials admitting them to the procession.

"What, only a bishop? I can't be a cardinal?"

"Okay, I be right back," Sergio said. He started for the crowd again.

"I'm just kidding, Sergio," Eddie said, stopping him. "A bishop from South Africa will do just fine. I take it you exercised your pickpocket skills."

"These two bishops, they easy. I even get their cash. If they know we here to help *Il Papa*, I'm sure they understand."

"I wouldn't bet on it," said Bishop Eddie as he donned the *zucchetto,* wrapped the sash around his waist and hung the credentials from his neck. He hoped the statues, wherever they were at the moment, would come through as well as Sergio.

The newly-minted bishops made their way into the crowd. Sergio created a path with a series of lightning-quick kidney and spinal punches. They moved toward the front of the procession that was assembling behind a car that would transport Celestine the Sixth.

A guard examined Eddie's and Sergio's credentials carefully before admitting them to the procession, just a few yards behind the pope, who was mingling with the locals. Eddie looked at his new name.

"Hmm, Bishop Von Jorgensen. Wonder where he's going to be watching the parade from?"

"Maybe from the jail, *Signore.* Turn around and look, but no laugh." Sergio motioned in the direction of two loudly indignant clerics surrounded by a half-dozen Mexican army troops. The recently defrocked bishops resisted the efforts to move them away, no doubt for some vigorous questioning. Eddie suppressed a smile.

Eddie and Sergio took their places in line with a couple dozen other high-ranking clerics. Again Sergio used his fists to work their way closer to Celestine's vehicle. Eddie spotted Bishop Sacchi, who stood just a few yards from them. Sacchi also spotted him; the bishop seemed confused but he took no action.

"The big ugly bishop over there is Sacchi. He's the one who I think may have had something to do with my brother's death," Eddie said to Sergio over the crowd noise.

Sergio surveyed the situation. "He the one you think might be *Santo Cane*, the Saint Dog of *La Mano di Cristo*?"

"Yes. Have you ever seen him before?" Eddie said.

"No, I never see him before."

Sacchi said something to one of the men with him. The man looked at Sergio and Eddie and grinned. Not a happy grin by any means, thought Eddie, but a grin that said I know your future and you don't.

"*Signore* Eddie, the ugly bishop see you. He know you and maybe me no belong here. Why you think he not say something?"

"Maybe he thinks he can kill three birds with one stone," Eddie said. "You, me and the pope."

"I hope you wrong," said Sergio.

"Me too."

Celestine the Sixth, wearing a black cassock without adornment, took his place in the back of an open car. A dozen papal guards, all wearing the same gray Italian-cut suits, stood a discreet distance away.

"Sergio, you're the expert here. What's gonna happen?" Eddie asked.

"We wait and see, *Signore*."

The procession began to slowly move.

"We have to get closer, *Signore*," Sergio said.

"We get any closer and we'll be in the car with the pope! You think something's going to happen with this many people around?"

"And it happen soon, *Signore*!"

"How do you know that? Do you recognize any of your old buddies?"

"Just one, *Signore*. Someone I work with one time."

"Which one is he?"

"The driver of the car where *Il Papa* ride is *La Mano di Cristo*."

"What? Why didn't you tell me that before now?"

"Because you worry too much, *Signore*."

"With good reason!" said Eddie.

Eddie and Sergio worked their way closer to the car carrying Celestine the Sixth as it inched through the crowd. Locals lined the road and showered the pope with flower petals, pushing past dozens of law enforcement and army troops attempting to hold them back. A steel door on a large warehouse along the pope's route opened from inside, pushing spectators out of the way.

Eddie thought it nothing more than the occupants of the building desiring a closer look at the pope. Hardly anyone except the papal guards—and Sergio—realized the opened door meant danger.

"Get ready, *Signore*," said Sergio.

"For what?"

The pope's vehicle abruptly accelerated and turned into the warehouse. It happened so quickly that few in the procession had time to react. The doors began to close rapidly.

"Is time, *Signore*," Sergio yelled.

Sergio, many of the papal bodyguards, a number of police and military and even a few spectators made it through the doors as they closed. Eddie, not knowing what else to do, followed. He was the last person to get inside the building and was almost crushed by the closing doors.

A large number of armed men inside the warehouse shot and stabbed the papal guards, police, military and even the few spectators that had entered. All fought bravely to help the pope but were outnumbered and were soon dead. Two men attacked Sergio, Eddie and the pope. Eddie fought, more gutsily than he thought himself capable, but a sharp blow to his head dropped him to the floor unconscious. Sergio and the pope were also subdued. The three men were thrown into a metal container in the back of a truck and driven away through a series of back alleys.

When the authorities broke down the doors, they found the abandoned papal vehicle and twenty-three dead bodies, eight of which appeared to be members of the group that had staged the brazen ambush. There was no sign of the pope nor of the two bishops last seen rushing into the building. The entire operation had taken less than three minutes. A police spokesman later told the media that the crime had been committed by "the most organized, determined and cold-blooded killers" his department had ever encountered.

TWENTY ONE

Eddie gradually regained consciousness. He couldn't see anything inside the darkened container but heard two voices. One was that of Sergio and the other, he soon realized, belonged to the very man they had come to save: His Holiness Pope Celestine the Sixth.

"*Signore* Eddie, you okay?" Sergio said. "*Il Papa*, this is my friend Eddie. He also come to protect you."

Eddie could think of nothing to say. He wasn't the least bit surprised at how their mission to save the pope was progressing.

"I'm okay," Eddie said, after a few minutes. "But I feel like I was beaten up pretty good. How about you two?"

"We okay, *Signore*," said Sergio. "But we have all been beaten, even *Il Papa*."

The pope spoke, calmly but with detectable skepticism, in English. "It would seem we are locked in a metal box of some sort and traveling somewhere unknown. Your friend Sergio claims you have both come to rescue me. Is this part of the plan?"

"Holy Father, I wish I could say there was a plan to save you. And us, too. But, sadly, there is no plan. We are counting on others to help and we do not know how or when they will do it."

"That is not encouraging news," said the pope. "Sergio told me there are statues that will rescue us. Is this the case? Statues?"

"Yes, Holy Father, our lives are in the hands of statues," said Eddie.

"Do we know where these statues might be?" the pope asked.

"They in Cleveland, Ohio, Holy Father," said Sergio, who had no other answer for *Il Papa* except the truth. "But they come pretty soon I think."

"We shall be patient and pray then," said Celestine, whose voice betrayed more than a hint of despair. "Do you know who did this?"

"Sergio, this is your department. Tell the Holy Father about your old gang."

"Holy Father, do you ever hear of *La Mano di Cristo*?" Sergio said.

"The Hand of Christ? No. What is that?"

Sergio spoke in Italian for a half hour, explaining everything he knew about the clandestine organization. When he finished, the pope asked many detailed questions concerning Vatican and papal security. Sergio never stumbled with the answers. His knowledge on the subject was comprehensive and convincing.

"We believe the assassins are led by Bishop Sacchi, the head of Vatican security," Eddie said.

"Nonsense! I know Bishop Sacchi. He was close behind us today when we turned off the road into that building," Celestine said. "Sacchi made the trip to *ensure* my safety."

"He made the trip to ensure you were *taken*, Holy Father. He has also shown an interest recently in killing me," said Eddie, who related the recent events in the Church of Martyrs, including a full account of how the statues had saved his life, killed two *La Mano di Cristo* assassins and spared Sergio.

"I'm afraid I don't believe your story. How can I? You are two men pretending to be bishops, who were abducted along with me and you have no idea what is going to happen," the pope said. "We are doomed if we're waiting for statues to save us. I would much prefer to see Bishop Sacchi."

"That will not happen. Holy Father," said Eddie.

Eddie knew he would never convince the pope. He quit trying. The three assessed their situation: their abductors had taken everything from them. They had no identification or money. Escape seemed beyond hope.

As they traveled, the three spoke for hours about many subjects. The pope, calm and resigned, described his dream to distribute the Vatican's wealth, the dream he never got to tell to his audience in Mexico City and the dream that he was now certain would never happen.

"I do not fear death," said the pope. "What I fear is that with my death will die my plans to do what Christ expected of us."

Sergio asked the pope to hear his confession—just in case.

"I fear no one will rescue us," said Celestine. "It is perhaps best to hear your confession now."

Speaking in Italian, Sergio confessed the sins of a lifetime: murders, torture, beatings, kidnappings and every other evil imaginable. Eddie tried not to listen but it was impossible to ignore. Until that moment, Eddie really did not appreciate just how much the statues had transformed his friend.

The pope absolved Sergio of his sins and prayed for him.

"And you, Eddie? Would you like for me to hear your confession?"

"Holy Father, I was once a priest," Eddie said. "I'm not certain exactly what I am now, but I can't be a hypocrite."

"I understand," said the pope. "But I think you'll enter God's world despite your doubts. I should also like both of you to know how grateful I am for your courage, no matter how this ends."

Many hours later, the vehicle came to a stop. The three kidnap victims heard two doors open and close and then nothing. A short while later they heard what sounded like a large propeller-driven aircraft land. The aircraft taxied close to where they were being held.

"I think we go for airplane ride," said Sergio.

"Why do you think that?" said Eddie, not really wanting to hear the answer.

"Is how *La Mano di Cristo* do when it want no bodies found. They will drop this box into the ocean."

"Couldn't you have just let that be a surprise?" said Eddie.

"Believe, *Signore,* believe!" said Sergio. "Holy Father, you too must believe."

"In *what* should I believe? Your friends in Cleveland, Ohio? Statues!?"

Eddie answered. "Yes, Holy Father, I'm afraid our...*friends* in Cleveland, Ohio are our only hope."

The container moved. Someone unlatched the lid and opened it. Sergio prepared to lunge and strike. He stopped when he saw a familiar robed man, a very large man with a hideously burned and blistered face, a face framed by fire set within a black cowl. The man didn't speak but instead made a gruff motion with his right hand, also ablaze, directing the three men to climb out.

The three obeyed the silent command and emerged from the container. Their rescuer stood by motionless, his fiery body lighting up the inside of the truck like a blast furnace. The flames radiated no heat.

"Is this one of your...friends?" the pope said, barely able to voice the words. "Who is he?"

"He is...Lawrence, *Saint* Lawrence!" Eddie said in a voice that was a mixture of relief and delight.

"Where did he come from?"

"Holy Father, he came from a rat-infested deserted Catholic church in Cleveland, Ohio. The West Side!"

"*Madonna mia*! Saint Lawrence? This is Saint Lawrence!?"

"Actually, it is a *statue* of Saint Lawrence," said Eddie.

"But he moves! It is a miracle!" proclaimed the pope.

"I agree, *Il Papa*," said Sergio.

Eddie didn't quite agree but he wasn't about to start a theological argument over miracles with Sergio and certainly not with Celestine the Sixth. Not just then, at any rate.

Lawrence climbed into the empty container and lay down. The three men watched the statue incarnate transform, the flames and charred flesh once again only paint and stone.

The pope, making the Sign of the Cross, asked, "Does he live?"

"We don't know," Eddie said. "Lawrence was a statue for seven hundred years and only recently showed an interest in human affairs."

"We talk about statues later. Is time to go!" Sergio said. He thanked Saint Lawrence before replacing the lid and latching it. Sergio looked out the back of the truck. When he saw no one outside, he and Eddie jumped to the ground. They tried to help the pope but he waved them off.

"I can do this myself," he said. "I am a young pope. And strong!"

The three were in what appeared to be a shallow valley surrounded by mountains. It was nighttime, enhanced by a full moon. The men moved to a brushy area to hide and wait, unsure of what would follow. The aircraft they heard land was parked a short distance away, its engines idling. A few minutes later, five men exited the aircraft and came with a forklift for the container, which they removed from the truck and loaded on the aircraft. All the men remained in the aircraft. It took off a few minutes later and headed west toward the Pacific Ocean.

The pope, Eddie and Sergio watched the aircraft climb into the night sky. They got into the truck. The ever-resourceful Sergio was able to start it without a key and the three drove off. They had no way of knowing that the pilot at that moment was making a frenzied radio call to a secret frequency, screaming into the microphone that a statue of a "man of fire" was burning everyone inside the aircraft to death, one by one. The panicked pilot reported that it was unbearably hot, so much so that the glass on the instruments was cracking. In the middle of the transmission, the radio went dead.

Sergio happened to glance at the departing aircraft as he drove. "Holy Father, *Signore* Eddie, look!"

The three intended victims saw the aircraft begin to glow red, then white before exploding. Flaming bits of wreckage fell from the night sky.

"May God have mercy on their souls," said Celestine. Yep, Eddie thought, the pope was a hell of a good sport and a man definitely worth saving. Personally, Eddie did not share the pope's concern for their abductors' souls.

"What will happen to...Saint Lawrence?" the pope asked.

"He's probably back in Cleveland already," Eddie said. "But please, Holy Father, don't ask me how that is possible. The statues share very little with me."

As Sergio drove in a more or less northerly direction, the pope said, "Now, I would like to know much more about your exceptional... *friends* from...Cleveland, Ohio?"

"*Il Papa*, we have seven friends!" Sergio said.

"Seven? Like him? Like Lawrence?"

"*Si, Il Papa*," said Sergio, who looked at Eddie, expecting him to continue the explanation. Eddie did not have the strength nor the inclination. He gave a nod to Sergio, who talked about the statues as they traveled.

Now that they were free, Eddie faced several new problems, not the least of which was determining exactly what the statues wanted him to do. As he had come to expect, it was up to him to fill in the blanks. He assumed that the pope's long-term welfare was the goal; this meant destroying Sacchi and his *La Mano di Cristo,* or at least as many of them as possible. He had to somehow lure Sacchi and his gang of killers to the Church of Martyrs, where the statues could finish what Eddie imagined would be some very nasty business. To get Sacchi to Cleveland meant convincing the pope to keep his rescue a secret and return with them. He'd also have to convince the pope to act as bait. Eddie's most immediate problem, however, was how in the hell they were going to get out of Mexico.

"Sergio, do you know the story of Saint Lawrence?" the pope asked.

"I know this story, Holy Father," said Sergio.

"Please tell it to us," said Celestine.

"The emperor tell Lawrence to bring to him all the treasure of the Church and he no kill him. Lawrence come back with the crippled children, blind people and lepers. He say 'this is treasure of our Church.' That when emperor throw him on the fire."

"You never cease to amaze me, Sergio," said Eddie, who decided it was as good a time as ever to ask the pope to remain in hiding and return to Cleveland with them.

"I see no reason for it," said Celestine, after hearing Eddie's case. "We are now free. We will stop at the first place we come to and report that we are safe. The entire world will be looking for us. It is not fair to keep everyone in suspense."

"Holy Father, if I'm right about Bishop Sacchi, you will not survive as long as he and *La Mano di Cristo* exist," said Eddie.

"How do you suggest we handle the bishop if indeed he is a threat to me?" said the pope. "What can we do?"

"We can do very little," admitted Eddie.

"Then who will stop him?" said the pope.

Sergio answered. "The statues, Holy Father. They no like *La Mano di Cristo*! The statues kill two of my friends the night we come to kill *Signore* Eddie."

"Tell me why the statues need us?" said the pope.

Sergio took the question, knowing that Eddie would not answer honestly. "Holy Father, the statues no need you and me. They need *Signore* Eddie. I not sure why, but he their big deal. They only do what they do when he in on the job. *Signore* Eddie not smart enough to understand this at first but now I think he understand."

Celestine turned to Eddie. "Then please explain why I am necessary?"

Eddie stumbled for an answer so Sergio spoke. "*Il Papa*, please forgive me but you are the...bait to lure the big fish Bishop Sacchi."

Desperate to get the pope's cooperation, Eddie related every unsettling detail of the last few days: Father Louis' journal, the message carved on the altar and Saint Stephen's tearful plea to end the martyrs' suffering and give them peace.

"The martyrs still suffer?" Celestine said. "How could this be possible? Did they...tell you this?"

"No, much worse," said Eddie. "One of the statues planted an image of their perpetual martyrdoms in my mind. They would have no reason to deceive me."

"Do we know who made these statues?" the pope said.

"An Italian sculptor named Cuccio," said Eddie. "Holy Father, you should know he made them at the cost of his own life to protest the murder of the pope whose name you took."

"Celestine the *Fifth*," said the pope. "He was Pietro Angelerio. History has not been kind to him but no one can refute that he was the most genuinely humble and pious person to ever sit in the chair of Saint Peter."

Eddie filled in the remaining blanks for Celestine. He explained how he had learned from Father Louis' journal that Cardinal Viviano was his father and how his twin brother had died under mysterious circumstances.

"I am truly sorry about your brother, Eddie," said the pope. "I am not so shocked to hear that Cardinal Viviano is your father. Alas, we are all human. What is unpardonable is that he turned his back on you. I spoke with the cardinal before I left for Mexico City. I'm afraid he does not share my views nor my concern for the impoverished. He desires only to be pope and keep the Vatican Bank full of money."

"We too need money," said Sergio, pulling off the road into a truck stop. "We need to get money for gas and food and clothes."

"Are you going to use your secret ATM code, Sergio?" said Eddie.

"The world is big ATM if you know code," said Sergio. "You and Holy Father stay here, please. I go find the ATM. Maybe I get lucky and see some Americans. They the best ATM."

"Sergio, don't you feel bad picking pockets while wearing a cassock?" Eddie said.

"Oh no, *Signore*. Priest is best cover. I dress like this many times when I pickpocket in Rome long time ago. You and Holy Father stay in truck."

Eddie pleaded with the pope not to follow Sergio into the truck stop and inform the world of his rescue. He asked for time to see if Bishop Sacchi would show his hand. The pope agreed to wait a while longer. When Sergio returned he carried two large bags of food, clothes and, most important, all the evidence Eddie needed against Sacchi.

"It say here 'Holy Father Safe!'" said Sergio, reading the headline from a Spanish language newspaper. "It say Holy Father call Vatican this morning."

The article quoted a Vatican spokesman who said the abductors had allowed the pope to call the Vatican to report that he was unhurt and being well-treated. The spokesman said the kidnappers promised that as soon as the ransom was paid, the pope would be released. The ransom was five hundred million dollars, the largest ransom in history. He did not reveal where the pope was being held nor did he mention the two clergy taken in the attack.

The spokesman was Bishop Lorenzo Sacchi, head of Vatican security.

"I had some apprehensions before I left for Mexico City," the pope admitted. "But it is difficult to accept that I was surrounded by conspirators. It is a great disappointment."

"Sacchi must think we're all dead or he would not be so bold," said Eddie. "That gives us an advantage."

"I will return to the United States with you and Sergio and help the statues do what they need to do," the pope said. "But how do we do this? How do we first get out of Mexico?"

"That little detail we're going to leave to our driver, whom I suspect has experience in such matters. He has not failed me yet," Eddie said.

"Is easy. I have the plan already in my head, Starsky," said Sergio.

"I can't wait to hear it, Hutch."

"We drive to border and we turn ourselves in," Sergio said.

"That's your plan?" said Eddie. "We turn ourselves in? I was hoping there'd be helicopters and secret tunnels and stuff."

"No make joke. Wait till I finish, *Signore*. We tell customs of Mexico that we escape from jail in Cleveland and come down here. Banditos beat us up and take our ID and money. We starving and now want to return, even to the jail in Cleveland."

"And then?" Eddie said.

"Before we surrender we call you fat cop friend. We tell him fake Italian names. He make fake, how you say?...the warrant and come down to get us. It will work if he will help us. I do this once before. No, *twice* before. No one want criminals in their country. Mexico get rid of us like the hot tomato."

"I'm sure Nick will agree to help us even though it's not legal, *especially* because it's not legal. He's been a closet felon his entire life. But where's he going to get the money? This will cost a ton," said Eddie.

"I have lots money, *molto soldi*, I hide in the priest's house before we leave. *Signora* Pat get the money and give it to you fat cop friend," said Sergio.

Eddie turned to the pope. "What do you think, Holy Father?"

"I am only the pope. I do not know about such things. But I will pray for Sergio's plan."

"It's settled then!" said Eddie. "What'd you get us to eat, Sergio? I'm starving!"

Sergio had cash, burritos, drinks, a pack of cigarettes and new clothes for all, including colorful T-shirts. The pope delighted in choosing a T-shirt with a portrait of himself on the front, Sergio's idea of a gag. Luckily, the image did not resemble him in the least. To Eddie's chagrin, the pope smoked a cigarette with Sergio. Eddie spared them his standard lecture on the evils of tobacco.

The three changed and put their cassocks behind some bushes; the garments were visible from the road. It was Sergio's idea. The clothes were meant to be discovered and keep the search, which continued despite the assurances of the Vatican, well south of the United States border. Sergio fueled the truck and headed north again.

"Now we go to America, to the Cleveland, Ohio," Sergio said. "Border town Reynosa only seven hundred kilometers from here." He handed the cash he had taken out of the pockets of three Americans to Eddie and asked him to count it.

"There's almost twelve hundred bucks here, Sergio. Didn't you get a little carried away?"

"Oh, no, *Signore*, we have no ID. We need money for the bribe if we stopped. Money make people not see things. Happen all the time in Mexico. Happen everywhere! You not know too much but I take good care of you. And you too, *Il Papa*."

Celestine, spiritual leader of a billion Catholics worldwide, nodded his gratitude to the ex-assassin and silently absolved him of the theft.

"Sergio, I have something to tell you," said Eddie.

"What is that?"

"On that first night, when you told me that I needed you, well, you were right. I would not have gotten very far without you. Thanks."

"You welcome, *Signore*. I know things they not teach in priest school, huh?"

"You could say that," said Eddie.

Sergio pulled into the next truck stop they came to. He asked Eddie to call Pat and give her three made-up Italian names which Nick would use on the faked extradition warrants. Sergio also told Eddie where he had hidden the money in the rectory. If all went well, Nick could be in McAllen, Texas, across the border from Reynosa, in less than twenty-four hours.

Eddie called Pat.

"Where are you?" said Pat. "Your friend in the church, the one with the flames, has been back for a long time."

"Did you by chance see him come or go?"

"No," said Pat. "I went to check and he was gone. A half-hour later he was back."

"How nice for him," Eddie said. "It goes without saying that we're stuck in Mexico."

"Of course!" said Pat. "You don't expect the statues to do everything, do you?"

"I'm beginning to think it's their idea of a joke," said Eddie. "But not to worry. Sergio's cooked up a plan to get the three of us home."

"*Three* of you?"

"Uh, yes, three of us," Eddie said. "We picked up a hitchhiker along the way, a real nice guy."

Eddie told Pat a few sketchy details of their escape and explained Sergio's plan, including Nick's part.

"Isn't this a bit...illegal?" said Pat. "You think Nick will buy into it?"

"Only because it *is* illegal! Nick has always longed to be on the wrong side of the law," said Eddie, who spelled the made-up Italian names for the fake warrants and gave Pat Nick's phone number. He also told her where Sergio had hidden the cash in the rectory.

"So...the hitchhiker's coming home with you?"

"Yes. He's always wanted to visit Cleveland," said Eddie. "He'll be safe there until we can figure something out."

"Okay, I'll call Nick and go look for that money in the rectory right now."

"Goodbye, Pat. I love you and miss you so much I can't tell you."

"Never mind the goodbyes. I'm more interested in hellos. Lots and lots of hellos with no clothes on!"

Pat hung up and called Nick.

"Mexico!? What the hell's he doing in Mexico?" Nick demanded.

"What else? He and Sergio went down there to rescue the pope from his abductors. They did it! They have the pope with them."

"The pope!? Maybe you haven't heard, but it's all over the news that the pope is being held by kidnappers. He has called the Vatican and said he'll be released when the ransom is paid."

"I heard that, too," said Pat. "But if Eddie says he has the pope, that's good enough for me."

"Me too! How did they do it? Why are they keeping quiet?"

"It's the biggest secret in the universe right now," said Pat. "Eddie didn't say exactly but I get the idea that the danger to the pope's life is not over. They've somehow convinced him to come to Cleveland."

"The pope's coming to Cleveland?" said Nick. "To Briggs Hill?"

"That's the idea," she said. Pat told Nick as much as she knew about what the boys had been through, sparing him the part about the statue, before explaining the role he was being asked to play. She wasn't sure he'd agree but, as Eddie had predicted, Nick jumped at the chance.

"Why not? I've been looking for a good excuse to retire for a couple years," said Nick. "This ought to guarantee it. What better way to go out than with a major league caper? They'll remember ol' Banjo Ass for a long time!"

"Banjo Ass?"

"That's right! I'll explain it to you later," said Nick.

"Well, Banjo Ass, c'mon over," Pat said. "I'll go to the rectory and find the money where Sergio stashed it. And I'll give you the fake names."

"I gotta admit it, Pat, I'm damned proud of Eddie and his little buddy...Sergio for pulling this thing off," said Nick. "I'm a little pissed, however, that they didn't take me along. I love Mexican food. I'll be right over."

Pat left the shelter and crossed the courtyard on her way to the rectory. A lone man approached her and called her name.

"Pat? Is that you Pat? I've been waiting out here for hours to see you."

Pat knew the voice. It triggered an escape response. She started to run but the man caught up with her. He spun her around. It was her ex-husband.

"Let go of me," Pat said. "Please let go of me! It's all over and you know it!"

"You shouldn't have run away. You knew it'd piss me off," he said, clenching a fist.

"Please don't hit me," Pat pleaded.

Pat's ex held her arm with one hand and swung his fist at her face. Pat recoiled. But her ex's fist did not land where he intended. A hand, a very large hand, an ancient hand, grabbed his wrist and re-directed the blow with enormous force to another entirely unexpected face, one not of soft flesh but of hard stone.

Pat's ex-husband, his fist bloodied and broken, fell to the ground. He looked up and saw a seven-foot-tall robed man standing over him: the martyr Stephen. Pat's ex groaned in pain as he got up on his hands and knees. Stephen raised his shackled hands, one of which held a sizable stone; he mercilessly slammed the stone down on his victim's hands, first one and then the other. Pat's ex fell on his face, shrieking.

Pat watched Saint Stephen slog back to the darkened Church of Martyrs, each heavy step accentuated by the woeful clanking of chains.

Still on the ground, Pat's ex studied the remains of what had been his hands. Blood ran from ripped flesh and opened veins. Several of his fingers remained attached by mere threads of skin. All were smashed. He looked at Pat.

"My hands! My hands!"

"You don't deserve hands, you son-of-a-bitch!" Pat yelled. She was shaking. "You want to hit me? Come on, hit me! Or why don't you try to rape me? Let's see what the boys in the church do about *that*!"

Pat's ex-husband stumbled out of the courtyard, moving as fast as possible, howling in pain and crying for help.

"What's going on here? Who the hell are you?" It was Nick, who lived a short distance from the church. "Pat, who is this? Someone you know?"

"He's my ex, or what's left of the asshole."

"What happened to the poor bastard's hands?"

"He touched the wrong person."

"If he touched you, I'll arrest him right now," Nick said. "I'll make a lot of trouble for him, bloody hands or not."

"Not necessary, Nick. He didn't hurt me. And I don't think he'll ever come back."

"You sure of that?"

"Seems I also have some tough friends in that old church," Pat said.

"Are we talking those damned statues again?"

"Yes, Nick, those damned statues again."

"Next you'll tell me the statues helped Eddie save the pope's life in Mexico!"

"Do you want to hear the story?" Pat said.

"No, I don't!"

Pat felt doubly gratified. Saint Stephen had not only rescued her from a severe beating and perhaps death, but she now knew she was part of the plan, whatever that plan might be. For the first time, Pat fully appreciated Eddie's situation and loved him all the more for it.

TWENTY TWO

Eddie, Sergio and Pope Celestine drove into Reynosa the day after their escape. They abandoned the truck after neatly stacking the remainder of their money on the seat for the first lucky passerby and walked a short distance to Mexican Customs. Sergio did the talking, explaining in Spanish how they were Italian citizens that were being held on a variety of charges in Cleveland, Ohio before they escaped and fled to Mexico. He said they had been robbed by banditos. With no food, money or identification, the three had no choice but to give up. Eddie added actor and con man to the list of Sergio's unique talents.

The Mexican Customs agent called the U.S. Customs office across the border. Nick had already contacted the American side and told them he had spoken with the fugitives. He would come for them as soon as he got the extradition papers, which he held in his hand.

Mexican Customs, after strip-searching the trio, gave them papers to sign for their extradition. The desperados were escorted across the International Bridge into the hands of waiting U.S. Customs agents. Eddie learned from an agent that Nick had cautioned them to be especially wary of the tall one, who was leader of a Cleveland gang called the *Dago Bombers*.

They were allowed to shave, shower and were given a meal. The pope thought it best not to shave to help disguise himself. The boys were locked in a holding cell for the night. While an anxious world prayed for Pope Celestine, he and his unlikely traveling companions spent the night on uncomfortable cots at the U.S.-Mexican border.

Nick arrived in McAllen, Texas the next day late in the afternoon. He wasn't happy when informed that he would have to wait until morning to serve his papers. His best Cleveland detective bullying technique did not go over well with the U.S. Customs agent, who told him to come back in the morning.

The next day, after Nick served the bogus, but quite official-looking extradition papers, an agent led him to the holding cell and the dangerous fugitives from justice.

"That tall one," Nick said, pointing to Eddie, "he's the real bad ass. May have to drug and chain him to get him home."

Eddie was very relieved to see his old friend, even if Nick overplayed his role.

"Yeah, but the one I wouldn't turn my back on is the little guy on the right," said the agent, pointing not to the former professional killer and expert pickpocket Sergio, but to His Holiness Pope Celestine the Sixth!

Nick grunted his agreement, somehow kept from exploding into laughter, handcuffed his runaways and left with them in the compact car he had rented. On the way to McAllen Airport, Nick found the nerve to speak to the pope.

"I believe I should call you Your Holiness, Your Holiness," Nick began, awkwardly. "I am very sorry about the handcuffs. Would you like me to remove them?"

"How 'bout us, Nick?" said Eddie. "Sergio and I would like ours taken off, too."

"Nah, I don't think so. You can't send me to hell. But the Holy Father can."

"My new good friend Nick, you know in your heart that only you can send yourself to hell," said the pope. "Perhaps we should all stay in our handcuffs. It will make us more believable."

Many long hours later Nick and his prisoners arrived in Cleveland, Ohio. It was cold and the boys had nothing warm to wear. Pat anticipated the problem and brought jackets she found in the rectory. The one that fit the pope advertised "Fiocca's Bakery," a local business that had once sponsored Eddie's softball team.

"This is most appropriate," said Celestine. "Perhaps you have heard that I am also a baker. Is this Fiocca's a good bakery?"

"The best!" said Eddie and Nick together.

Eddie and Sergio rode with Nick to the Church of Martyrs. Pat drove the pope. She could not think of a conversation starter. She wasn't Catholic and wondered if she should even speak.

The pope had his own conversation starter. "Dear lady, have you seen these statues move with your own eyes?"

"Yes. Yes, I have," said Pat.

"I saw Saint Lawrence when he saved our lives," said the pope. "I will never get it out of my mind. It was the most frightening and exhilarating moment of my life."

Pat related the latest human interaction with the statues, how Saint Stephen had mangled the hands of her abusive ex-husband.

"The statues kill and maim without a second thought, it would seem," said Celestine, contemplatively. "Even though I am alive now because of that violence, I have trouble reconciling it."

"As do I," said Pat. "Please tell me how I should address you. I'm not Catholic and I don't know."

"Most say Holy Father, but I like *Il Papa* also."

"Then I shall call you *Il Papa*. I am Pat."

"Then I shall call you Pat," said the pope, sounding pleased. "Now, Pat, tell me what you think of all this."

Pat paused to collect her thoughts. Pope Celestine had just asked her opinion!

"*Il Papa*, while Eddie and Sergio were gone, and when I wasn't worrying myself sick, I gave a lot of thought to what's been happening. At first, the statues' actions seemed disconnected and arbitrary. But it gradually became clear they were collecting us like pieces of a puzzle for one purpose: your survival."

"I cannot tell you how glad I am the three of you came to that conclusion," said Celestine, with a smile. "I have much I want to do with my life. But it seems we have something most unpleasant to do first."

"I wish it were over, *Il Papa*," said Pat. "I very much wish it were over."

"So you understand that I am here to help Eddie and Sergio lure Bishop Sacchi and his assassins to their destruction?" said the pope.

"Yes, I assumed as much," said Pat. "And I am terrified by what may happen!"

"I have great faith in God and great trust in the statues with the miraculous powers, but I must admit I too am terrified," said the pope. "I would give anything and do anything in my power to prevent more killing, but I feel it is now out of our hands."

That evening Celestine entered the Church of Martyrs carrying only a candle. He walked from statue to statue, examining each closely and taking time to thank Saint Lawrence. Though he tried to fight it—indeed, he felt as pontiff he should have been above such trepidation—the statues unnerved him. He knelt and prayed and asked for guidance. Should he attempt to draw out those who had tried to kill him and perhaps put an end to the villainy that had infected the Catholic Church for centuries? And, though it was beyond human understanding, bring peace to the martyrs?

In the end, it was the statues' eyes, eyes that seemed to petition Celestine from an unknowable world, which convinced him of what had to be done.

At the first opportunity, Pat told Eddie about her experience with her ex-husband and Saint Stephen.

"I actually felt a little sorry for the bastard," she said. "Those statues don't play around."

"Sounds like your ex got what he had coming! Now, speaking of playing around...."

"I'm glad to see you've lost your bashfulness," said Pat. "You've certainly caught on to this sex thing in a hurry."

"I don't think one has to be an ex-priest to understand it," said Eddie, mimicking Pat's comment of a few days earlier.

"Very funny. I suppose I had that coming," she said. "Did you miss me as much as I missed you?"

"Pat, all I thought about was getting back to you. That is, when I wasn't getting beaten up or worrying about dying some horrible death. Thinking about this moment helped me more than anything, with the possible exception of a much-needed statue intervention and Sergio's assorted criminal skills."

"So what's going to happen with the statues now?"

"I'm not sure," said Eddie, "but based on our experiences with them, I will guarantee we won't know what's going to happen until the moment it happens. They like to surprise people."

"Meanwhile," said Pat, "what do you say we find a place where we can surprise one another?"

"Thought you'd never ask," said Eddie.

The former convent was out of the question, though Eddie had not forgotten how much it added to the excitement the first time Pat and he made love there. Nor did Eddie feel comfortable doing anything in his room since the pope slept next door and Sergio, rearmed by Nick, insisted on sleeping in a chair outside the bedroom door. With no other option, the new lovers happily—and quietly—availed themselves of the lumpy couch downstairs in the rectory.

In the morning Eddie, Pat, Sergio and the pope ate breakfast and discussed their situation. They knew that Celestine could not conceal himself from the world for long and that the only reason they had gotten away with it thus far was because Bishop Sacchi kept insisting to the media that the pope was safe and would soon be released when the ransom was paid. They also knew they had an edge on Sacchi because he more than likely assumed the pope had been killed in the aircraft that went missing in Mexico.

Others behaved as if they were *certain* Celestine was dead. The pope read with simmering anger a story in the *Plain Dealer* reporting that his cardinals and bishops, along with the Curia, freely discussed scaling back and perhaps dismantling his "unworkable" wealth distribution program. The Curia had put an "indefinite hold" on Celestine's planned new Office for the Distribution of Christ's Wealth.

"I am reading that those running the Vatican in my absence want to end my plans," said the pope. "It seems many would much prefer to have me dead rather than alive."

"I'm afraid so, Holy Father," said Eddie. "I have the feeling that when you return to Rome, there are those who will have much to explain."

"Adversity always defines one's friends, does it not Eddie?" said the pope. "I will do my best to be charitable to those who have taken advantage of my situation. Although I must admit that the Italian in me begs for a little revenge."

"I know the feeling," said Eddie. "Holy Father, do you have someone in Rome you can trust?"

"I have such a man," said Celestine.

"May I ask who he is, Holy Father?"

"His name is Gesa Danku. He is a blind Gypsy priest who has spent many years working in the rainforest with the Pygmies of the Congo."

"Of course he is," said Eddie, with a deep sigh. "Holy Father, at this point I would have been shocked and even a bit disappointed if your trusted man in Rome was *not* a blind Gypsy priest from the Congo!"

"Before I left for Mexico City, I sent my aide Father Villalobos, a loyal and trustworthy man, to find Father Danku in Africa and bring him to Rome. I named Danku my secretary of state. He should have arrived by now."

"Maybe it is time to contact your new secretary of state," said Eddie.

"I agree," said the pope. "I will call Father Villalobos tonight, when it is morning in Rome, and give him a message for Danku. I will use a code no one but Danku will understand."

TWENTY THREE

Father Danku and the two Jesuit messengers arrived at their offices in the slums of Rome early in the morning three days after the pope had been abducted. They only knew what the world knew, which was what Bishop Sacchi wanted the world to know.

Before leaving on his ill-fated trip, Pope Celestine had left detailed instructions for Father Danku. Among other things, the pope wanted his secretary of state to interview perspective managers for the new Office for the Distribution of Christ's Wealth. He relied on Father Danku's Gypsy talent for assessing character, or lack thereof. Anyone who could get past Gesa Danku was good enough for Celestine the Sixth.

That job could wait, however. Father Danku immediately set to work seeing what could be done to help his friend the Holy Father. He prayed for just a few clues. His finely-tuned unerring logic would take it from there.

A delegation representing the College of Cardinals and the Roman Curia insisted on seeing Danku within hours of his arrival from Africa. They had some news for the Gypsy: he was *not* the Vatican secretary of state. The College of Cardinals had named one of their own in the position, pending Father Danku's expected resignation. They had learned Danku was blind and feared he could not handle the job or, worse yet, prove *too* loyal to the pope. The delegation requested that Danku meet with them in a Vatican office, rather than in Danku's office in the Rome slums.

"Tell them that if they wish to see me, they must come here, where the Holy Father wishes all of us to be," Danku said to Father Villalobos, whom he had asked to be his aide until the pope's return. "And caution them to be careful where they park their expensive Vatican automobiles. God forbid they should have to walk home."

Villalobos grinned. The Jesuit had quickly learned to admire this Gypsy priest from the rainforest, whose good humor spread to all around him. "Should I remind them of the Holy Father's directive to live and work among the poor?"

"No, don't be hard on them. The little mice always sneak back into the cozy house when the cat is away, especially if they believe the cat might be dead," said Danku.

With no other choice, the delegation of high prelates and Curia arrived at Danku's office a few hours later. A bishop opened the meeting by explaining to Danku that he had a choice: he could voluntarily resign from his position as secretary of state or he would be forced to resign. The bishop assured the Gypsy that he would find some suitable job for him in the Vatican if he wished to stay or that he could return to the Congo. The bishop also offered Danku the services of a seeing-eye dog.

"That is very kind of you, bishop, but surely Your Excellency knows we Gypsies *eat* dogs. We don't follow them around," Danku laughed.

No one laughed with him. All were too amazed at how this priest without eyes knew the person offering him a seeing-eye dog held the rank of bishop.

"With all due respect, Father Danku," a cardinal in the group began, "we must demand your immediate resignation on a number of grounds."

"And what would they be, Your Eminence?" asked Danku.

The cardinal did not reply right away, openly surprised that Danku also knew *his* rank. "For one thing, and I mean no disrespect, you are blind!"

"Your Eminence acts as if I'm unaware of my blindness," Danku said.

"No, I say that because you won't possibly be able to perform the function of papal secretary of state. For one thing, you will have many complex documents to read in the course of a day. The workload will surely increase with this tragedy to our Holy Father. We can't be expected to translate hundreds of documents into braille or read them to you."

"Do you have one of these 'complex documents' that I may see?" said Danku.

The group appeared baffled by the request. One of the Curia officials, however, pulled a spread sheet from his briefcase and handed it to Danku, who took it and, rubbing it delicately with his fingertips, began to read aloud and explain the long list of numbers, even pointing out an error.

The delegation was astonished, all except Father Villalobos, who had already learned what a great mistake it was to underestimate Hatti Hashi, "he who sees nothing and sees all."

A bishop in the back of the room reached into his cassock for a cigarette and lighter. He put the cigarette to his lips and was about to strike the lighter when Danku spoke.

"Bishop, would you please not smoke in my office? Cigarette smoke, especially that harsh Italian brand with which you punish your lungs, dulls my sense of smell. I would not be able to tell if a wild animal was stalking me. Thank you, Your Excellency."

The bishop, clearly annoyed and amazed at the same time, complied.

"Could you read another document, Father Danku?" a Curial official asked, impatiently.

"Of course," said Danku, who walked into the group and took the paper from him.

Villalobos noticed that the official handed Danku the paper face down. The Jesuit was about to object to the unfairness of the test when Danku, without hesitation, said, "Don't you know that this paper is upside down? Maybe your sight is not so good, eh? Maybe the kind bishop, or your own Curia, could supply *you* with a dog. And, oh my, it's in Latin."

Danku did not bother to turn the paper over. He ran his fingers under it and began to read, first in Latin and then with a translation to Arabic, then to Greek. When finished he said, "Would you like it translated into any other language? The soulful tongue of the Hittabbe perhaps?"

The bishop who had been asked not to smoke stepped to the front of the assembly and protested loudly, "This is Gypsy sorcery! All my life I have distrusted you *zingari*! We will not abide Gypsy sorcery in our Church! You blaspheme!"

Danku aimed his non-eyes directly at the bishop. He spoke slowly and deliberately, as if to end his trial at the hands of fools. "No, dear bishop, it is not sorcery. What you have witnessed is a skill that I learned with much patience, practice and God's merciful help over many years. If I were to use my Gypsy sorcery, I could make you shrink and, perhaps, even disappear. Would Your Excellency like a demonstration?"

The bishop did not call Danku's bluff; he offered a weak apology and left. One by one, the other inquisitors followed, unsure of what they had just seen but no longer willing to challenge this strange priest. Nor did they voice their demands that Father Danku cut his long black ringlets, stop wearing golden earrings and begin wearing shoes.

"Now that our visitors have departed to do whatever it is they do," Danku said to Villalobos, "we must devote ourselves to helping our Holy Father. The pope's kidnappers have sent a ransom letter to the Vatican Bank. We will visit the bank to see how it intends to handle the payment. Would you call ahead and tell them we are on our way? I would also like the person in charge of the pope's security to be present."

"Bishop Sacchi is in charge of all security, including that of the bank," said Villalobos. "He and Cardinal Viviano, president of the bank, are friends. I'm told Sacchi spends a good deal of time with the cardinal."

"Hmm, that is interesting. I read in today's paper that this Bishop Sacchi was in Mexico City with the Holy Father when he was abducted," said Danku, thinking out loud. "The article said that Sacchi has been back in Rome for several days. Seems he would have felt obligated to remain in Mexico to conduct the investigation."

"I had that same thought," said Villalobos.

"Perhaps you have some Gypsy in your Jesuit blood!" Danku speculated.

"I think, after knowing you a few days, that would not be a bad thing," said Villalobos.

Several hours later, Danku and Villalobos arrived at the Vatican Bank. At the entrance was a bronze plaque that read, "OFFICE OF RELIGIOUS WORKS," the official name of the bank. Danku ran his fingers over the letters. "My friend Prala wants nothing more than for this bank to someday live up to its name. I pray he gets the opportunity."

Danku turned to Villalobos. "I have a request of you."

"What would you like Father Danku?" Villalobos said.

"I will be playing the fool in this meeting. It is something I am good at, comes to me quite naturally," Danku said. "Please play along. Take my arm and lead me."

On their way to the meeting, Villalobos turned down the wrong corridor. Danku caught the mistake and redirected him. When the two entered Viviano's office, Danku nodded his head in the presence of the cardinal but in the wrong direction. Bishop Sacchi, who was known to hate Gypsies, sized up the new barefoot secretary of state from a comfortable chair in the corner.

"Will the head of security be meeting with us today?" Danku asked, as he fumbled to find the chair behind him.

"I am here, Father Danku," Sacchi said. The bishop sat with the confidence of a spider tending a web no one dared vibrate. He seemed amused at Pope Celestine's ridiculous choice to fill such a powerful position.

Father Villalobos stifled a grin. Sacchi was not well-liked among Vatican staffers due to his intimidating manner. Villalobos enjoyed watching him fall for Danku's ruse. He knew that the priest from the Congo could easily have told Sacchi what he had eaten for breakfast, much less where he sat. None of them, however, could know that Danku detected the scent of predation in the cardinal's office.

"I know only that we have received a ransom letter from the kidnappers and that they demand five hundred million American dollars. Will that be a problem for the bank, cardinal?" said Danku, looking past Viviano.

"It is quite a large amount of money but it has already been done," Viviano said. "The kidnappers are holding the Holy Father in Brazil. The cash was flown there yesterday and transported to the kidnappers by truck. Except for the amount of the ransom, the outside world knows nothing of this. The Holy Father's life depends on maintaining great secrecy."

"I agree," said Danku. "Bishop Sacchi, do you know if the Holy Father is still unharmed?"

"The kidnappers allowed His Holiness to call a few hours ago," said Sacchi. "He told me he is well and confident he will soon be set free, now that the ransom money has been paid. All we can do is pray."

"This is indeed good news, Bishop Sacchi. I feel much relieved after meeting with both of you. The fate of our Holy Father is in good hands," Danku said.

Viviano had ordered lunch for the four men. Throughout, Danku fumbled with the condiments and could never seem to remember where he had placed his drink or set down his fork. After they had eaten, Danku and Villalobos left.

When Villalobos returned to his office, his secretary told him that there was a message from the United States. She said the caller was a woman and the message came in on a phone line known only to a very few.

"What is the message?" Villalobos asked.

"I could not understand it, Father Villalobos. It's in some kind of code. The woman asked me to write it down as she spelled it. She said you were to give it to Father Danku."

Villalobos brought the message to Danku, who read it with his fingers and beamed.

"The Holy Father is free!" said Danku.

"How do you know that?"

"This message is from him. It is in Romani. Part of it reads, 'Prala laso sim.' It means my best friend in this world is safe and well."

"Where *is* the Holy Father?"

"He is in...Cleveland, Ohio, of all places on Earth," said Danku.

"Why is the Holy Father there? How did he get there?" said Villalobos.

"He did not explain," said Danku. "He merely said he is safe and staying with those who rescued him."

"What of the pope's abductors?" Villalobos said.

"We just had lunch with them."

"Cardinal Viviano and Bishop Sacchi? Why would they lie to us? Why would they pretend to send money to kidnappers in South America?"

Father Gesa Danku considered the question, then spoke. "Simple logic tells me it is because there was no money in the Vatican Bank to send."

TWENTY FOUR

Father Gesa Danku walked to a small park not far from his office and called the number provided in the message he received from the pope. It was late in Cleveland but Eddie and the others stayed awake waiting on the call.

"Church of Martyrs Women's Shelter, this is Eddie, can I help you?"

"I am Father Gesa Danku. I believe we share a great secret. No?"

"Yes, Father Danku, we do," said Eddie. "I am going to give the phone to him."

"Gesa, you have received my message. Good. Are you free to speak?" said the pope, who suggested they speak in Romani.

"I am in a park in the middle of the poorest section of Rome speaking an almost unknown dialect of Romani. Yes, I am free to speak, my Holy Father," said Danku. "First, I must know. How did you escape from your abductors?"

"With the help of a saint," said the pope.

"A saint?" said Danku. "Where did you find a saint in these unholy times?"

"He is not from these times, Gesa."

"Not from these times?"

"No, Gesa, he is not. I myself will never fully believe what happened but there will be much to tell when this is over and we meet again. My story is far better than any story of marvel and wonder and terror you ever heard from the old men in the Gypsy camps."

"That is saying quite a lot. I shall look forward to it," said Danku. "Please tell me why you are in the United States and why you remain in hiding?"

"My rescuers believe that the danger to my life has not passed and that if I return to Rome my enemies will not rest until I am dead. My death seems to be imperative to some people who may have worked under my very nose."

"Holy Father, I believe your rescuers are correct about your life being in danger still."

"Why do you agree with them?" said the pope, sounding surprised.

"I have just come from the Vatican Bank," said Danku. "Bishop Sacchi was there with Cardinal Viviano. Sacchi claims he spoke with you a few hours ago. Has this happened?"

"No, it most certainly has *not* happened!" said the pope. "Sacchi is the one we suspect may want me dead."

"Probably Sacchi *and* Cardinal Viviano. They claim they have sent the five hundred million dollars in cash to kidnappers somewhere in Brazil, where they told me you are being held," said Danku. "I don't believe there was any money in the bank to send. They will use the ransom as an excuse for the bank's insolvency. I also believe they think you are dead."

"Why do you say that?" said the pope.

"Cardinal Viviano's office had the smell of a village preparing to celebrate a successful hunt."

"I am very glad you are back, Gesa," said the pope.

"I am also glad I am back. What would you like for me to do?" said Danku.

"We need to lure Bishop Sacchi to this old church where I am staying."

“This I don’t understand, Holy Father. Please explain why you would take such a risk?”

“We have good reason to believe Sacchi is the leader of a group of Vatican assassins known as *La Mano di Cristo*. This ‘Hand of Christ’ kidnapped me and two men who tried to help me. One of those men is a former member of *La Mano di Cristo*. We were all about to be killed when we were rescued.”

“Vatican assassins? The Hand of Christ?” said Danku. “If this is true, all the more reason to return to Rome where we can protect you!”

“No!” said the pope. “I will not live looking over my shoulder for the rest of my life! Sacchi must come here!”

“Why? What will happen?”

“He and anyone who comes with him will be destroyed if they are determined to kill me.”

“Who will do that, my Holy Father?” said Danku.

“I told you I was rescued by a saint,” said the pope. “That saint is a statue in an abandoned church where I am staying. It is one of seven statues that will kill Sacchi and anyone else who tries to harm me or my friends. It was one of these statues that saved our lives in Mexico.”

“Statues!?” said Danku. “Holy Father, did you say *statues*?”

“Yes, *statues*!” said the pope. “Gesa, for the first time in our long friendship, you know less than I do. If you can lure Sacchi here, his assassins will follow. May Almighty God forgive me, but this is necessary. Help me lure Sacchi, please. Tell no one and send no one. Believe in me, Gesa. And believe in these statues of which I speak!”

“It appears I have no other choice, Holy Father. If you insist on getting Sacchi to you, it is as simple as calling him. Tell him to come and secretly escort you back to Rome, where you will announce to the world that you are safe.”

“That sounds too simple, Gesa,” said the pope.

“Simple deceptions are best. They don’t appear to be deceptions at all. Ah, but every deception must have a hook in it.”

"And what is that hook?"

"When you talk to Sacchi," said Danku, "tell him to call me immediately. If he does as you instruct and calls me with the news you are safe, then we will know he is just another unpleasant bishop among many unpleasant bishops in Rome. If he does *not* call me, then you should fear for your life. I will, of course, warn you."

"We will do as you say, Gesa," said the pope.

"Also tell Sacchi about this *La Mano di Cristo* and that one of its ex-members helped you escape and remains with you. If the bishop controls such an organization, he will be doubly anxious to come to you so that he can eliminate you *and* the traitor."

"There is one more bit of information you should know," said the pope. "Cardinal Viviano fathered twin boys when he was a young priest at this church where I am staying. One of the sons, who worked at the Vatican Bank, died mysteriously a short time ago. There was a recent attempt to kill his other son. The statues intervened and saved his life. He is one of the two men, along with the statue, that helped me escape."

"Ah," said Danku. "*Three* good reasons for Sacchi to come to Cleveland. I will pray for you, Prala, and for your friends and these...statues. I have the number to Sacchi's office for you when you are ready."

After the pope had written down the number, he ended the conversation.

Danku explained the situation to Villalobos but did not mention the statues at first.

"The Holy Father does *not* want us to tell the world he is safe and return to Rome?" said a stunned Villalobos. "Church assassins? Could this be possible?"

"Everything is possible," said Danku. "The Holy Father all but begged me to do this his way. He must have good reasons."

"Danku, if we are successful and lure Bishop Sacchi and these... assassins to the Holy Father, what then?" said Villalobos. "Did the Holy Father tell you what would happen? Who will protect him?"

"That is the part that frightens me," said Danku, who took a deep breath before telling Villalobos of the statues. "The Holy Father claims there are statues in an old church that will protect him and his rescuers."

"Statues!?" said Villalobos.

"That was my reaction, also," said Danku. "I fear for the Holy Father. I wish I knew more but I do not. Logic will not play a part in any of this."

When the pope explained the plan to Eddie, he was skeptical. Celestine tried to reassure him.

"I have spent much time with the Romani," said the pope. "They are proud of their ability to deceive non-Gypsies. They believe it is compensation from God for the curse of having to wander the world."

Sergio approved of the plan.

"Why Sergio?" Eddie said.

"This Father Danku is clever man."

"How do you know that? Do you know him?"

"No," said Sergio, "but every pickpocket in Rome know it is not possible to steal the wallet from a Gypsy. They steal your wallet instead."

"Sergio, you're pretty good at these things," said Eddie. "Why don't you try to call Sacchi? But be careful, he might be a little harder to con than those U.S. and Mexican Customs agents at the border. You get Sacchi on the phone and give it to the Holy Father."

After several attempts, Sergio reached Bishop Sacchi's office. The bishop's secretary, one of a tier of three that screened the bishop from the outside world, finally agreed to give a message to her boss.

"Tell him someone who know about the pope on the phone," said Sergio. "Very important I talk to Bishop Sacchi."

The secretary asked Sergio for a number. The message got to Sacchi, who immediately went outside and called.

"What is this nonsense?" Sacchi demanded. "Do not waste my time! Who are you!?"

"My name not important. What is important is the Holy Father. He is here in the United States, in Cleveland, Ohio."

"The Holy Father? The United States?" Sacchi spoke so loudly that several persons close by turned. He lowered his voice. "That's not possible!"

"You want to tell this to *Il Papa*?"

Sacchi looked around to make sure no one could hear the conversation. He allowed his voice to settle. "Yes, if the Holy Father is with you, let me speak with him."

Sergio handed the phone to the pope.

"Holy Father, can this really be you? Are you safe?" said Sacchi, in as caring a voice as he could manage.

"Sacchi, why did you tell the press that you have spoken with me?" said the pope.

The question caught Sacchi off guard. He fumbled for an answer. "Holy Father, I told them that...only to calm the world. I knew in my heart you were all right."

"Sacchi, it is no thanks to you that I am 'all right.' Your security failed me."

"I thank Almighty God that you are safe, Holy Father," said Sacchi. "I will regret my failure for the rest of my life. How did you...escape, Your Holiness?"

"With the help of two men, an ex-priest and an ex-assassin who was until recently a member of a secret society of killers known as *La Mano di Cristo* that operates from the Vatican," said the pope. "Do you know of such a group?"

"No, Your Holiness, I have never heard of it," Sacchi said. "You were rescued by only two men?"

"There was also a statue," said the pope.

"A statue, Your Holiness?"

"Remind me to show it to you when you arrive," said Celestine. "How soon can you be here to escort me back to Rome?"

"I will be there within twenty-four hours, Your Holiness," said Sacchi. "You will be back here soon."

"I do not want the world to know that I am safe until I am back in Rome! Do you understand?"

"Yes, Your Holiness, I understand."

"If a ransom has not yet been paid, do not pay it."

"It is too late for that, Holy Father," said Sacchi. "When we received the ransom note from those who said they held you, we sent the money as soon as we could. The cash has already been delivered to Brazil. I'm afraid we've been duped."

"So be it. I also want you to immediately call my secretary of state, Father Gesa Danku, with the news that I am alive. He is to remain in Rome. Tell him not to try to contact me. It is too dangerous. Do you understand?"

"Yes, Your Holiness," said Sacchi, "I will not fail again."

The pope gave Sacchi the location of the Church of Martyrs before ending the call.

"No, Holy Father," said Sacchi coldly, replacing the phone in his pocket. "I guarantee you I will not fail again!"

TWENTY FIVE

Bishop Sacchi realized how foolish it was to travel to the United States to personally direct the murders. Not only did he risk being exposed, but there were many threats to his future that needed attention at the Vatican. He knew that opportunists, empowered by the pope's misfortune, maneuvered behind the scenes; they would have to be dealt with. But, Sacchi reasoned, he would be back in Rome in a day. Besides, the trip seemed somehow irresistible.

Sacchi had not become *morte domina* of the most dangerous and secret group of assassins in the world by his timidity. He had taken many chances and risked his life numerous times as a young man with *La Mano di Cristo*. His bosses noticed; they encouraged and sponsored his decision to become a priest. Later, he became one of the youngest bishops ever raised to the rank, the benefit of knowing people with whom he shared many dark secrets. Assuming control of Vatican security when the job became available was a given.

The bishop had lost five of his best men in the unexplained missing aircraft in Mexico and two more the night he ordered Eddie Russo killed. The death of his assassins meant little to him. What bothered Sacchi was how the "cargo" on that aircraft, the box containing the pope and two others, was not destroyed.

He knew that the pilot of the doomed aircraft made a last radio call describing a statue of a "man on fire" killing all on board. A statue? And hadn't Pope Celestine told him a statue had saved his life? Bishop Sacchi was puzzled but far from intimidated.

"Celestine, you will need more than statues to save you this time!" said Sacchi.

Sacchi had three operatives already in the United States. He dispatched them to Cleveland. Three more would fly from Portugal and join them.

Before Sacchi departed Rome, there remained an unpleasant item of business. He had to deal with his friend and accomplice Cardinal Viviano, who had lately become dangerously scrupulous. Sacchi had to be certain that the cardinal would not expose the plot to abduct and kill the pope. The bishop made a call that he had hoped would never have to be made; he sealed the cardinal's fate with just a few words.

Late that evening, Sacchi drove to Rome's DaVinci Airport and boarded a chartered private jet to fly him non-stop to his destination. He would arrive in Cleveland after dark, the preferred working environment of *La Mano di Cristo.*

As Sacchi ate a fine meal on route to the United States, a lone assassin entered Cardinal Viviano's apartment as he slept. He crept past Viviano's favorite painting, a Renaissance rendition of Jesus Christ chasing money changers from the temple. The painting was on long-term loan to Viviano from the Vatican museum. When the cardinal showed it to people, he liked to jest, "Jesus chased the money changers from the temple and they ran straight to my bank."

Fear of being found out as an accomplice in the pope's kidnapping had kept Cardinal Viviano from sleeping for the past few nights. That evening, on Sacchi's recommendation, he took a strong medication and slept deeply. The cardinal may have been praying in his dreams for God to show him a way out of his predicament when the Hand of Christ assassin fired one shot from a small caliber pistol into his brain.

Viviano's maid found his body later that day, the pistol in his hand. The cardinal had been "suicided," a variant of the classic Italian Solution. There was no note. Viviano's death drew relatively little attention because the world was fixated on the whereabouts and welfare of Pope Celestine the Sixth.

When Gesa Danku did not hear from Sacchi that the pope was safe in the United States, he phoned Celestine to tell him that their suspicions about Sacchi appeared warranted.

"Prala, please let me send armed men to escort you back to Rome," said Danku. "I insist!"

"My dear friend Gesa," said the pope. "We have already covered that. I have seven armed men that have been waiting centuries for what will happen here. You wouldn't want to disappoint them, would you?"

"I don't understand, but it will be as you wish, Holy Father. May the Lord keep you safe," said Danku.

"And you also, old friend," said the pope. "I will see you back in Rome soon. I promise."

Danku walked to Father Villalobos' office. "It is in God's hands," he told Villalobos. "We must begin a vigil and pray for the safety of the Holy Father and his brave rescuers."

Villalobos was incredulous. "And the statues the Holy Father speaks of, is his fate in their hands as well? Should we pray for the statues? Are we to take the Holy Father seriously?"

"Yes, the statues too. I will pray especially hard for the statues," said Danku. "Villalobos, you and I have believed in the power of miracles our entire lives. Now we must pray for one."

TWENTY SIX

Nick sensed a showdown was near. He sweated the details out of Eddie and insisted that he be allowed to form a welcoming committee for Sacchi and anyone else the bishop might bring with him. Nick wanted to stack the Church of Martyrs with SWAT teams. He had far more faith in automatic weapons than in statues.

"You won't need the statues," Nick said. "We'll blow that bastard to kingdom come if he so much as hiccups! And those assassins he supposedly has, they ain't seen shit until they see how good The Great Piccione shoots!"

"If there's even a Boy Scout here when Sacchi shows up, he won't do anything," said Eddie. "You know that. The only way he'll show his cards is if he thinks we don't suspect him and that he has a chance of killing the pope, Sergio and me and getting away with it."

"I hate to hear you talk like that," said Nick.

"Nick, you're not going to like this, but I need you to do something for me."

"I haven't even heard it yet and I already don't like it," said Nick. "What is it?"

"Bring Pat and the other women at the shelter to your house tonight. Give us time to handle this. Make the ladies your famous spaghetti and meatballs. You could play your accordion for them."

"If this Sacchi prick turns out to be who you think he is, he'll bring a ton of firepower. You're setting yourselves up. You'll all be killed while I'm home stirring the sauce and playing *'Funiculi, Funicula.'*"

"Please, Nick. It has to be like this and, if I'm right, Sacchi won't waste time. He'll be here soon, just as he promised the pope."

"Okay, I don't like it but I'll go along. Who am I to question someone with the balls to rescue the Holy Father? But I'll only stay away until I can't stand it."

Eddie asked the pope to also stay with Nick and the women. Celestine would not hear of it.

"Bishop Sacchi is the problem of the Catholic Church, which means he is *my* problem," said the pope. "I pray we are wrong about him, but I will not allow you and Sergio to do this alone."

Eddie reluctantly agreed, although he was pleased that the pope was willing to put his own life on the line with them.

Pat also asked to remain at the Church of Martyrs. She pleaded her case to Eddie. "I finally get a chance to see my sexy hero in action and you don't want me there."

"Let me be clear about a few things, Pat," said Eddie. "First, I will be trying hard to avoid *any* action while setting Sacchi up for whatever the hell those playful statues have in mind. Second, I very much *want* to have you, Nick, every cop in Cleveland and the United States Marine Corps in that church. But the fewer of us here when Sacchi shows up, the better."

"Do you have any idea what's going to happen?" said Pat.

"Of course not! If I did, I'd probably be a thousand miles from this place. If something does happen here tonight, chances are it won't be pretty. You've seen these statues in action. Please get the women together and stay with Nick. I promise to show you some hero action later."

"That's mighty big talk from someone who just recently learned about women," said Pat. "But you can bet I'll hold you to it."

When Sacchi's three intended victims were finally by themselves, the pope announced he was going into the Church of Martyrs to pray. Sergio, who had not let the pope out of his sight since the rescue, accompanied him, though unarmed. Celestine had convinced Sergio that bringing a weapon into the church would show a lack of trust in the statues.

"Sergio and I will say two prayers," said the pope, "one that Sacchi is not coming here to hurt anyone and one for Sacchi's soul if his intentions are evil."

He wasn't about to mention it, but Eddie thought it might not be a bad idea for Pope Celestine to throw in a few prayers for the three of them also. Just in case.

To distract himself, Eddie caught up on some women's shelter business for a few hours. He was nervous and ambivalent. He feared Sacchi would come and he feared he wouldn't. He had no idea what to do in either case. Eddie had long since given up trying to second-guess his friends in the transepts. He found a dusty bottle of *Four Roses*, took a gulp, remembered he didn't drink hard liquor, laughed about it and took another. After waiting for about an hour, Eddie stepped outside for some air.

"Where is Celestine?" A voice, severe and impatient, came out of the dark the moment Eddie left the rectory. Even though he had only heard it once, Eddie recognized the voice as that of Bishop Sacchi.

"I had just about given up on you," said Eddie, trying to control the panic brought on by Sacchi's sudden presence.

"But I have not given up on you," said Sacchi. "Again, where is Celestine?"

"He's in that old church, the one with all the broken windows," said Eddie.

"What's he doing in there?"

"He's waiting to hear your last confession."

"Has he heard yours?"

"No, he hasn't."

"That's unfortunate because I can't spare the time and you'll soon be dead," said Sacchi. "Tell me something first. You escaped my men last week, even managed to kill two of them. Then you and that traitor escaped with the pope and I lost five more good men. And an aircraft! How did you do it?"

"Statues!" said Eddie. "Magic statues!"

"These statues! Where are they?"

"You'll meet them soon enough," said Eddie. "You're about to pay for your sins, Sacchi!"

"Someone is going to pay," said the bishop, "but it won't be me."

"Tell me, before you die, did you kill my brother?" said Eddie.

"Your brother was about to tell of certain embarrassing inconsistencies in the Vatican Bank," said Sacchi. "Your father was also killed last night in Rome. He was too weak for his position in this Church. You would have been proud of him."

"You're a no good bastard, Sacchi!" said Eddie. "Or should I call you 'Saint Dog?'"

"I consider that name a compliment," said Sacchi. "Men like myself keep this world running smoothly, my friend. We are not afraid to face reality."

"Your idea of reality will be forever challenged if you enter that church," Eddie warned.

Sacchi turned away and walked toward the Church of Martyrs. He issued a summary command over his shoulder to "make it quiet" to a person or persons unseen by Eddie. The bishop entered the church, which was dark except for the bit of light that seeped in from the Brewer Avenue streetlamps and some votive candles Sergio had lit.

"Where are you, Celestine?" said Sacchi.

"I am here, bishop, by the statues," said the pope. "Have you come to escort me back to Rome? Is that why you have come, Sacchi?"

"It is *not* why I have come!" said Sacchi. "I have come to end the madness that is your papacy. Your plans threaten the future of our Church. I have come to stop you! This is not personal."

"I believe that is what they told Jesus Christ and every other man and woman ever put to death for their beliefs," said the pope.

"Don't flatter yourself," said Sacchi. "Why have you made this so easy? You have only one traitor and a pathetic ex-priest who is now dead. Four men, all experts at killing, have entered this church with me. Two more will join us shortly. You should have returned to Rome when you had the opportunity. You would have lived a while longer in Rome."

"If it is God's will that I die in this church, then so be it," said Celestine. "But if it is God's will that you be killed, then I wish you a quick death."

"Who is going to kill me?"

"The statues," said the pope.

"Statues! I keep hearing about statues!" said Sacchi. He approached the three martyrs in the south transept. "Are these the statues that I should fear?"

"They are. It may not be too late, Sacchi," said the pope. "Believe what I tell you."

"I believe in God and myself, not you and certainly not statues," said Sacchi. "It is a measure of your madness that you believe these statues will help you!"

Pope Celestine spoke loudly in Italian to Sacchi's men, a blanket warning and plea for them to give up and save themselves.

They answered him with laughter and insults.

"I will show you how much I fear these statues," said Sacchi.

One by one, Sacchi's assassins came out of the shadows to watch. They turned on their flashlights. Four beams of light appeared from different sections of the church, all aimed at the statues. Sacchi picked up a wooden plank from the floor and walked behind Saint Lawrence.

"I believe this sad excuse for a statue is Saint Lawrence, is it not?" Sacchi said.

"It is indeed Saint Lawrence," said Celestine. "He is the one that saved us in Mexico."

"Then he should save you now, no?" said Sacchi. He stepped behind the statue, placed the plank on the saint's back and pushed hard. The statue toppled from its plinth. When it hit the floor it did not simply break apart. Instead, it burst into many pieces, as if the stone was under pressure from within.

"Why don't you kill me and my men and save the Holy Father?" Sacchi shouted at the pieces of broken stone. He laughed and kicked one of Lawrence's large sandaled toes across the floor.

Sacchi moved to the statue of Saint Bartholomew. "Perform for me, statue! Why don't you do something? Cut me with your knife!"

When the statue of Bartholomew didn't react, Sacchi scoffed and stepped behind it. He pushed Bartholomew off the plinth. The statue hit the floor and also seemed to explode, same for Saint Elmo. The bishop crossed to the north transept and destroyed the statues of Stephen, Sebastian and Blaise in the same manner. The statues with the unimaginable powers that had so effortlessly killed and had for so long given pause to so many were gone, smashed to bits, in minutes. Without a fight! The pieces mixed with the broken glass, dirt and trash on the Church of Martyrs floor.

"Are you certain these were the statues?" Sacchi said, approaching Sergio and the pope. "Why don't you and your friend look worried?"

"Because we have a faith that you will never know," said the pope.

"Misplaced faith, I would suggest," said Sacchi.

"You miss this one!" one of Sacchi's men yelled. He had discovered the statue of Saint Dionysius in the corner chapel. Following the lead of his boss, he pushed the heavy martyr to the floor. Dionysius, too, broke into pieces no longer recognizable as a statue. The assassin picked up a portion of the saint's head and rolled it to the back of the church in the direction of the bell tower. "Like the bocce ball, eh?"

"Your statues have forsaken you, Celestine," said Sacchi. "They didn't protect your friend in the courtyard and they won't protect you!"

"Did someone mention my name?" said Eddie, walking into the church. "Have I missed anything?"

The four beams of light redirected at Eddie. Sacchi squinted, as if to convince himself who it was.

"How are you still alive?" Sacchi demanded, his voice lacking a good deal of its previous condescension. "It's not possible!"

Eddie began to answer Sacchi but stopped when he saw the broken statues, including that of Saint Blaise, who had just minutes before made quite a mess of two *La Mano di Cristo* assassins in the courtyard.

One of the bishop's men, apparently wanting to gloat before killing the helpless victims, picked up the capstan Saint Elmo had held in his hand for centuries, the capstan around which pagan torturers had wound the saint's intestines. "I think I take home a memento," the killer said.

The capstan proved an unfortunate choice of souvenir. As the man held it up and used his flashlight to show the others, the capstan, bits of Saint Elmo's fingers still attached, slammed into his stomach, striking with such force that he buckled over. The assassin slowly straightened and stood motionless, his face blank. He looked down, as if wondering what was to come next.

Three flashlight beams illuminated the capstan as it emerged from the assassin's stomach, trailing steaming intestines. The capstan hovered before its victims face as Elmo's fingers began to move, rotating the capstan and winding the intestines around it. The souvenir hunter, clutching his entrails, fell to the floor screaming.

The remaining killers shined their flashlight beams around the church like erratic searchlights in an anti-aircraft battery, looking for clues that could explain what had happened to their comrade, whose dying screams echoed through the Church of Martyrs.

The killer closest to Eddie threw down his light, produced a knife and backed Eddie to the altar steps. He pounced on Eddie, knocked him to the altar floor, raised the knife and drove it at Eddie's heart. Eddie felt a powerful blow to his chest but not the knife blade he expected. His attacker no longer had a knife. Nor a hand.

The killer, still on top of Eddie, studied a bloody stump where his hand had been. The hand, amputated at the wrist, lay on the altar, twitching and still grasping the stiletto. The assassin tried to stand but was unable. His legs, cleanly severed above the knees, lay on the altar. In apparent denial that he no longer had legs, the killer made repeated attempts to stand, causing his torso to trace a circle in blood. A small bloodied object lay near Eddie's head. There was no mistaking it: the tip of Saint Bartholomew's stone butcher knife.

"Why is it necessary to scare me first?" Eddie said, as he got up from the altar.

The Martyrs Bell, forgotten and unheard for years, began to toll its poignant chorus, the moans and sobs of a thousand men and women martyrs.

Eddie, rattled by the bell that should not have been ringing, searched for Sergio and the pope in the semi-darkness of the church. He ducked under a flashlight beam that shined straight ahead. He saw that a man held the flashlight in one hand, a pistol in the other. The man, like the beam, was motionless, frozen in mid-stride. If it meant life itself, Eddie had to see why the figure did not move. He approached carefully, in a crouch, below the light beam. Eddie soon regretted his curiosity. A bloody arrow tip stuck out of the man's head; the end of the arrow was visible where it had entered between his legs.

"*Il Papa*, I think the bell a sign that the statues want us in the tower," Sergio hollered to the pope. "Follow me!"

Sergio and the pope climbed the steep stairs to the bell tower's narrow catwalk, which encircled the huge timbers that supported the Martyrs' Bell. The last of Sacchi's men gamely followed and reached the catwalk. Sergio stepped in front of the pope. The killer fired blindly at shadows, by chance hitting Sergio twice. Sergio dropped to the catwalk. The killer spotted Celestine, stepped over Sergio's limp body and raised his pistol.

Sergio, drawing on what life remained in him, grabbed the gunman's ankles and pulled his legs out from under him. Sergio rolled off the catwalk and fell to the church floor, taking the gunman with him. The assassin fired his pistol all the way down.

From below Sacchi watched the scene in the bell tower, lit dimly and unevenly by flashlights on the church floor, flashlights dropped by dead *La Mano di Cristo* assassins. It was left for him to kill Celestine, now alone on the catwalk. Sacchi, apparently believing that he could commit the murder and make it back to the safety of the Vatican on the jet waiting for him, began the long climb.

Eddie had heard the pistol shots and ran for the bell tower. He caught up with Sacchi on the stairs and jumped on his back. The bishop reached around with a knife and stabbed wildly at Eddie, inflicting several deep cuts along his ribs. Eddie loosened his grip to protect himself from the blade. Sacchi turned and kicked him down a dozen steps to the floor.

"Sacchi, can't you see what's in store for you? This ain't your day!" Eddie yelled, getting to his feet. "Give it up!"

The bishop turned and looked at Eddie but said nothing. He soon reached Celestine. The pope, small but with the strong shoulders and hands of a baker and the instincts and resolve of a fighter, met the much larger and more powerful Sacchi head on.

Sacchi quickly gained the advantage and pinned Celestine by the neck. Sacchi raised his knife but the pope grabbed his wrist and held it at bay with one hand while he delivered blows to the bishop's face with the other. As they fought, the pope tried to convince Sacchi to quit, shouting at him in a choked voice over the Martyrs' Bell, which swung so violently it shook the bell tower timbers. The moans and sobs within the bell had turned to screams.

Eddie, bleeding from his side, again climbed the stairs and reached Sacchi and the pope. He pulled and pounded on Sacchi but feared interfering too much lest all three of them fall to their death. Eddie grabbed the knife blade, which cut a savage wound across his palm; he did not let go. He wrapped his other arm around Sacchi's thick neck and pulled but could not budge the bishop.

Far below the mortal combat in the bell tower lay the face and part of the head of Saint Dionysius, the "bocce ball" tossed by one of the now-dead *La Mano di Cristo.* The saint's eyes, closed for seven hundred years, snapped opened. The head scanned the floor before rolling toward a length of discarded steel cable. When it reached the cable, the head grasped an end in its teeth and began to spin, slowly at first, but soon increasing the speed. As the head of Saint Dionysius spun, the cable lifted into the air, rising like a lariat toward the bell tower.

Eddie, still holding the knife blade that cut to the bone, pounded on Sacchi's head with his other fist but with little effect. He watched helplessly as the pope began to succumb to the bishop's strangling hand.

"You will be next," Sacchi snarled at Eddie.

The steel cable Dionysius spun from the church floor had risen to the bell tower. Eddie watched it bump against Sacchi's shoulder, as if sizing up its victim. Sacchi removed his hand from the pope's neck and pushed the cable away. The cable stopped spinning, seemed to take aim, looped around the bishop's neck and tightened in one quick movement.

Sacchi released the pope. He dropped his knife, stood and frantically pulled at the cable with both hands. The bishop lost his balance and fell backward, draping himself over the catwalk.

The pope reached down. "Take my hand, Sacchi!" he yelled in a weakened voice. "Take my hand!"

Somewhat reluctantly, Eddie also offered a hand to Sacchi, who accepted the men's help. As Eddie and Celestine lifted the bishop, he showed his gratitude by yanking the pope off the catwalk while keeping the cable slack by not letting go of Eddie's hand. The pope caught a timber below the catwalk and held on with both arms. Sacchi made desperate last grabs at Celestine's dangling legs.

When Eddie finally broke free of Sacchi's grip, the bishop's weight instantly tightened the cable and constricted the noose. Sacchi dropped out of reach of the pope.

Eddie could not help Celestine from atop the narrow catwalk. He climbed down onto the timbers and, carefully skirting the swinging, deafening Martyrs' Bell, helped the pope back to the safety of the catwalk. Eddie and Celestine watched Sacchi tug at the noose until, surrendering to his fate, he swung both arms out. The bishop stared at his adversaries through red, bulging eyes, a look not of despair, or fear, or even hatred but of iron will and pride, the look of a person about to gladly die for something in which he truly believed. When Sacchi's neck, nearly severed by the cable, could no longer sustain the weight of his body, his head detached and fell, along with his torso, to the church floor.

The Martyrs' Bell stilled, punctuating the end of the statues' long and difficult journey, a journey begun seven hundred years before at the hands of a hack sculptor in Italy.

Nick had heard the Martyrs' Bell begin to toll. He knew the bell had been broken for many years and that it had no *gong* in it! It was too much for him. He and Pat ran to the church; they reached the scene just in time to watch the partial head of Saint

Dionysius release the cable from its mouth, close its eyes and revert to stone.

"What the fu...!? Did I really see that!?" said Nick.

All rushed to Sergio, who was still alive.

"Sergio, hang on," said Eddie. "We'll get you help."

"Is okay like this, *Signore*. Too cold here," Sergio said before he died.

Pat leaned over Sergio. She listened for a heartbeat and felt for a pulse. "He's gone, Eddie. Sergio's gone!"

"Sergio told me when we entered the church tonight that he would not leave alive," said the pope. "He said it was the will of the statues, that he could do nothing about it."

Eddie sat down on the church floor and cradled his friend's body; he was unable to speak through his grief.

In death, Sergio wore the hint of a smile.

Celestine touched Sergio's face. "Only those who know love die with a smile," he said. "Thank you, Sergio."

The pope gave Sergio the Last Sacraments. He went from corpse to corpse, administering the Sacraments to Bishop Sacchi and the others killed in the church and the courtyard.

Police and medical personnel worked the next five hours in the Church of Martyrs, removing bodies and sorting through evidence. Nick called in every possible favor owed him over a long law enforcement career and somehow managed to sweep under the rug what had been a mass murder.

The *Plain Dealer* and local television reporters, blissfully unaware they were being cheated out of the most sensational news story of all time, reported what Nick told them: a drug gang had attacked a rival gang operating out of the old church. Bizarre ritual executions had taken place, same as what had happened to the two men killed in the same church a week before. No more comments, no more questions!

Nick somehow neglected to mention to the Cleveland media that His Holiness Pope Celestine the Sixth, wearing blue jeans, a sweatshirt and sneakers, was in the secluded corner chapel at that very moment. Celestine was on his knees, giving thanks, praying and begging God's mercy on the souls of all those who had died.

TWENTY SEVEN

Nick secretly escorted Celestine the Sixth to Rome the day after the bloody conflict in the Church of Martyrs. The pope traveled on the last of Sergio's passports. They bought tickets with the last of Sergio's money. Eddie stayed behind, wanting no part of what he knew would be a circus.

When Nick and Celestine arrived unexpectedly at the papal offices and living quarters in the Rome slums—by taxi, no less—the pope was saddened and chagrined to see the place was largely vacated. Most of his staff, believing he would never return, had gone back to their former plusher accommodations and offices in Vatican City. Father Danku, Father Villalobos and a few others had remained. Also, to Celestine's great delight, the papal baking staff had been loyal to him and stayed. Danku called a press conference and announced to the world that the pope was safe and back in Rome, apparently having materialized out of thin air!

Media from around the world rushed to interview Pope Celestine and, of course, his deliverer and spokesman, Lieutenant Nick Piccione of the Cleveland Police Department. Nick was suddenly a celebrity and gloried in it. Though he had once sworn to never talk to reporters again, Nick gave a drawn-out, mind-staggering account of how the pope had been rescued in a cowboy-type shootout with kidnappers in South America. Flagrant contradictions overflowed in the question and answer session that followed. Nick had street reporters and famous news anchors alike talking to themselves. He would later tell Eddie that "it felt real good getting even with those bastards."

Pope Celestine sat quietly to the side during the press conference and nodded in agreement with everything. All involved would take the story of the statues to their graves. What choice did they have?

At the Church of Martyrs, Eddie began the task of burying the statues. He called Johnny Izzo, a neighborhood friend who ran an excavating business. Eddie asked him to bring a backhoe.

"What do you need, Eddie?" said Johnny, as he unloaded the equipment.

"I need a hole big enough to bury seven guys, seven very big customers."

"You're talking like a real Italian," Johnny joked. "These guys wouldn't be the statues, would they? I heard they got broken. How'd it happen?"

"There was a wild party in the church," said Eddie. "A little too much vino, I'm afraid."

"Yeah, sure. At any rate, wouldn't it be easier to just let them stay where they are? There's already so much junk in that old church, who'd notice?"

"I would notice, Johnny," Eddie said. "The statues need a place to rest in peace."

"Whatever you say. Don't suppose you're going to tell me what *really* happened the other night, are you? I heard Pope Celestine was here. Is that right?"

"Johnny, get serious. What would the pope be doing here in Briggs Hill? Trying to recruit me again? There's nothing to tell."

"I heard that the bodies they dragged out of the church were pretty messed up."

"Maybe a little," said Eddie, drolly. "Like I say, it was a wild party."

"And how in the hell did Nick Piccione get into the act? He's a freakin' superhero, Batman and Robin all in one. His ugly mug's all over the television and everywhere else you look. I almost fell over when I saw him standing next to the pope! In Rome! And that story he told! Holy shit!"

"To the best of my knowledge, the Cleveland cops got involved in a secret mission to rescue the pope in South America," said Eddie. "Naturally, they assigned their best man to the job. That would be Nick. Just a nice kid from the neighborhood doing well. I always knew he had it in him."

"Yeah, right. The police chief claims he knew nothing about it. He wanted to fire Nick but ended up promoting him to captain!"

"A long-overdue and well-deserved advancement, I should add," said Eddie, wishing Johnny would drop the subject.

"When Nick gets back, we'll have a few beers and he'll tell me what happened."

"Don't count on it, Johnny," said Eddie, becoming serious. "There are some secrets in this world bigger than all of us, bigger even than *Captain* Nick Piccione."

"All right, keep silent like a good Italian boy," said Johnny, as he began digging with the backhoe in a secluded area behind Father Louis' greenhouse. Eddie stood by and stopped him when the hole was deep and wide enough to hold the statues.

"How much do I owe you, Johnny?"

"Forget it, Eddie. I owe *you*. You helped me out once or twice."

After Johnny departed, Eddie began the process of burying the statues—what was left of them. The stitches in the stab wounds on his side and his deeply cut hand pulled and stung but Eddie hardly noticed. He declined Pat's help. This was something he would do alone.

Eddie gathered every piece of statue he could find, some covered with painted blood, others with real blood. He swept the church floor and sorted out all traces of broken stone weapon and torture device, every sliver of limb, beard and clothing and even small chips of paint. He placed the pieces outside on the ground, reassembling the statues, now mosaics, as best he could.

The saints held one last surprise for Eddie, a pleasant one. Saint Bartholomew's lips, which had snarled in a crate for six centuries and for a century longer in the Church of Martyrs, showed the faintest of smiles. Same for the others, as far as Eddie could tell from the fragments. He remembered the words the pope had spoken over Sergio's body, how only those who know love die with a smile.

"So, at last, you guys get to smile," Eddie said. "I'm happy for you. Maybe we can all smile now. Okay?"

Eddie carried the statue fragments down a ladder and laid the saints softly, piece by piece, on white cloth. He arranged them in the same order they had stood in the Church of Martyrs. Saint Dionysius was a short distance from the others, as he had always been. Eddie placed Father Louis' disinterred journal among the statues and covered everything with more white cloth. He filled the grave using only a shovel. It took all day. Afterward, he said a prayer of farewell and thanks, his first prayer in many years. There was no marker. Eddie didn't think the statues would have wanted one. Besides, he thought, who would be foolish enough to try to find words to describe the indescribable?

As Eddie walked away from the grave, he had one last request of the boys: "Stay put, damnit!"

Inevitably, stories spread of the strange events in the Church of Martyrs. Skeptics and believers alike traveled to Briggs Hill to see where statues had come alive! Where statues had killed! Where statues had saved the life of Pope Celestine the Sixth! Eddie discouraged the curious and denied everything but they still came.

To kneel uninvited on the dirty floor of a cast-off church and ask silent questions for which there are no answers. To pray. To wonder.

THE END

CLOSING NOTES

Pope Celestine the Sixth, unhindered at last, launched his dream of disbursing the entire wealth of the Catholic Church to provide food and a better life for the impoverished of the world.

Eddie and Pat married and continued to run the Church of Martyrs' Women's Shelter. Eddie eventually got to Disneyworld, which he found boring.

Sergio was buried in Italy on a warm sunny hill in his home town cemetery with all his Cleveland friends in attendance. Pope Celestine the Sixth gave the eulogy. He called Sergio "a guardian angel who lived among us."

Father Gesa Danku, his uncommon abilities no longer required in Rome, returned to his idyllic life among the Hittabbe—as he had promised them.

The pope named Father Villalobos a bishop and appointed him Vatican secretary of state and president of the new Office for the Distribution of Christ's Wealth.

Captain Nick Piccione retired from the Cleveland Police Department and moved to Florida. He never mentioned the statues again.

No one claimed the bodies of Bishop Sacchi and his assassins. Lacking identification, they were buried in unmarked graves in a county cemetery in Cleveland.

The surviving *La Mano di Cristo* members around the world disbanded, fearing not death but death in the horrific manner of their comrades. They continue to operate as freelancers and will kill for anyone—except the Catholic Church!

The Church of Martyrs remains in ruins.

45272060R00143

Made in the USA
Lexington, KY
23 September 2015